MEG GEORGE

About the Editor

BEN GEORGE is editor of the literary journal *Ecotone*. His work has been nominated for a Pushcart Prize and for the *Best New American Voices*, and has appeared in *Ninth Letter*, *Tin House*, and elsewhere. He lives with his wife and daughter in North Carolina, and teaches at UNC Wilmington.

THE BOOK OF DADS

THE BOOK OF
DADS

*Essays on the Joys, Perils, and
Humiliations of Fatherhood*

EDITED BY BEN GEORGE

AN ECCO BOOK

HARPER PERENNIAL

NEW YORK • LONDON • TORONTO • SYDNEY • NEW DELHI • AUCKLAND

HARPER ● PERENNIAL

An extension of this copyright page appears on page 273.

The lines in quotation marks and within parentheses at the beginning of the section titled "[The Pond]," on page 133 of Nick Flynn's essay, "Here Comes the Sun," are taken from George Oppen's poem "Sara in Her Father's Arms" and are used with permission of Linda Oppen.

HarperCollins books may be purchased for educational, business, or sales promotional use. For information please write: Special Markets Department, HarperCollins Publishers, 10 East 53rd Street, New York, NY 10022.

FIRST EDITION

Designed by Ruth Lee-Mui

Library of Congress Cataloging-in-Publication Data is available upon request.

ISBN 978-0-06-171155-8

09 10 11 12 13   OV/RRD   10 9 8 7 6 5 4 3 2 1

This book is for

my daughter,

Lucy,

who likes to swing.

How do you like to go up in a swing,
Up in the air so blue?
Oh, I do think it the pleasantest thing
Ever a child can do!
—ROBERT LOUIS STEVENSON, "THE SWING"

And

for my father,

Daniel.

Ah! yes, his children are to every man as his own soul; and whoso sneers at this through inexperience, though he suffers less anguish, yet tastes the bitter in his cup of bliss.

EURIPIDES, Andromache

Contents

IX

CONTENTS

CONTENTS

Introduction

For Mother's Day, a few months before my daughter, Lucy, was born, I bought my wife, Meg, a copy of Anne Lamott's *Operating Instructions*, which charts Lamott's first year with her son. Meg waited till Lucy was born and then read the book bit by bit throughout our daughter's first year. Almost every night, propped on my pillow beside her in bed, I would hear the titters start.

"What?" I'd ask. "What's so funny?"

"Anne's son just grimaced and passed gas when he saw George Bush Sr. on TV," she told me. Or "Anne just called her infant son a 'little shit.'"

My wife (and I through her) was getting that feeling we all cherish when reading someone else's unafraid, honest observations: *I'm not the only one!* Though we hadn't admitted it to anyone besides each other, we'd certainly already felt that kind of deranged frustration when Lucy refused to be mollified even when it appeared that we had met every conceivable need. It no longer seemed unbelievable to us that someone, ravaged by fitful sleeplessness, might shake her baby. Incredibly sad and heartbreaking, yes, but unbelievable, no.

I cannot overstate how good it was for my wife and me to have those moments of laughter together as she read Lamott's book. Because we knew that in a few short hours (or less) we ourselves would be losing sleep. More than the laughs, though, or the insights, Lamott's book was providing Meg with comfort . . . fortitude, even. No parent we'd talked with before Lucy was born could give us what that book was giving Meg.

When Meg's twelve weeks of maternity leave were up, and I, with my half-time editor's job, found myself entirely alone with my daughter two days a week, it didn't take long to realize just how bankrupt the platitudes and assurances people had been offering me beforehand really were. Maybe the parents I'd talked with as a single man thought that if they let the real truth slip, I might be dissuaded from joining their club. (Once you're a parent, you understand this sentiment. You desire fellow sufferers, as well as others who get all the in-jokes. Would a recent *New Yorker* cartoon in which a ferocious, psychopathic-looking toddler in her jammies is taking a chainsaw to the family couch while her parents calmly confide to their guests, "She gets this way when she's tired," have been as funny to me before I was a father?) Nobody mentioned, for instance, that regular showering is the first thing to go. On any given day there might well be a few million new fathers masking their musk with enough deodorant to make it through undetected. It is hard to explain how a shower—that once rote morning activity—comes to be regarded as something you must *do*, an action that must be completed. But if you get a few minutes before the first wail emanates from behind your child's closed door, whether it's in the early-morning dark or during an afternoon nap, you're desperate to get something "accomplished," and in the hierarchy of pressing tasks a shower doesn't make the cut as often as it once did.

At some point in all of this, it began to dawn on me how much I wanted, like my wife, a book to bolster me, a companion that could plumb the numinous qualities of fatherhood. I'm not sure when I admitted this need for solace. Was it the long night that my wife and I awoke to the bleating baby monitor for the third time, around four a.m., and in an attempt to fuel myself I popped a cup of coffee into the microwave, only to discover the next morning, when the cup had been among the missing for several hours, that I'd put it in the freezer instead?

To be fair, it wasn't only solace I sought, it was also a chance to glimpse another father witnessing the wonder of a new life developing—and not just any new life, but one he himself had a hand in creating. These moments, too, were at the heart of my fatherhood experience: Lucy lifting her stuffed bunny to the bedroom window so the bunny could see outside, or her exuberant squeals and laughing jags as she chased soap bubbles across the backyard.

A book like *Operating Instructions*, despite its many pleasures, was, to state the obvious, written by a mother; also, my innate skepticism tends to prevent me from taking just one person's word on the matter, which made the idea of an anthology appealing. What's more, it wasn't only the early years of fatherhood that I wanted to know about. I'm impatient—I wanted to know about the whole shebang. Inveterate worrier that I am, already I cast ahead to the Drugs Talk, the Independence Talk, the Yes But You Can't Always Believe Boys When They Tell You They Love You Talk.

Whenever the need for this book first took hold of me, once it had me it became a permanent jones. I wanted a collection of essays that reached for what it *means* to be a father—from beginning to end. In what ways, for instance, was it different to be a father than a mother? What did it mean to be a good dad versus a bad dad? And why did there seem to be so much talk, and so many books, about motherhood, but not that much discussion, at least as far as I could tell, about fatherhood? (Witness, for just one example, the supposedly gender-neutral magazine *Parenting*, whose subtitle, unsubtly, was until very recently *What Matters to Moms*.) It couldn't be that fathers just weren't interested in fatherhood—the practice, the difficulties and the gratifications, the way it redirects a man's life—not according to the conversations I was having.

But when I started to look for a book like this anthology, my Amazon.com search for "fatherhood" returned this: "Did you mean 'motherhood'?" (On and off, ever since, I have heard this sentence in my head—like a catchy pop song I hate or the Tickle Me Elmo laugh—as some kind of tape-looped voice-over questioning whether fatherhood is really all that important an undertaking.) I scrolled down the page of results and saw that my hunt had yielded a gaggle of books purporting to instruct me on how to keep my baby alive until my wife got home and how to remain a mack daddy even in the grip of new fatherhood. There were plenty of sophomoric how-to or self-help guides masquerading as memoirs, all claiming, in general, to show me how to master the entire endeavor. But if there was one thing I'd learned in my brief stint as a dad, it was that fatherhood was never going to be something you mastered. And while I could understand the desperation of wanting to be rescued by the arrival of one's wife, that wasn't the book I was looking for, either. Sure, I wanted to know about the practical stuff. But most of all I wanted to read the writers I admired telling me something true about this new experience of fatherhood, a life change for which I grasped early on how poorly equipped I'd been. (And I had *chosen* to do this, I often reminded myself. It had been on purpose!) Of course there were great fictional examples to show me the kind of sacrifices this brave new world might entail. And I returned to some of my favorites—Andre Dubus's chilling "A Father's Story," for one. But what I wanted, ultimately, was something directly from the writers' lives: the pure, uncut, undiluted, unvarnished skinny. The nonfiction book that took fatherhood, in all its permutations, seriously, and that was seriously funny, didn't seem to exist.

But could I really trust the writers in this book (a number of whom, there's no denying, are mostly *fiction* writers) to do that? It's true, of course, that not all literary icons are fatherly exemplars. Hemingway's blunt advice was this: "To be a successful father . . . there is one absolute rule: when you have a kid, don't look at it for the first two years." Frederic Henry, Hemingway's character from *A Farewell to Arms*, compares his newborn son to a "freshly skinned rabbit" and supposes that he might someday "get fond of it maybe." There's a gallows humor in Henry's terminology, and a good-natured leave-the-nurturing-to-the-women smirk in the Hemingway observation. But the strong silent father type became déclassé a good while ago. Gone are the days when it was acceptable, maybe even desirable, for a dad to be remote, enigmatic, impenetrable, emotionally inaccessible, unknowable. The Provider. When your responsibility was little more than to secure shelter, food, clothing—to make sure your children did not maim or kill themselves before they reached legal age. Maybe fathers in prior generations didn't know better. Now we understand that if we don that well-worn coat we'll probably be the root of years of expensive biweekly therapy for our children. The job requirements for today's father seem to have proliferated. They are unique to the age: achieving a precarious balance between manliness and sensitivity.

Many, many dads, I discovered—as I talked with more and more of them—were trying to forge a fatherly identity, to determine what kind of father to be. The idealized family life, we soon figure out, often seems pitted against our own individual lives and careers and pursuits (even more so now that these careers frequently blow us around the country, away from family members and friends who might otherwise assist us in the exhausting child rearing we're doing). How did things fit together, your old life and this new forevermore life? Once a father myself, I could not imagine the chaos that ruled my life reigning in the lives of the literary personages I admired. It was impossible for me to conceive of a contemporary hero like Richard Ford—much less Hemingway, who talked of sitting down at his typewriter and bleeding—doing anything as depressingly pedestrian as standing over a changing table, elbow-deep in a tar-filled diaper, or hosing down a vomit-covered car seat in the backyard. Grace under pressure indeed. But such unglamorous things had become just a fact of life, a standard part of my existence.

Of course, to portray the opposite of the strong silent father, the "involved" hands-on dad, can be just as problematic. Such attempts can come across as stagy or contrived. We have a hard time believing them—or I do, anyway. Not long ago I came across a photo of the late and much-beloved George

Plimpton sitting near his disarrayed desk, rolling a sheet of paper into his typewriter. He gazes out his Seventy-second Street apartment window into the apotheosizing bars of bright sunlight. Meanwhile, behind him, on a plush rug, lie his two young twin daughters, head to toe, each contentedly sucking on a bottle of milk as Plimpton goes about his important work. The skeptic in me could almost hear Plimpton, as soon as the photo was snapped, calling out, "All right, that's a wrap," and asking the nanny to whisk the girls to the park. *Ha!* If it were me, as soon as I'd rolled in the fresh sheet of paper and Lucy had finished her milk, I'd have to make sure she wasn't poking the dog in the eye, or climbing the bookshelf, or playing in the toilet water.

Though a picture like the one of Plimpton and his twins may have accurately captured a moment, in my experience it's ultimately dishonest in what it suggests to the viewer, which is that one's own individual pursuits and the sacrificial nature of fatherhood somehow exist in unperturbed symbiosis. Parenthood will almost certainly provide the writer some new material, but it probably won't aid in getting that material written down. Ford, in fact (who doesn't happen to have any children), once quipped that he thought each child a writer had was probably equivalent to at least one fewer book in output. (Faulkner said, unapologetically, that Keats's "Ode on a Grecian Urn" was worth any number of old ladies. So how many children is *Independence Day* or *Rock Springs* worth?) But I've also heard Ethan Canin say that anything the writer loses in terms of time or creative output by having children is offset by a tremendous gain in his own depth of feeling.

Bearing these various complexities in mind, the essays in this book have pleased me in both their honesty and their balance. They're full of the joy, the pleasure of being a dad, the incomparable kick of it, the profligacy of a father love that cannot be contained or summed up. But there's also the humor, the pain, the self-doubt, even the desire, at times, to be anything other than a dad. Fatherhood, to borrow a phrase from Vince Vaughn's character in the movie *Swingers*, isn't all "puppy dogs and ice cream." Raymond Carver, for instance, while conceding, in his tour de force essay "Fires," that there were some good times in his fathering years—certain "satisfactions that only parents have access to"—also claimed he'd "take poison" before reliving that time. He describes the influence his children exerted on his life as "a negative one, oppressive and often malevolent," "heavy" and "baleful." When he finds himself stymied in a Laundromat one Saturday afternoon, he reflects that fatherhood, for him, is a job of "unrelieved responsibility and permanent distraction," a situation that has formed his life into "a small-change thing for the most part, chaotic, and without much light showing through."

You won't find any essays here with a vision quite so bleak. But even those of us with the most generous outlook on fatherhood have known dark moments, times when a one-room cabin in the Yukon Territory begins to sound very appealing. Still and all, I'll wager everything I have that not one of the writers here would give it up. Not for love or money.

There's a final thing I want to recall. It's the weird unexpected sadness I had after my daughter's second birthday, when we no longer measured her age in months. Saying your daughter is seventeen months old—that can be deceptively reassuring: you think you'll have forever to get to know her. It comes as a tugging pang when you remember that you won't. One outward reminder is that every time you gain command of the fatherly skills needed for a period in your child's life, she's on to the next stage, and everything you just painstakingly figured out is now mostly obsolete. Even though it happens slowly enough that I can't quite tell, every day my daughter is a little bit taller, she's a little bit smarter, and almost every step she takes now is another step away from me. Slow down, I want to tell her. What's the big hurry? Stick around a while. For once she was born, I now had my prime yardstick for time's inexorable progress. I understood on a more visceral level how it wasn't going to slow down for me, much less be stopped. If my sojourn on the planet goes as it should, there's a lot of Lucy's life I'm going to miss. I wouldn't want it the other way around—unthinkable—and yet it's still a little bit crushing to think of the years she'll have that I'll know absolutely nothing about. Because even though I realize I can't know everything about her, I want to learn whatever I can.

That's the trick of fatherhood. We tend to think that, in the father-child bond, it's the dad who does the teaching. But in fact it's fathers who learn from their children. Peter De Vries, the seldom-remembered comic novelist (and father of four children), put it this way: "The value of marriage is not that adults produce children but that children produce adults. Who of us is mature enough for offspring before the offspring themselves arrive?" De Vries is certainly right.

And yet children do more than make us grow up. They make us grow down. Before Lucy was born, I had long ago forgotten what it was like for each day to be brand-new. Her wonder, her insuppressible curiosity, helped me to remember. Whenever we would head out to the car to go somewhere, she would stop every couple of feet along the walkway to finger a flower petal or a bush. This capacity is what Wordsworth is getting at when he declares the child to be the father of the man. The world is something by which we ought to be en-raptured. This is what the child teaches the man. Wordsworth wanted to keep this feeling his whole life. He wished for his heart never to stop leaping up when he beheld a rainbow. "Or let me die!" he proclaims, if he should lose that way of seeing things.

During most of the time I spent putting this book together, I lived in Portland, Oregon, and it's one autumn Saturday there, on the first day of rain in what often turns out to be seven or eight months of mostly unrelieved, mood-darkening wetness and gray, that I have to learn this lesson again. In a lull I decide to walk the dog to the park. We're almost there when the rain kicks up again, lightly, at the same time that the sun is pulsing luminously just above the horizon—a paranatural event in Portland, which is almost never cloudless once the rain sets in. The park has a wide flat field, and when the rain pauses again, an entire dazzling rainbow, stem to stern, appears off in the distance. I can't remember whether I've ever seen a whole one before, maybe once or twice. But I know I've never seen two simultaneously. And there above the first rainbow is another, a pale doppelgänger, almost like an afterimage, but visible nonetheless.

When I get home with the dog, there is just enough light to rush Lucy into the backyard for a peek. Once she's seen the pair of rainbows, she insists, for some reason, on bubbles. So Meg and I get out the giant purple dollar-store bottle and take turns blowing soapy orbs out across the lawn. "Bubbles!" Lucy erupts. Chasing them seems to be just as much fun for her as the first time she ever did it. The dog gets in on the act, too. There the two of them are, prancing after the bubbles, sometimes making it in time to touch one before it bursts, but usually not. That doesn't stop them. Dusk is coming on but there is time for a few more rounds. All the bubbles, I notice, have a life, a trajectory of their own. They float up. They hover on a gust, teasing, right at their zenith. Then they drift down, vanishing when they're pricked by a leaf or a blade of grass. But oh how brilliant while they rise.

—Ben George

THE BOOK OF DADS

THE NIGHT SHIFT

BEN FOUNTAIN

It's a blur, a lot of it, those first few years, and so much of it seemed to happen in the dark. There is truth to the rumor that children do occasionally sleep through the night, but they also get thirsty, get hungry, go to the bathroom, have great ideas, throw up, and get the willies just as grownups do, and anyone who thinks that children aren't attuned to the more insidious forms of longing and dread simply hasn't been paying attention. They feel everything, and one way or another we usually hear about it.

There was a night that first summer when our son John could not be consoled, and it played out like a kind of baby opera: he howled, and the more he howled the more desperate he became, and so he howled even louder. His rookie parents, twelve weeks into their first season, quickly ran through their thin bag of tricks, so sometime after midnight

I said to my wife, "Hook him on." "*Now?*" "Now." We slid him into the baby pouch and attached him to my chest, and I set off into the night to walk him to sleep.

It was summer, which in Dallas, Texas, means night temperatures just shy of molten and the roar of bug life like tinnitus in your ear. When John realized what was happening he fell nearly silent and had a look around. "What's this?" he as much as asked, and having registered that it was an awfully odd hour for a walk, he went back to howling. And so we roamed the leafy sidewalks of suburban Lakewood, chest to chest, his head snug just beneath my chin, the two of us sweating like miners. The hiss of lawn sprinklers tracked us through the neighborhood. The streetlights threw my pregnant-lady silhouette fore and aft, a shifting blob of protoplasmic mass. I think I blushed, tramping the sidewalks with this screaming child. I was as embarrassed as a person can be in the dark; it was like parading a siren around the neighborhood, or a small bomb with a very loud fuse. Surely somebody was going to call the cops, but no, only the occasional civilian car cruised past, yawing and weaving as the driver processed this very strange sight, a man walking the streets at two a.m. with a baby strapped to his chest.

With time John's howling began to lose conviction, but freight trains and ocean liners don't stop on a dime. It took miles for him to wind down completely, and even then he stayed awake, calm but alert, gravely looking about with the large, liquid eyes of a sensitive sea creature. His thoughtfulness made an impression on me; we tend to ignore the huge amounts of time that babies spend quietly contemplating things, but like monks or fakirs that's mostly what they do.

I want to think, and maybe there's a chance I'm right, that we came to a kind of understanding on that walk. The moist night seemed to cup us in its hands—the heat, the softly roaring cicadas, the meditative rhythm of footsteps and breath all aligned in such a way that life made sense. John's baby-sumo body gradually sagged into mine. We both seemed to know a little peace just then, and because we came to it together, through each other, the joint nature of it seemed significant. Even after he fell asleep I kept walking, as if by going a couple of extra miles I could lock in this good thing between us.

Much of life, fatherhood included, is the story of knowledge acquired too late: if only I'd known then what I know now, how much smarter, abler, stronger I would have been. But nothing really prepares you for kids, for the swells of emotion that roll through your chest like the rumble of boulders tumbling downhill, nor for the all-enveloping labor of it, the sheer mulish endurance you need for the six or seven hundred discrete tasks that have to be done each and every day. Such a small person! Not much bigger than a loaf of bread at first, yet it takes so much to keep the whole enterprise going. Logistics, skills, matériel; the only way we really learn is by figuring it out as we go along, and even then it changes on us every day, and so we're always improvising, which is a fancy way of saying that we're doing things we technically don't know how to do. In my early twenties I watched my sister with her two young daughters and thought, "Forget it, I'll never be able to do that." The skill set was daunting enough—changing a diaper, say, while the kid's thrashing around like a rabid ferret, or extracting a splinter with a surgeon's finesse—but it was her nonstop selflessness that intimidated me, how she gave so much of herself, always, every day, a perpetual gusher of soul and spirit that left me exhausted just watching it.

I was in awe. I wondered where she found the strength, and what kept a person from being emptied out. When my own turn came, I learned that a person can, in fact, get emptied out, but I also found some measure of that selflessness, a deep behavioral pull that took hold of my life and made it a very different thing. After those first few weeks of burping and bathing and midnight feedings I realized with a shock that I could do it—*was* doing it, and more or less automatically, as if the mechanics were wired into me. Your own child is a force of nature, maybe the strongest you'll ever encounter; if you want proof, see what happens when you and your spouse are leading up to sex and your kid starts crying in the next room. So here was an instinct that trumped even the mighty sex drive, and it started working on me in a weirdly backward way.

At that particular time in my life I had a law job with an office, secretary, bosses, clients, the whole bit. I doubt the job was any more soul killing than most such jobs, but it did give me a better sense of my father, of what he'd dealt with and become during all those years of being a man out in the world, working for a living. So I was that salaryman now, but like virtually all salarymen everywhere I had secret ambitions to be something else. When John was born, more than one colleague clapped me on the back and cried: "We've got you now!" And I assumed they were right, that with a kid to support I was locked into the salary life for good. But in time that assumption got turned on its head. Food, clothing, shelter, *stuff*, the material things of life do matter, and they all cost money, but I began to sense other, equally pressing obligations. These other obligations, they seemed to have something to do with ultimate choices, with living genuinely, seriously, not treating life as a game. I began to realize that it's possible to lead an eminently responsible adult life and still be doing nothing more than marking time. The harder choice—the one we resist—that's usually the choice required of us, and becoming a father put that home truth right in my face. I wanted my kid to have all the normal comforts of American life, but I was gradually coming around to the belief that the best thing we can do for our children, better than wads of disposable income or trips to Disney or the coolest technology that credit can buy, is for us, their parents, to be whole in ourselves. That was my inarticulate sense of it at the time, this urgent but notional ideal of wholeness or peace, and I guessed that it would come—imperfectly at best, intermittently if at all—only by living most of my days a certain way.

"What pattern of existence," as Toni Morrison once framed the issue, "is most conducive to honesty and self-knowledge, the prime requisites for a significant life?" I'd thought that becoming a father would excuse me from the harder choice, from the work, and by extension from a way of life that would require more of me than marking time, but I was wrong; seeing my son's face every day obliged me to try this harder thing. Because they know it, who we are; our children will find us out no matter what. To the extent that we compromise, fudge, live falsely, they feel it as surely as the weather on their heads, and sooner or later they'll dish it back to us in spades. It took time for me to accept the situation, and more time for my wife and me to gather our nerve and rearrange our lives, but eventually I quit the law and began a new career as a suburban house husband and unpublished writer. My wife would go off to work every day and make money; I would stay home, raise the kid, and run the house, and for a certain number of hours each day I would sit down at the kitchen table and try to teach myself to write.

Presently our second child arrived, a girl this time, Lee. Five years of practicing law had brought me to a better understanding of my father, and as I moiled through a second and then a third year at home I believed that I was starting to understand my mother. At the very least I was gaining a new appreciation for her, for how she managed to stay as sane as she did through her thirty-year saga as housewife and mom. Running a house, raising kids—this is hard work; maybe the hardest. The pay is abysmal, although I trust this won't be news to anyone. The hours are long, and you're always on call. It's not for the squeamish, not with all the bodily functions involved, and though there are people who make the job look easy, they're either insanely gifted or faking it. As I remember, my mother was exhausted much of the time, and so I became, too, to an extent I'd never been on the salary job, and if these depths of fatigue seemed strangely familiar to me, then that was the echo of my mother's life coming in range. I asked her once, "How did you do it?" She'd raised four children, yet I had all I could handle with two. She shrugged, snorted, looked out her kitchen window, simultaneously pleased and impatient with the question. "There was no other choice," she finally answered. "It had to be done." No, I reflected later, there is always a choice, and she made hers every morning for thirty years, regardless of whether it crossed her mind.

I'm inclined to believe it's a good thing, young fathers gaining a better appreciation of their mothers. Where you were seeing the world with one eye, now you start to see with two, and for me doing the work was what it took, undertaking the endless rounds of meals, baths, diapers, doctors, walks, games, naps, and everything else about children you can cram into a day, along with the comic subplot of keeping the physical plant of the house marginally functional and intact. Something was always breaking down, something else limping along, and some third or fourth or fifth thing merely a pain in the ass. There were plenty of weeks when the yard had to fend for itself. Laundry was an ongoing phenomenon, the sheer tonnage of dirty clothes that could appear overnight. I reflected on our modest family of four and decided that a couple of extra people were living in our attic, that was the only explanation for why the hampers were always stuffed.

For all the fullness of these days, they could be lonely. My children were good company, but they were still children, and maybe the isolation was somewhat more acute for me as a man. By the time Lee was born we'd moved to north Dallas, where the dominant culture is hard-core conservative and luxury consumption always in style. In the aggressively upscale world of north Dallas, house husbands were about as rare as igloos or rappers, and though people were generally nice, they didn't know what to make of me, those churchgoing soccer moms, those hard-charging executive dads. Was I a pedophile? a drug dealer? a Democrat? It probably didn't help that I drove a bright gold 1970s muscle car.

So mostly I hung out with my kids. I'm lucky, I was there to watch them grow up, but as full and demanding as the days were, it's the nights my mind goes back to, all our wanderings through the house fetching water, hunting medicine, fleeing nightmares. There's nothing fun or sexy about sleep deprivation, but I can't say that I was unhappy, most of those nights. I felt useful. I was serving a need. In a world filled with unimaginable pain and suffering, here were a few small problems I could do something about. We had all the usual troubles that keep families awake at night, the earaches, the coughs, the bouts of throwing up, the strange noises and fears of burglars and ghosts. Sometimes John would call for water, but what he really wanted was comfort of a different kind. "What happens when we die?" he would ask, eyes drilling me over the rim of his tippy cup. "What if there's nothing after we die, what if it's all just black?" During Lee's first winter her energy would surge precisely at eleven o'clock at night, and the only way to get her to sleep was to put her in the stroller and do laps through the house. I had a route: den, living room, dining room, kitchen, den again, and onward—we had so little furniture in those days that it was clear sailing the whole way. Eventually she would sleep, but if I stopped too soon she'd snap awake when I moved her from the stroller to the crib, which meant starting the long march all over again. And so around and around we went, a bit like characters in a Beckett play. Can I stop now? Should I put in ten more laps? I suspect that Beckett was peculiarly attuned to the tedium inherent in domestic chores.

Meanwhile my daughter's internal clock kept to its nocturnal track, and as a toddler she formed the habit of climbing down from her crib in the middle of the night and trotting out to the den, ready to start the day. Such a strange, funny, busy little kid; it seemed not to occur to her to be scared of the dark. If I managed to roll out of bed and follow her down the hall, I'd find her perched on the couch with her passy in her mouth and one of her stash of stuffed bears in her arms, patiently waiting for the rest of us to join her. So I'd gather her up and carry her back to bed; I don't remember us ever speaking, those nights, only a sweet, comfortable silence, a hush halfway back to sleep. She seemed to understand when I held out my arms that it wasn't yet time to be awake, but if I didn't go right away, if I hesitated in my bed and fell back asleep, she would still be in the den the next morning, slumped over asleep on the arm of the couch.

Lee was the night owl, John the early riser; whipsawed as we were between the two, those early years passed in a haze of exhaustion. I wonder now if I was fully conscious some days, just as I wonder why I think of those nights as much as I do, why they seem so close, so essential. Maybe it has something to do with the sensory imprint of the memories, the shadowy blues and grays, the deep quiet, the way we always spoke in low voices, whispers. In the silence, the soupy, pixelated dark, things seemed not so much stripped down to their essence as terrifically compressed, charged with an extra density and weight. That sense of compression, of space reduced to a pressurized niche, seemed to stop the normal drift toward numbness and distraction. A small space just large enough for a parent and child, where even the slightest gesture mattered.

No, I wasn't unhappy those nights, but then you have to get up and deal with the day. Sleep, like any other necessity, takes on the allure of the most extravagant luxury when it's in short supply, and since a good night's sleep was often beyond my means I became a master of the stealth nap. I stole sleep when and where I could, though this was sleep lite, more in the nature of low-grade dozing or a semi-sentient trance, consciousness simmering along on autopilot. Making indoor tents and forts was usually good for a nap, a few minutes of "pretend" sleep while the kids were making improvements to the tent. Getting shot in the war could lead to a couple of blissful minutes, and I was always willing to be buried beneath whatever came to hand, leaves, Legos, sofa cushions, shoes. Once they made me disappear under a mound of (unused) Huggies. Or we could do some slow-motion wrestling, where I'd lie on the bed and make myself as heavy as possible, the very paradigm of passive resistance as John and Lee strove mightily to push me onto the floor.

These were some things a young father did to get through the day. Lack of sleep is a flu you can't shake, the funk that comes of eating junk food for a week. If it persists you go a little crazy—time speeds up and slows down, brain function reverts to reptilian levels, and your body aches all over. Maybe this is how the elderly feel all the time. When we'd see our DINK friends—double income no kids—they seemed like beings from another world. They looked so fit, so rested. Their hair was perfect. They were perpetually tanned and mellow, and always seemed to have just returned from vacationing in some far-flung, paradisiacal place. With so much time and energy to lavish on themselves they began to seem childlike to me, stunted, not quite adult. I could feel pretty holy in those days about my chronic frazzlement and lack of sleep, and not a little resentful—do all young parents carry around this sort of galled pride?—but even now I wonder how many of us ever truly grow up until we have kids of our own. Maybe it takes parenthood to force us out of ourselves; maybe that's what maturity is in the deepest sense, living and doing for someone else, practicing the forms of empathy day in and day out. Maybe that's what it takes to be whole in ourselves—first we have to be forced out of ourselves.

Some years ago I came across an anecdote about Flaubert, how he was taking a stroll with friends one Sunday afternoon when his group passed a bourgeois couple with young children. They were an ordinary French family, nothing remarkable, and yet the sight rocked Flaubert with a sudden revelation. *"Ils sont dans le vrai!"* he exclaimed to his companions, turning to stare after the family. Then, as he and his friends resumed their walk, he began shaking his head and muttering to himself as if struggling to absorb what he'd just seen, *"Ils sont dans le vrai . . . Ils sont dans le vrai . . ."* They're in the real. They're living the true life. Flaubert led as full a life as any man could reasonably hope for: he worked hard at his art, traveled widely, had a circle of brilliant friends, enjoyed affairs with beautiful women and lots of exotic commercial sex. But the sight of that bourgeois family staggered him; it was as if he realized that his lifelong bachelorhood, however pleasurable it might have been, had barred him from some ordinary yet profound truth.

I suppose I've lived that truth, although I couldn't tell you exactly what it is. Perhaps it lies in the dailiness of family life, in the unspectacular accretion of weeks and years of being a married man and father, and the fact that we'll fail, the whole premise of "family" will fail, unless we're consciously, diligently trying to give more than we take. And to the extent that we fail or succeed in this, that's the world. Somewhere in that gray area between the extremes lies the difference between making a good life and making a bad one, and so much of it gets determined when we're tired, when we don't feel well in ourselves, when we're distracted or numbed by the daily grind and too many nights of short sleep. Those memories are as vivid as any I have, the times I needed to be a better person, a better parent, and even as I was doing the best I could, I knew it wasn't very good. We're always falling short, so it's a question of degree—of where in that gray area we fall. But when we do come through, that's as close a brush with grace as many of us will ever have. I failed a lot, but sometimes I did all right, and again my mind goes back to those nights when I managed to do some good. Fetching a glass of water, stroking a fevered brow. "What if there's nothing after we die?" But holding hands, talking softly in the dark—this was something. At least this.

THE CHAOS MACHINE

An Essay on Postmodern Fatherhood with Footnotes
by Daniel Baxter

CHARLES BAXTER

Late spring in southern Minnesota, 1998: the days
build from deceptively clear mornings to damp
overheated afternoons. I have driven from Michigan
to pick up my son at college and to take him home
for summer break. As I enter Northfield, Minnesota—a sign announces the town, modestly boast-
ing of its "Cows, Colleges, and Contentment"—I
open the window and smell the faint receding scent
of farm fields and the stronger cardboardish odor of
the Malt-O-Meal plant just inside the city limits.

A strange mix, a pleasantly naive Midwestern
smell. Our minivan, emptied of its benches and
rear seat, should accommodate all my son's college
paraphernalia, but the van, too, has an aroma—of
Tasha, the family dog, a keeshond, and of the coffee I have been drinking mile after mile to stay

awake. In fact, the van smells of all the Baxters. In Michigan the previous day I witnessed an accident near Albion, a woman driving suicidally into a bridge abutment; as a result, today I am shaky and still unnerved, and I am giving off a bad odor myself.

Daniel meets me in his dorm room. My spirit lifts when I see him. We hug. He is smiling but preoccupied and quiet, as he often is. Typical college kid? How would I know? He's the only son—the only child—I have. We arrange to go out to dinner at some air-conditioned Northfield bistro. Later, eating his pasta, a favorite food, he tells me that, yes, he will help me load up the van tomorrow, but, well, uh, he also needs to work with his friend Alex on a physics project the two of them have cooked up and have almost finished, a "chaos machine," as he calls it. He tries to explain to me what the chaos machine is, and I manage to figure out that it's some sort of computer randomizer. Much of the time when he explains anything technical to me—he has a brilliant mind for physics and engineering—I am simply baffled. I try to disguise my ignorance by nodding sagely and keeping my mouth shut. One's dignity should ideally stay intact in front of one's adult children.

So, OK, I will load the van tomorrow myself.*

I drop him off at his dorm and go back to the motel to get a night's sleep. All night—I suffer from insomnia, and the motel's pillow seems to be made out of recycled Styrofoam—I smell the production odors from the Malt-O-Meal plant, the smell of hot cereal that I was served every winter when I myself was disguised as a child.

---

* I'm fairly certain that I had told my dad that we would both load the van after the chaos machine was complete. My dad, however, decided to load the van on his own before the machine was finished.

My own father died of a heart attack when I was eighteen months old. I remember nothing of him, this smiling mythical figure, this insurance salesman, my dad (a word I have never been able to speak in its correct context to anyone). Said to have a great sense of humor, grace, and charm, John Baxter, whoever he was, withdrew his model of fatherhood from me before I could get at it. It's not his fault, but there's a hole in me where he might have been. There's much that I don't know and have never known about parenthood and other male qualifiers, such as the handyman thing. I once tried to assemble a lawn mower by myself, and on its maiden voyage across the lawn, it sprayed screws and nuts and bolts in every direction, an entertaining spectacle for the onlookers, my wife and son.

Lying in the Northfield Country Inn, wide awake, I wonder if my father would have driven to my own college to help me move myself back home. Maybe yes. But somehow I doubt it. Growing up, I did not live in a universe in which such things ever happened.

In college, I was vaguely afraid of parenthood myself, as many young men are. Indeed, fatherhood, that form of parenthood specific to my gender—and which should be avoided at all costs, according to Donald Barthelme in *The Dead Father*—rose up before me during the early years of my marriage as a cloud of unknowing. What, past the conception stage, do fathers actually do? How should they behave? No usable models had presented themselves to me, though I had been given a good non-model, an intermittently generous, Yale-educated, martini-drinking, Shakespeare-quoting stepfather, a successful attorney, gardener, and quietly raucous anti-Semite who had loved me and taken care of me in a distant Victorian way. Stepfathering, however, is not identical to fathering, at least in my stepfather's case; for him, it was largely a peripheral occupation.

It gave him the right to make pronouncements, his favorite being, "Life is hard."

Recently, reading an account of Senator Jim Webb of Virginia, I noted that he believes that a father's duty is to teach his sons to fight and to hunt. I haven't done either, nor will I. I am a traitor, it seems, to my gender. Once my wife said, "All you're teaching Daniel is irony."

Martha, my wife, always appeared right from the start to have a clear idea of what motherhood required, and she set to it with determination and alacrity. "Women don't need the manual," I thought irritably at the time; "they just know how to do these things." Me, I needed the manual. But the manual cannot be found in a book. So I was an ironic parent, a chaos machine myself.

Rules to live by:

1. WHEN THE SERVER BRINGS THE BILL, ALWAYS GRAB IT BEFORE ANYONE ELSE DOES.
2. LIFE ISN'T PARTICULARLY SERIOUS UNTIL IT BECOMES SO.
3. TRY TO BE KIND TO PEOPLE. BE GENEROUS.
4. A GOD NAMED LARRY IS THE GOD OF PARKING. DON'T ASK ME HOW I KNOW THIS. PRAY TO LARRY FOR PARKING SPACES WHEN YOU NEED ONE, AND YOU WILL BE REWARDED.

The next day, Daniel and I have breakfast together. Then I begin loading the van. It's getting hot. Daniel's room is cluttered with clothes (a tropical-colored shirt* for his performances in his cult rock band, Grätüïtöüs Ümläüt,† for which he plays

---

* The shirt was red and shiny but was by no means a "tropical shirt" in the Jimmy Buffett sense of the term.
† GÜ was best known on campus for covers of "Psycho Killer" and "Jump" and for the original mini rock opera *Astronaughty*.

keyboards), amplifiers, CDs, a VHS copy of *Repo Man*, and books, including *Moby-Dick*. Easy things first: I'll start with the blankets.

Following his birth, my son had a fearsomely difficult infancy. In those days, he had a different name: Nathaniel. He came out of the womb jaundiced and stayed jaundiced for longer than is usual. He could not breast-feed and lost weight following his birth. "Failure to thrive," the doctor said, darkly. When he was finally able to nurse, he proved, in time, to be colicky and irritable. The doctor prescribed phenobarbital, which helped, briefly. Then the house was filled, morning until night, with the sound of desperate crying from the nursery. This production of noise from babies is not unusual, and many parents get used to it. Martha did. I didn't. I would take Nathaniel outside under the crabapple tree, which sometimes calmed him down, but I was criticized for not letting him cry himself out.* We took Nathaniel off milk and supplemented his breast-feeding with soy, in the hopes that he would find it more digestible, then from soy to a manufactured protein called Nutramigen. Often when I hugged him, he bent backward away from me, as if in pain.

As Nathaniel lies in his crib, I watch him. I am afraid of him. I am afraid to pick him up; he looks so breakable. What if I drop him? What should I do, as his dad? On one occasion, I try to cut his baby fingernails and make a mistake, cutting into a bit of skin, and he begins to howl, and I am besieged with guilt over my carelessness. Martha comes upstairs. "What happened? What did you do?" she asks me, distraught.

On another occasion, I am feeding him with a baby bottle

---

* My dad was often able to quiet me down by playing Brian Eno's *Music for Airports* while we drove around in his car.

full of Nutramigen, and Martha comes upon me and is completely overcome with jealousy; she tries to talk it through but cannot defeat this emotion. She will feed Nathaniel from now on, she says. She cannot bear to see me feeding him. It does not occur to me to fight over this.

Heavier things now: I pack up Daniel's keyboard. One of his keyboards. He has several. Now his cello. The cello rests inside an enormous protective black case, lined inside with what looks like velvet.

More rules to live by:

5. MUSIC MAKES LIFE EASIER AND OFTEN JUST PLAIN BEARABLE.

6. MOST GOOD WORKS REQUIRE OBSESSIVE DETAIL.

7. LOSING YOUR TEMPER, THOUGH SATISFYING, USUALLY DOESN'T GET YOU ANYWHERE, AND IT CREATES MORE TROUBLE THAN IT'S WORTH.

8. TAKE LONG WALKS, ESPECIALLY ON WEEKENDS. NATURE RESTORES THE SOUL.

Long after most children started speaking, Nathaniel continued to stay silent, or his words were so garbled that I could not understand them, though his mother usually could. She played with him, the blocks and the trains. But he was prone to sudden white-faced rages: once, carrying him into Lord & Taylor, I found myself, with Nathaniel in my arms, in front of the escalator, a device that seemed to frighten him, and he began to claw at my eyes. Around that same time, my wife's back had bite marks and scratch marks, where he had clawed at her. I carried my own wounds around, especially near my eyelids.

But I liked to carry him around anyway, anywhere, on my

shoulders, a daddy thing to do. On Saturday night, we danced together to music on NPR and tumbled around on the living room floor, roughhousing. "I am inventing fatherhood," I told myself. Like most grand concepts, fatherhood appeared to be made up of small, mosaic-like blocks of activities. In Hawaii, it means taking Nathaniel around to see the pop-up lawn sprinklers, which he adores.* Or forcing him to try chicken coated with honey. Or, back in Michigan, singing to him as he falls asleep, particularly "You Are My Sunshine." Or taking him to McDonald's, for the hamburgers (not the buns, which he will not eat). Trying to understand his speech, I give him a microphone attached to nothing and pretend to make him into a network correspondent, or a guest on a talk show.† I sit him on my lap so that he can pound the keys on the typewriter, and I sit him on my lap again, downstairs, so that he can pound the keys on the piano. This habit of playing the piano stays with him.

Nathaniel is obsessed with fountains, with elevator doors and escalators, and with gaps that divide and then close, such as screen doors that he can open and shut repetitively, all afternoon. He adores trains.

A young woman wearing a Carleton College T-shirt comes in asking for Daniel. I tell her that he's not here, that he's off with Alex working on the chaos machine. She nods, smiles, and disappears. She has a pleasantly absentminded expression freighted with intelligence, very much the norm at this college; I have rarely seen so many intelligent and physically awkward

---

* Unfortunately this is true. I remember getting in trouble in Hawaii after I snuck out early one morning to watch the pop-up lawn sprinklers in action.

† My dad's short story "Talk Show" was based on this and the aforementioned Hawaii trip, although I don't remember there being anything about pop-up sprinklers in the story.

students in one place.* Seeing Carleton students playing Frisbee is like watching a convention of mathematicians out on a dance floor.† The sight is touching but laden with pathos.

I am physically clumsy. Daniel is physically clumsy, or was. Instead of shooting hoops, on almost every Sunday afternoon, winter and summer, he and his mother and I, along with Tasha, the dog, if she is up for it, go out walking in one of the Michigan parks. These walks constitute one of our family rituals—walking on a path in the woods affords both togetherness and privacy: you can be pensive, and in solitude, but you're being pensive and solitary in the company of your family, and you're being active, too. Families sometimes give the appearance of three or four solitudes living under the same roof. Ours certainly does. Did.‡

Now I am carrying out Daniel's chair, purchased by us at ShopKo, and his computer, a giant lumbering old Macintosh. Is it already afternoon? Sweat is pouring down my face and soaking my shirt.

Gertrude Stein, in *Everybody's Autobiography*, said that the

---

* None of my Carleton friends appeared physically awkward, at least not to me anyway.

† In fairness to Carleton it should be noted that the women's and men's top-level ultimate Frisbee teams won the national championship in 2000 and 2001, respectively.

‡ The weekends followed a pleasant routine. My parents and I went out to dinner on Fridays. My dad, Tasha, and I would always go through the drive-through line at the nearby Taco Bell to get lunch on Saturday, where we (except for Tasha) would always order the same things we ordered every Saturday. After we ordered, Tasha would start to growl if the drive-through line was slow, which it usually was at that particular Taco Bell. When we got home, Louis the parrot would squawk until he was given a nacho from my Nacho Supreme, and I would sneak a second nacho to Tasha. On Sunday afternoons we would go walking, as my dad mentioned, and we always had spaghetti for dinner afterward. My efforts at the time, however, to convince my parents to extend this system and have a different preset dinner for every night of the week were not successful.

twentieth century was the era of bad fathers. She noted that bad fathers would appear on the scene locally, within families, and, nationally, as bad political fathers—Hitler and Stalin—and that the appearance of these tyrants was an effort to reintroduce a dead God (He had died in the nineteenth century) and to put Him in charge of the state apparatus. There has already been too much fathering in the twentieth century, Gertrude Stein said. My own parenting lacks a certain authority; I am a somewhat insincere and doubtful father, having never quite become accustomed to the role.

One morning when he was four years old, Nathaniel came downstairs, and when Martha called him "Nathaniel," he said, "Not Nathaniel. Daniel." And he became Daniel from then on.* He named himself. My brother Tom was frightened and appalled by our son's self-naming and worried about what would happen if he tried to do so again. What if he kept renaming himself? Chaos. Napoleon crowned himself—a blasphemy—and Daniel renamed himself, as hippies in my era did. So, OK. Why shouldn't children name themselves, particularly if they can't pronounce their given names? So we let him do it, and Martha went down to city hall and had the birth certificate altered so that "Daniel" would appear on it instead of "Nathaniel."

Despite the normalization of his name, Daniel felt slightly different (to me, to others, maybe to himself) from other boys: obsessive, brilliantly intelligent—those shockingly intricate sentences! that diction level!—and physically at odds with himself. Other kids noticed, and eventually we took him out of public school and placed him in a Waldorf school, a Rudolf Steiner school, where many of the kids were oddballs (even his

---

* I'm not in a rush to let people know about the name switch, but I suppose this essay would be incomplete if this were omitted.

teacher called them "oddballs," and the teacher himself was no slouch, either, when it came to oddballdom) and where Daniel was accepted and loved by everybody.*

I dismantle the desk and take it to the van. Or do I?† It's almost a decade later, now, as I write. The past is beginning to smear together, the years taking their kindly toll.

More rules to live by:

9. WHEN DRIVING, RESPECT THE ORDERLY FLOW OF SPEEDING TRAFFIC.
10. USE THE LEFT LANE TO PASS. BUT DON'T STAY THERE.
11. LIFE IS REALLY VERY SIMPLE; BE OPENHEARTED AND TRY TO LIVE FOR OTHERS. AVOID PRETENSE.

Throughout his childhood and adolescence, we travel; we see the world, we view the United States (by car, by train), the three of us. Daniel and I both love Virgil Thomson and Gertrude Stein's opera *Four Saints in Three Acts*, especially to drive to. An odd love for a father to pass down to a son, but it makes us both laugh.‡ Once, following a case of pneumonia, he says

---

* My favorite years before Carleton were when I was at Steiner, from third through eighth grade.

† Probably not. The desk was included with the furniture that came with the room.

‡ *Four Saints in Three Acts* is still funny and is good driving music. Along with *Four Saints*, tapes of the NPR incarnation of the *Bob and Ray* radio show were a staple of my family's annual summer road trips to Minnesota's north shore. Growing up, I'm pretty sure that I assumed that both *Four Saints* and *Bob and Ray* were also being listened to in many of the vehicles we passed on the freeway, but when I think about it now I can't remember the last time I've heard either of these mentioned in conversation or the media. I hope this is because I'm not talking to the right people or reading the right magazines, and that there are, in fact, plenty of people driving around with *Four Saints* and *Bob and Ray* in their CD changers and iPods.

he wants to see New York City, and he and I take a slow train there and back; in the dining car we meet the lead singer for Herman's Hermits, who tells us about a "great novel," one of his favorites, Ayn Rand's *Atlas Shrugged*. As Daniel's father, I explain to my son after we have returned to our compartment why the famous singer in the dining car is full of shit. This, too, is a parental responsibility.

Daniel begins playing. He plays keyboards. From first grade onward, the house is full of music, morning and night. Mozart, Hummel, Beethoven, and then, later, Virgil Thomson's *Louisiana Story* and Ravel's Piano Concerto in G. Have I had anything to do with this? I played records and CDs constantly, but I can't play the piano, not really; classical music is simply one of the atmospheres Daniel has grown up in and breathed.

On short notice, I write lyrics for his rock band.

> *You're from Banana Republic*
> *You look like J. Crew*
> *You're a victim of fashion*
> *I'm a victim of you.*

Adolescence is supposed to be a scary time for parents. In America, at least, the norm is for boys to turn into sweaty sticky hostile monsters, full of rage against the world and their parents. They are full of alcohol and drugs; it is the time in life of projectile vomiting. My wife and I await this change. We wait for yelling and slammed doors. It never happens. Daniel becomes a bit quieter but remains sweet and affable.

He did, however, along with a few of his adolescent chums, have a few other artistic ambitions, which included an intentionally ironic art video entitled *Mr. Scary*. This feature, made in black and white, combined the moody expressionism of

Bergman's middle period with the outsize silent-film theatrics of Eisenstein. Daniel, playing the eponymous Mr. Scary, accompanied by our dog, Tasha (who played herself),* walked through a forest, raised his eyebrows, answered the door speechlessly (Mr. Scary does not ever speak) when a salesman came to call—all these scenes shot in a pretentious, over-the-top High Art style.† A lighthouse served as a recurrent symbol of something. The tone of the film was jarring: think of *Alexander Nevsky* in the suburbs. Like Orson Welles's *Quixote*, this work of cinematic artistry was never completed. It succumbed to its own irony.

I take his clock radio to the van. The vehicle is almost filled with the detritus of a young life.

When children are small, time often crawls. Then they grow, and time speeds up; once you couldn't get away from them, and then they're never around.

What do you mean, he's ready to apply to colleges? He was just born! He studies late, to the wee hours, and I cannot sleep myself until he turns his lights off and goes to bed. He struggles through the college applications, bitterly complaining every step of the way. One late afternoon, while he is laboring to complete the application for Northwestern University, which includes the demand that the prospective student write an essay explaining why he or she wants to go to Northwestern, I slip into my study and write a goof version of this essay for him, for laughs.

---

* In the closing credits, Tasha is credited with the role of Cerberus.
† For example, the last scene featured close-ups of Mr. Scary's face, onto which 8-mm home movies were being projected, intercut with footage of imploding buildings from *Koyaanisqatsi*.

WHY I WANT TO GO TO NORTHWESTERN
by DANIEL BAXTER

Many is the time I have thought of the pleasing location of Northwestern University, situated on the shore of picturesque Lake Michigan. The campus, I have noted, is close enough to the rocky shore of this Great Lake so that students, carrying their heavy textbooks on the way to classes, can be pleasantly diverted by hearing the sounds of waves crashing on the rocks. These sounds are almost always mixed, in damp and rainy weather, with the sounds of muted foghorns, which make their way into the liberal arts classrooms where Shakespeare's plays are being taught by bearded and grizzled scholars. Foghorn sounds are like the lowing moos of anxious herds of cows, waiting to be milked. Certainly, from time to time, one must also be able to hear the muted clash and clang of freighters colliding. With the right kind of police scanner, you might also hear the radio distress calls. Perhaps, as Lucretius says in the second book of *On the Nature of Things*, it is pleasant, even sublime, to see ships sinking in the distance if you yourself are on the shore, that is, at Northwestern, safe in a sort of "ivory tower" from danger. Lucretius calls this the sublime experience of beauty, and so it would be on the campus of this great institute of higher learning, home of the #1 business school in the United States.

But the beauties of Lake Michigan are not the only advantages of which Northwestern can boast, and there are many other reasons why I wish to attend this fine Big Ten center of erudition. The architecture of the buildings varies from Gothic Revival to 1950s Bauhaus to Frank Gehry Las Vegas–style "postmodernism." This distinctive brand of eclectic architecture, so different from the bland brand of monomaniacal "Ivy League" architecture favored by our so-called "prestige" universities, gives to Northwestern a more democratic and populist "grab-bag" appearance. Moving from one building to another on the Northwestern campus, from the threatening appearance of the music building to the turreted castlelike appearance of the humanities build-ing (where many damsels are possibly in distress), the stu-dent hardly knows what to expect from one moment to the next. Call me an eclectic student, if you will, but I must say that Northwestern's unpredictable appearance, whether you approach it by bus, truck, train, or family car, is one of the particular sources of my interest in it.

On my two visits to Northwestern, I have noticed that most of the learnèd professors are quite mature. Their gray hairs and beards (not on the women, of course) are signs of learning and experience. Walking about on campus, one cannot but be impressed by their slow pace, their hands on their canes, as if they were thinking about "thoughts that lie too deep for tears." I was impressed by the colossal lecture halls and huge classes, and the Wildcats who were listening and dozing through the lectures, knowing that the profes-sors would cover material that they had missed, their voices echoing in the immensity of the lecture chambers.

Northwestern has lately achieved a bit of a renaissance. I refer, of course, to the superlative record of the Northwest-ern football team. The school fight song (I have learned it) is the most memorable tune associated with any great public American university that I know of. Any school worth its reputation must have a football team to keep up its manly institutional pride, and Northwestern has lately improved its athletic skills so that it is no longer known as the "whipping boy of the Big Ten." Now it is the Northwestern Wildcats that are doing the whipping!

In summary, Northwestern has much to offer me in its location next to Lake Michigan, in its surprisingly successful and bowl-headed football team, in its always surprising architectures, and in its wise and aging faculty speaking to crowds of attentive youths. I can imagine myself dressed in the school's colors of purple and white, waving a school banner displaying the word NORTHWESTERN with pride. I hope you will agree.*

What kind of father would do such a thing? Write a mockery of such an essay? I would. That's the kind of father I am, the kind of father I have always been.

Daniel got into Northwestern, by the way (without ever visiting it), but did not go there. He went to Carleton instead, which is full of students like him.

Here he is. The chaos machine is finished.† He's taller than I am, has longish brown hair that used to be blond, and has widely spaced brown eyes that radiate interest and intelligence. He walks with his head slightly bent, as if he were ducking under a doorframe. (Later, in his twenties, he begins

---

* This essay still makes me laugh. Another Northwestern demand was to list my least favorite word, which was then, and still is, "potpourri."

† The chaos machine, when completed, was an analog electrical current waveform generator that consisted mostly of a small circuit board and several electronic instruments from the physics department attached to a metal rack and connected together with cables. It was capable of generating waveforms with chaotic properties, the details of which I have since forgotten. The machine worked as planned, and Alex and I made a poster (which either has been thrown away or is gathering dust somewhere in the physics department) that explained its inner workings and reason for existence. Over the following summer, the machine was probably dismantled by members of the physics department who needed its parts back.

to straighten up. But I am still trying to break him of the habit of walking with his hands clasped together in front of him.) He helps me finish loading the van, and we make it as far as Rochester, where we find a Mexican restaurant where we have dinner.* We drive that night as far as La Crosse, Wisconsin. He asks about Tasha, the dog, and Louis, the family bird, who also helped raise him.

These days he works as a successful structural engineer, a bridge designer, in downtown Cleveland. He has published papers I cannot understand. He's a fine and wonderful young man.

The next morning, with Daniel sometimes driving (the person who does not drive is responsible for directions and what gets played on the van's audio system), we head toward Michigan. He instructs me on how to get on to the Chicago Skyway from the Dan Ryan. We both admire the sublimely sinister industrial magnificence of Gary, Indiana. I am proud of him. I love him. And he is a better driver than I am, much more alert, as the young should be, as they must be, to get where they're going.†

---

* I remember that we ate at the somewhat oddly named Mexican restaurant Carlos O'Kelly's.
† Except where I've noted previously, this essay is fairly accurate. It is probably worth mentioning that this is my first, and probably last, writing collaboration with my dad, unless my editing assistance for his last three novels counts. All in all, my dad is a nice guy. You'd like him.

IN TEN YEARS HE'S GOT A CHANCE TO BE THIRTY

JIM SHEPARD

My father bought me a boat when I was about eleven. He got it used, and it looked safe enough to him. It was nothing America's Cup-ish, just something he thought even I couldn't get into too much trouble with. It resembled a Sunfish, only tubbier and slower. It was called a Skate. The sail featured an "SK" and an "8." The first day I had it I trundled it down to the shore on its little hand-trailer, mushed it through the deep sand to the water's edge, hoisted the sail, sat in the thing, and pooled around in little ovals in knee-deep water near the shore. The second day I took it straight out into the Sound—the wind had picked up a bit—and in ten minutes I was so far out that I could no longer identify any landmarks on the shore.

We lived in Lordship, Connecticut, on Long Island Sound, five minutes from the beach by foot, and my father, one of the great covert worriers anybody's ever known, dropped by whenever he knew I was down there, just to, you know, check and see if the kid was doing anything stupid, or was still alive.

In this case, of course, the kid was both. I was so far out by then that my father scanned the horizon from east to west and thought maybe I'd decided against going out after all. He turned to leave but as an afterthought asked the lifeguard standing nearby if a kid had gone out that morning on a sailboat with a pale blue hull and a red and white sail. The lifeguard said, "Yeah, that's him there," and pointed to a speck-sized triangle.

My mother, who'd followed my father to the beach with a thermos and some sand chairs, entertaining quixotic hopes of maybe a nice family outing, later told me that when she arrived the lifeguard came over to her and said, "Can you get this guy out of here, or take him home? Because he's scaring everybody."

What her husband had been doing, in his helpless panic and maddened inability to reach me, was striding up and down the beach uttering oaths, as they used to say in nineteenth-century novels, and carrying on an exasperated monologue that featured the bottomless brainlessness of his son's decision-making capabilities. "Saying the rosary," is how my mother usually put it.

At some point during my sail I realized, in my own open-mouthed eleven-year-old way, that the Long Island shore looked much closer than the Connecticut one, and that black clouds were blowing in. These realizations led to the single prudent decision I made that day: I brought the boat around, for just about the first time in my boating career—nearly tipping in the process, but what the heck; I *was* only fifteen miles from shore—and sailed it right back in on the same tack I'd taken out. I was still very far from the beach when I noted one tiny figure in particular, stomping back and forth, gesticulating.

I wasn't allowed back to the beach for a week, and for most of that time whenever we crossed paths my father would look as if he'd just smelled something dismaying, and shake his head. But by the following Saturday, when he found me sitting in the grass doing nothing in particular, he asked why I didn't take the sailboat out. "Because all you do is get mad," I told him. "Well, maybe if you stopped playing Magellan, I wouldn't get mad," he told me. I took the boat down to the beach that day, and he helped me get it into the water. The wind was blowing onshore, which meant I could only tack back and forth parallel to the beach fifty or so yards out, and I'm sure he misunderstood and appreciated my doing this as a concession. I cruised past him in my tubby little slowpoke of a boat and loved that he was even happier than I was.

I've always loved that paradox in my father—the tension between his anxious sense on the one hand that almost anything his kids could do was a potential source of disaster, and his sense on the other hand that wouldn't it be great if his kids did some of the things *he* always wanted to do: sail a sailboat, for example, or take a long trip. Take some chances.

He grew up in the Depression with a father who seemed unapproachable on good days and a mother who was solicitous but fearful, and at eighteen, like most everyone else his age, he trooped off into World War II—another effective way of honing your capacity for anxiety—flying ground-attack missions in Burma and cargo over the Himalayas. The attrition rate on the latter missions was around twenty percent. He survived that and contracted malaria, survived malaria and made it back to Connecticut.

By the time I was sentient, it was the early 1960s. We all had our health. His job situation was stable and we lived on a fairly quiet street. What was there to worry about? His kids.

My brother was five years older, and between us we did lots of stupid things, sometimes together, sometimes apart, and those little bits of narrative, once uncovered, always lopped a few years off Shep's life. (From a very early age we called our father "Shep." One of my aunts heard me do so and remarked, "Did you just call your father 'Shep'?" "Yeah. That's his *name*," I explained to her.)

He kept a particularly sharp eye out for anything that seemed like more than the usually intractable unhappiness or instability on our parts. At about the same time I received the sailboat, I remember moping around the house at one point and finally being questioned about it by an exasperated Shep. What was the matter with me lately? "I don't know," I told him. "I guess I'm depressed." I'd gotten the term from *Peanuts*.

"*Depressed?*" Shep exclaimed. "What do you mean, 'depressed'? How can you be depressed?"

"I just am," I told him.

"You're not *depressed*," he told me. "You're eleven years old. Eleven-year-olds don't *get* depressed."

I dropped it, but he didn't. For months afterward, he'd peer at me closely every so often and then say to himself, "Depressed. He's depressed."

My mother would ask me something like whether I wanted to go to the beach, and Shep would say, "Don't ask *him*. He's depressed."

"I could be," I told him. Which of course caused him to watch me all the more carefully.

Both of his boys kept to themselves a lot and may have seemed to him moody, but I turned out to be the one who, given half a chance, always seemed to get myself into life-threatening situations, and despite all that, Shep never denied me a chance to attempt the kinds of activities that always ended up making him wish he'd never been born.

For example: he countenanced, a year after the sailboat fiasco, my scuba diving, and bought me everything I needed for that hobby except the tanks and regulator, which I borrowed from friends. There was a group of four of us, three of whom had tanks and regulators, and only one of whom had actually been through a certification course. We all had bought spearguns. We did a lot of spearfishing. Long Island Sound, where we did this, in most conditions had all the visibility of iced coffee. How much trouble could four twelve-year-olds get into with scuba gear and spearguns in murky water?

One kid, pursuing an eel, put his spear through the main part of one of my dive fins. Another kid accidentally hit someone else in the chest—but at the very outer limit of the spear's range (they lost momentum very rapidly underwater) so that the kid who'd been hit turned out to have only a red mark on his sternum once we peeled off his wet-suit top.

"How was diving?" Shep would always say once we got home and were washing everything off. He took the assiduousness with which we took care of our equipment as a good sign.

"Good," we'd say, as noncommittally as we could.

"I hope you're using your head out there," he'd warn us.

"We're pretty careful," we'd tell him.

"That's not stuff you want to screw around with," he'd remind us.

"It sure isn't," we'd agree.

And then as if to prove his point we developed a new game, on a day in which the Sound seemed so empty of life that cruising around with spearguns trying to shoot something seemed pointless. In about thirty feet of water we conceived of the idea—actually, I think *I* conceived of the idea—of having just one person don everyone's weight belts, so that that person could be like Deep Sea Diver Dan, galumphing around on the bottom and making slow-motion leaps from spot to spot, like Neil Armstrong on the moon. Everyone instantly recognized it for the innovative idea that it was. I bandoliered on everyone's belts—my own around my waist and the other three crisscrossing my shoulders and chest—fixed my regulator in my mouth, took a few deep breaths, and allowed myself to be pushed overboard. We used my sailboat, minus its mast, as our dive platform.

Down, down, down I went, and landed in a little cloud of murk. I struggled to my feet. The regulator made its Darth Vader sounds. I hopped around, floating back down to the bottom in a pleasing imitation of weightlessness.

I craned my neck up and could see my three friends twenty feet or so above me, the sunlight filtering down from the surface. (Visibility was a little better than usual.) And here was something funny: because they were in full wet suits and no longer had their weight belts, they were too buoyant; they couldn't get down to me. I could see them struggling to do so, straining to dive to get a better look at all the fun I was having, and failing to get more than five or six feet deep.

But there's a detail about diving equipment in the early 1970s that you need to know to appreciate fully the idiocy of what we were doing. In those days you could pay extra to have what they called a J valve: a valve that held five minutes of your oxygen capacity in reserve, in order to let you know it was time to get to the surface. What happened was, your tank stopped providing air, abruptly, and you were supposed to pull your J valve (a metal rod running out of the regulator and down along the cylinder of the tank behind you) to release that last five minutes. But those who wanted to save a few bucks could buy tanks *without* J valves. Which was, of course, the kind of tank that I had on at that point.

You see where this is going. The boys above me cavorted; I lurched around from spot to spot, happily, and then my air shut off. Mid-breath. I reached behind me for the J valve, but of course there was no J valve. I shed my weight belt from my waist, but that didn't matter, because I had three others crisscrossing my torso. Where were *those* belts' release buckles? Well, that was hard to say. My hands scrabbled all over my chest. I found one and released it, but since it was pinned to my body by one of the others, it didn't fall. Since I hadn't had any warning, I hadn't been able to take a deep breath in preparation for this. I waved frantically for my friends. They waved back. I seemed to them to be having fun. Or was I pretending to drown?

At some point my friends did realize that something was wrong, but there was no time for them to shed their wet suits and no way for them to get down to me without doing so. Eventually I did get the other three belts off me—partially by just ripping one off my shoulder and down over my torso—but my lungs had already given out and I was taking in water before I reached the surface. I spent the rest of the day recuperating, and we were all shaken up by what had happened, but not nearly as shaken as we should have been. I'm sure, at least up to now, that this is the closest I've come—consciously, anyway—to killing myself.

It makes sense to me, then, looking back, that my father would have seen the main challenge of fatherhood not in terms of some issue of nurturance but more in terms of just trying to get us through our childhood alive and mostly undamaged. I sometimes find myself thinking of fatherhood in those terms, too. Of course I want to be emotionally present for my kids, and a good provider, and all the rest of it. But first things first: did Aidan, our sixteen-year-old, get home all right from his class trip? Is our eleven-year-old Emmett's croupy cough anything more than a croupy cough? And what if Lucy, our six-year-old, got too close to where the big kids were limbering up with the baseball bats?

I suppose the good news was that this hypersensitivity to the possibility of a baroque kind of disaster turned out, at least in Shep's case, to translate into an intuitive empathy that could not have been more emotionally intimate, finally, in those moments when it did peep through.

Some years before the sailboat and the scuba diving, maybe when I was five or six, I woke in the middle of the night petrified: giant blocks of the darkness around me seemed to be detaching from one another and spiraling slowly toward me and away. I huddled under the covers hoping this would go away, but it didn't, and eventually I crept downstairs. I had no words for what was happening to me. "The dark's moving," I told my father. "I can't get the dark to stop moving." "You'll be OK," my mother, exhausted from a day of doing everything to keep the household running, assured me. "Just close your eyes and try to rest." But my father quizzed me more closely. He couldn't get anything more eloquent out of me, but he sat up with me and the next morning brought me to an ear, nose, and throat specialist, who discovered that I had a severe inner-ear infection.

It was in moments like this that the logic of Shep's worldview seemed to pay off. The darkness itself is moving? Well, it has to be something. Let's check it out, and immediately.

Now that he's a grandfather, he's transferred some of his anxiety about me as a child to my role as a father. At times after witnessing what he considers especially egregious examples of the casualness of my parenting style—like, say, my snuggling up for the evening with a four-year-old Lucy in front of *Jaws*—he'll comment to my wife Karen with a wry resignation, "What chance do these kids have?"

So far, thank God, our kids haven't pushed the envelope at all, in terms of courting disaster. But maybe we can construct the intuitive empathy and emotional intimacy on other terms. It's like I'm simultaneously hoping for the moon and hoping for not very much at all.

And I'm reminded at such times of a comment made by the New York Mets' original manager, Casey Stengel, who memorably articulated just how minimal his expectations for one of his outfielders were by telling a reporter about that outfielder, "And Greg Goosen, he's only twenty, but in ten years he has a good chance of being thirty."

For my father and for me, it's not much, and it's everything, in terms of our hopes for those entrusted to our care. Those twenty-year-olds: in ten years, they've got a chance to be thirty.

THE JOB, BY THE NUMBERS

CLYDE EDGERTON

BEFORE BIRTH

1. Before the baby is born, go ahead and install the car seat and put together the crib. This will take four to seven days. For safe installation of the car seat, certain hooks are located out of sight in the backseat where you'd slide your hand if you were looking for something lost. If your car doesn't have these hooks, you are required by law to buy a different car. One of your cousins or a brother or a sister-in-law will eventually inspect the installation of the seat and will get very, very upset because it's too loose or not hooked up right, and they will call the authorities. This relative will be a vegetarian.

2. Children cannot sit in the front passenger seat of an automobile until age twenty-four. Else the front-seat air bag will kill them. If the front air bag happens not to kill them, then the side air bag will try to. After they are eighteen they can sit in the front seat if they face backward.

3. If you decide to get your car seat installed at a fire station, you will be required to ask the firefighter for a fire lecture. After the lecture you are required to buy chain ladders to hang from each window of your house—first floor included; and the firefighter will show you how to grab your baby and roll on it if it catches fire. A nurse will be on hand to tell you how to resuscitate a smothered baby.

4. For the first few months, before using the crib, you'll be using a bassinet. Most people buy expensive white wicker ones with little handles and a satin pillow and all that. My cousins Caleb and Cindy realized that a little baby can't half see and couldn't care less, so why not use an ice cooler? With the top removed. Not the Styrofoam kind. You know, the hard kind.

5. When you need the crib, about three months after the child's birth, you will be so sleep-deprived you will not recognize your baby, and will be falling down a lot. That's why I'm saying assemble the crib before the baby is born. The crib comes in a big cardboard box with staples so deep that you' will need pliers and a flashlight to get them out. Most of the instructions for crib assembly say things like, "Assemble Part B into upper part of Part B with plier." I assembled our crib in our living room over a number of days, and when at four

a.m. one morning, on the last day of assembly—having just heard the morning paper slap onto the driveway—I started rolling the thing to the child's room, I found that it *would not fit through the hall door.* So, listen: put the crib together *in the baby room.* Remember, the baby room will be relatively empty because for the first three months the baby is in your bedroom in the cooler.

6. While you're preparing car seat and crib, you can bet on one thing: your wife will be cleaning the house. Mother Nature tells her to do this like she tells trees to grow leaves. Your wife, on hands and knees, will wash spots off baseboards with Q-tips. And when she asks you to do something, do it. In responding to her requests, don't ever use the word "logical." Before my first son's birth, my wife asked me to get a wire clothes hanger, put chewing gum on the tip end, and go deep inside the lint holder in our clothes dryer and get every speck of lint out so the clothes dryer wouldn't catch fire and burn the house down on our first night home from the hospital. You know what I did? I did it. You know what I said? Nothing.

BIRTH

1. When your wife's water breaks, she will tell you. Your job is then to call her doctor's office. When the recording says, "If you are a doctor or pharmacologist, press one," press one. You will get a recording that says to press eight if your wife's water just broke. That recording will say to stay at home until you can see the baby's head between your wife's legs. The recording will also

say that your wife, in that condition, should not operate a motor vehicle. So you will need to drive her to the hospital.

2. When you get ready to go into the birthing room at the hospital, a nurse will hand your wife a gown with snaps and will say, "The snaps are so that if there's an emergency, the doctor can rip your gown off."

3. You do not have to worry about the birth part. That's taken care of by your spouse. You just have to be there to embrace your wife (unless she says, "Don't you dare touch me") and quietly accept her cursing and screaming. Sometimes at you. You will forget the names she calls you just as she will forget the pain of birth. Within a few months home from the hospital, she'll be saying, "Giving birth was a wonderful miracle. It was one of the most wonderful experiences I've ever had." By the way, do not videotape the birth until after the birth part.

4. If the birth is by C-section, it's all quite different. In an operating room, you will be standing beside your wife's head—which is poking through a hanging green sheet—and she will be smiling the whole time, in spite of the burning smell from the searing of cut blood vessels in her stomach, and when it's over, both of you will be able to smile and cry and hold the baby. But next day, when the pain comes on sure enough, she may say ugly things to you. NOTE: Some wives do not talk this way. But they all think it. If only briefly.

5. If the birth is vaginal and your wife chooses to get an epidural, you need to understand that the nurse giving the epidural will be a very nervous man who sits behind her while she sits on the edge of the bed, and he will ask

her to be still while she is having contractions and he is trying to stick a very, very long flexible needle into the hollow part of her spine. Encourage your wife to get this done right away when she arrives in the admissions room of the hospital, where, by the way, she— with the baby's shoulders now in view—will be handed a number (around fourteen) and a magazine and will now have time for the epidural or a liver transplant.

6. About four hours after the birth, the baby and your wife will—because of insurance regulations—be rolled out in a wheelchair to your car. They're rolled out because your wife is too weak to stand. (In the 1950s, new mothers spent months in the hospital, and she and the child both walked out of the hospital.) All the nurses from the baby ward will come down, put the mother in the car on a stretcher, then gather around the baby's car seat like waiters waiting to sing "Happy Birthday." They will inspect the seat and then vote on whether it's safely installed. One "no" vote and your car will be impounded.

7. On the drive home from the hospital you will experience an odd combination of two feelings: (a) extreme ecstasy—about the birth, and (b) deep worry—about how the baby will keep breathing all night on that first night home, and how to keep large rats away from it. NOTE: Rats have a hell of an easier time eating through wicker than through a cooler.

AT HOME

1. Once you get the baby home, you will read instructions about safe practices for how your baby should sleep.

These instructions are written in a document signed
by a doctor from your practice. (Whom you have not
met because there are so many of them. Nor will many
of the other doctors in your practice have met him. He
will be from a small island in the Philippines and he
will have started out in India as a phone operator for
Sprint.) This paper he signed will say that if the baby
sleeps on his back then he will die from inhaling vomit,
and that if he sleeps on his stomach he will die of SIDS,
and that if he sleeps on his left or right side then his
heart will stop because of arrhythmia. There will be a
picture of a $535 device (along with a prescription) that
you can buy from most pharmacies. The device will
have three poles that fit together like a tepee and several
straps from which you can suspend your child by the
chin and knees for safe sleeping.

2. An older woman neighbor you've never met will come
by for a visit on the second day you are home. She will
have shingles. She will explain that shingles is not con-
tagious, but that her grandson has some skin disease
so bad he has to be bathed in Vaseline and wrapped
in pajamas soaked in kerosene, and that, whatever you
do, don't touch the umbilical cord, because it will get
infected—and needs to be covered in a mix of Vaseline
and iodine constantly—and she'll say that if the child
ever gets a fever over 104.5 it will never be right again.
And that a fever can shoot up in the middle of the night
in minutes. She will leave a gift—a small picture frame
with plastic animals glued to it, several of which have
fallen off.

3. You should share night feeding duties with your wife.
That means when the baby starts crying just as you're

falling asleep, you pick the baby up from the cooler and take it to your wife's side. Your wife's doctor will have instructed you always to keep tabs on which breast she used last by noting in a notebook "L" for left and "R" for right. But the best way is to sort of juggle both breasts to see which one is heavier. This will normally wake her up, fresh and ready to feed the baby. But if she won't wake up, whisper that you want to make love: she will try to escape, thus waking up. Unbutton her pajamas and prepare the baby for the appropriate breast. (No matter what that breast used to be like, it will now be great big.) The hungry baby's head will bob and jerk around while it looks cross-eyed for anything that resembles a nipple; you should keep it away from the bedside radio because it will suck the knobs off it. Your wife's nipples will be so sore that air hurts them, and the baby's gums are like brass knuckles. The baby will bite your wife's nipples for the first few weeks of breast-feeding, making your wife scream. But she loves the baby and will forget all this. When the baby finishes nursing, you take the baby from your wife, tell her to go back to sleep, and change the baby's diaper.

4. In the hospital a nurse will have taught you how to change a diaper. You look through the glass viewing window while she changes the diaper with one hand, holding somebody else's baby in the other arm. While the nurse was showing you how to change a diaper, you had to lip-read because of the thick glass window. If the baby had a bowel movement, then the nurse cleaned up the mess with a thick wet tissue called a "wipe," folding it six times with one hand in the process. You will have loads of fun learning about diapers and wipes on

your own. Don't worry. You'll learn. And listen, don't get one of those plastic cans, sort of like a covered trash can, with a hole and a revolving switchback device that is supposed to hold dirty diapers while not releasing a bad smell. Man, that thing is a big pain in the ass. It will start stinking because of stray feces that get hung in these cracks you cannot get to. The revolving top gets stuck all the time, and you will end up very frustrated, out in the backyard pressure-washing the crap from all the crevices. Here's what you do, seriously: ball up the pee diapers and throw them in any trash can in the house. Put stinky diapers in a plastic grocery bag, tie the opening shut, place them outside the back door, and next time you go to the outside garbage can, take them along. That's the best way to handle all that.

5. One of the most unfortunate aspects of fatherhood is *talking toys*. Whenever I turned out the lights at night in the playroom, one of my first son's toys would screech, "Good night!" I couldn't find it because it would talk only in the dark. One night I took the toys out of my son's two big toy boxes and put them on a table and cut the light out, and it wouldn't say a word. Then back in the toy box it started talking again a few nights later. "Good night!" After a week or so, I caught it—a little plastic man. It was rummaging in the desk drawer where I kept my prophylactics. I tied it up, put it under the back tire of our car, and backed over it. One of the most satisfying sounds of my life—the pop and scattering on the driveway. My suggestion is that the birth announcement say something like this:

It's a Girl

Born: 13 February 2010

Name: Jessica Danielle Dorsey

Weight: 7 pounds, 12 ounces

Length: 21 inches

Any Talking Toy Gift Will Be Burned or

Otherwise Mutilated

6. Discipline and all that. Don't tell children to do something and then ask, "OK?" The one-sentence question tells them who is in control. Children need clear direction, clear structure, and clear limits. Man oh man. When a father is afraid of what a very small child is about to do, and then asks the child to make some kind of decision—like, "Well, Johnny, would you like to go upstairs or stay downstairs . . . go to bed or stay up?"— then the father is about to age fast, and will soon be taking directions from worried and impatient children.

7. Sleep problems. Read and follow the suggestions in *Solve Your Child's Sleep Problems* by Richard Ferber. Best advice on babies I ever got.

8. Play. I'm trying to stay away from advice, but . . . after the first few months, act silly. Put odd things on your head. Talk goofy and make funny faces. Slobber. Pretend you are a dog, a turkey, a computer scientist. Get down on the floor with your children at least once a day. If you're very tired, then you can doze off and let them play on you.

9. Reading. OK, this is it on advice. The best way to handle some of those sentimental children's stories is to thumb through the book and ask the child where the

bird is, where the cow is, where the moon is, and all that. Wait until they're older to worry about reading the text. And then get the original Brothers Grimm. (a) That will hold their attention and (b) they damn sure won't get up and wander around the house after lights out. Also, please read Br'er Rabbit in its original (and beautiful) dialect, not in that god-awful Standard English text.

DOWN THE STRETCH

1. Family meetings. Have them. At one of them—after some sort of misbehavior or broken window—you will give a short meaningful talk, and then your wife will do the same. (Or she may go first.) You will then ask if your children have anything to say. This will be a serious meeting, somber tone, etc. Your two-year-old will say, "I want to speak." You will say, "OK. What do you have to say?" And the child will say, "Poopy butt." Freedom of speech is important.

2. Kindergarten. After the first few days, your child will—at the dinner table—say something like this: "Everybody in this family who has stuck your finger in your butt, raise your hand." For a second you will wonder what to do, but you should be honest with your children.

3. High school. If you come to believe your teenagers are never going to speak to you again as long as you live— and chances are they will tell you this—then you will be relieved. No, seriously, though they may tell you that, chances are that by their early twenties they will come around the bend and you'll be able to talk and

laugh with them again. And rebuild the trust that was always beneath the surface.

POST-NOTE (FOR FATHERS ONLY)

I'm sixty-four as I write this. I was thirty-eight when my first child was born. She's now twenty-six and brings me happiness and joy. My other three children were born five, three, and two years ago. They bring me happiness and joy. I am blessed with happiness and joy and children. So my wife and I recently decided that I'd get a vasectomy.

The preparation information and instructions I brought home from the doctor included orders to shave my scrotum— no more than twenty-four hours before the operation. My appointment was for two p.m. on a Thursday and somehow I'd put off the shaving until just before one thirty. I wasn't about to shave early and go in there with a five-o'clock shadow.

I didn't want to use an electric razor—*my* electric razor, anyway. It tends to pull. I needed a disposable razor. I asked my wife if she had one.

"Single blade or double?" she asked.

"Double, I guess."

I stood naked in the bathroom, holding the razor in one hand and a can of her shaving cream in the other. I looked around. Tub should work.

I decided the best thing to do would be to sit on the edge of the tub with my feet in, turn on the faucet (to my right), lather up, and proceed. But when I got situated and ready to go, I realized that my position wasn't quite right, so I straddled the tub wall, faced the faucet, and shifted to the left so that I could get at my job more easily.

I splashed on warm water and lathered up. Remember, I'm

just after the scrotum, no more. The lathering up was no problem at all. Plenty of lather. I took razor in hand, and was trying to remember if a razor was supposed to go against the grain or with, and then thinking which way the grain would be, when in wandered my three-year-old son.

"What you doing, Daddy?"

"Oh, just getting ready to go to the doctor."

"What are you doing?"

"I'm going to shave, and I need some privacy."

"Why?"

"I just do. I'll be out in a minute."

He walked out.

So. Now. I reached down and sort of stretched the skin like I used to when shaving my face with a razor, and started in, but a major problem was that I couldn't see down there . . . down under. I bent over some, shifted to the left a little more. Oops. Almost lost my balance.

"What about a handheld mirror?" I thought. But everything would be backward. But it was backward when I shaved my face, wasn't it? In this present case, though, I'd be looking down into the mirror at something hanging from above, and also, it would be backward, a reflection. My mind flashed to that phrase, "Objects in mirror are closer than they appear." Or was it "larger than they really are"?

I decided to forgo the mirror and proceed by feel. Slowly. I shaved a swath.

I wondered: If I stood and bent way over . . . could I see better? But I am not flexible. My wife can flatten her hands on the floor while standing. My wife . . . would she be willing to . . . ?

"Honey?" I called.

"Yes."

" . . . Nothing."

"How's it going?" she asked. "It's almost time to leave." She was not reluctant for me to get on with this procedure.

"Oh, it's going fine."

And the procedure did go fine. But I'm going to miss having babies—the great fun part of it all.

WHAT I CAN OFFER

NEAL POLLACK

When it comes to stuff that dads are traditionally supposed to impart to their sons, I'm a little
lacking. I don't camp or fish, and I can't tie knots.
Though I can tell the difference between a knife
and a gun, I don't know how to use either of them.
Maybe, in a serious emergency, I could change a
tire, but I wouldn't count on me for instruction.
My son isn't ever going to catch me working on an
engine block. The only way he'll see me covered
with grease is if I'm cooking bacon. It's hard for me
even to light a candle without burning myself. And
if I didn't learn how to ride a bike myself until I
was sixteen, how am I supposed to teach my kid?

Even when it comes to book learning, I feel de-
ficient. Thinking about fatherhood, my mind often
turns to John Adams and John Quincy, because I'm
a nerd. I remember reading an Adams essay where
he instructs John Quincy to read Terence, "for

the excellence of his morals." Adams also taught his children the basics of farming and animal husbandry. Well, good for John Quincy, who became a master statesman and a competent gentleman farmer, but I've never read Terence, and I don't know my way around a barn. I spend half my workday in my basement getting stoned and looking at porn with my zipper undone. I have no morals. My reading experience may be vast, but I'm not about to start giving my six-year-old son comparative literature tutorials about Jim Thompson and Patricia Highsmith. He's still reading the Frog and Toad books.

I share my troubles with a lot of postindustrial, media-age dads, who've spent their entire careers developing software or looking at spreadsheets, doing Web design or starting worthless Internet companies, or, in my case, working as a hack freelance writer for nearly two decades. We're not dumb (or at least some of us aren't), and we have some very specific skills, but they're not exactly skills that traditionally get passed down to children. What, then, does the contemporary dad, weak-minded and culturally neutered, have to offer his kids?

The following isn't a comprehensive list. Actually, it's not a list at all. Instead, consider the examples below as rudimentary guideposts for dads raising kids in a senseless world ruled by geeks. For that, we're all supremely qualified.

Let's begin with media literacy, by which I mean, "Exposing our kids to stuff that we like." From an early age, my child has lived in a media whirlwind, and I hate most of the crap our corporate masters have offered him. A steady diet of Baby Einstein, Dora, the Wiggles, Laurie Berkner, *Blue's Clues*, and, later on, *Ben 10*, would starve any brain. You wouldn't give your child Pepsi in a bottle, so why would you expose him or her to *Power Rangers: Ninja Force*?

Over the years, I've exposed my child to, among many other things, the following: *The Muppet Show, Animaniacs, The Tick*, all three Flanimals books by Ricky Gervais, Tintin, Asterix, Wallace and Gromit, *The Electric Company*, the Captain Underpants series, and *The Hoboken Chicken Emergency* by the then-called D. Manus Pinkwater. We've done comparative Superman viewing, from the Richard Donner movies to the Max Fleischer cartoon to the excellent Bruce Timm cartoons from the 1990s. We've engaged in Batman studies, but to a lesser extent, because some of the Dark Knight's iterations are still a little violent for the boy. I've explained to him why *Challenge of the Super Friends*, though definitely full of kitsch value, is far inferior to the "Legion of Doom" season of *Justice League Unlimited*, in quality of animation, depth of character, and plotting. I think he understands. At least he says he does.

I've done my best to impart a sense of ridiculousness to my son in his Fortress of Dorkitude. Mostly, this has worked. I showed him three-quarters of season 4 of *The Simpsons*, regarded by connoisseurs of such things as the best, and he now often says stuff to me like "I call the big one Bitey" or "Dad, it's funny when Homer has a toilet plunger stuck to his head." That's when I activate the lesson in humor appreciation and comic timing.

"You're right, son," I say. "It is. But can you tell me why?"

"Because he's not supposed to," says the boy.

"Good enough," I say.

Sometimes I've jumped in too eagerly, like when I tried to show him *The Naked Gun* before his fifth birthday. But I realized my mistake early on, and shut down the video before the scene with the full-body condom. Still, I'm watching the calendar for the day it's appropriate for me to show him *Airplane!*

And it's almost time for him to be able to watch *Top Secret!* I have so much to teach, and he has so much to learn.

About a month before Elijah turned six, we had a few dead hours on a Saturday. Regina refused to step away from the computer. She'd fallen into a heated argument with some totally misguided commenters on Daily Kos. The burden of weekend enrichment fell to me.

"Son," I said to Elijah, "I want to introduce you to one of my favorite movies."

"What is it?" he said.

"It's very funny. The movie is called *Young Frankenstein*."

"Are there monsters?"

"One monster."

"Is he scary?"

"No, he's funny."

"Why's the movie called *Young Frankenstein* then?"

"Because the doctor in the movie is the grandson of . . . Tell you what. Let's watch the movie, and then you'll learn."

So we watched. I had to turn down the sound only once. When Gene Wilder knees Liam Dunn in the nuts, he curses too much for six-year-old ears. Other than that, Elijah got most of the jokes. After the movie, we recapped.

"Hah hah!" he said. "Igor said 'walk this way,' and then Young Frankenstein had to take the cane and he walked that way."

"Yep," I said.

"And then the pretty girl said 'do you want to go for a roll in the hay' and she started rolling around, singing 'roll, roll, roll in ze hay!' "

"Uh huh."

"But then why did the horses make noise every time anyone said 'Frau Blücher'?"

"Because 'Blücher' is the German word for 'glue.' "

"Why?"

"It just is."

"No, why do horses make noise when they hear the German word for glue?"

"Oh, right. They used to make the hooves of dead horses into glue."

"Glue is made out of horses?"

"It used to be."

"So that's why the horses are afraid."

"Right."

"You know what my favorite part was?"

"Do tell."

"When the monster was on the seesaw with the little girl and her parents were running around worried about not being able to find her, and then the monster sat down on the seesaw and she flew up into the air through the window into her bed, and she was there when her parents came upstairs."

"Yes."

"That was so silly."

"Yes."

"Daddy? Why was the monster rolling around on the woman and grunting?"

"Because he likes her," I said.

Some lessons will have to wait until Elijah's eight.

We're also expected to teach our kids about religion. But my commitment to my boyhood religion doesn't go much beyond a love of Mel Brooks. As Jon Stewart says, "I'm Jewish because of the delicious snacks." It also doesn't help that I'm beyond skeptical, and leaning toward resentful, when it comes to some of religion's most dubious claims. Any intimation that man once walked with dinosaurs is met with a subtle fusillade of secular propaganda in the form of comic books about the theory of evolution. I must steel Elijah in case he ever stumbles upon a den of creationist thinking.

At the same time, while I don't care if my son ends up being atheist, it's never good form to *raise* a kid atheist. Kids need to believe in something.

Recently at the dinner table, Elijah asked, "Dad, do you believe in God?"

"Not really," I said.

"I don't either."

"OK."

"What do you believe in?"

"It's complicated."

"I believe in angels."

"Whatever."

But even if I don't teach my child Jewish theology, I think it's important that he learn something about his cultural background. I'm determined that Elijah will grow up appreciating the delicious snacks. One recent late September morning, I woke up to an e-mail from my mom, featuring a little backdoor Jewish New Year guilt. To be fair, she also wanted to let me know how much she was enjoying *American Wife*, which I'd given her for her birthday. Here's what Mom said:

Happy New Year. I know this doesn't mean much to you, but the combination of school starting, my birthday, and Rosh Hashanah has always been the start of a new year for me. I wish I could capture and explain how special this time of year was when I was growing up.

Yes, yes, I know. Things were so much better in New Jersey in the 1950s. As soon as I closed the e-mail, I did an abashed Google search for "shofar." A wise acquaintance of mine has said that a Jew need fulfill only one true requirement on Rosh Hashanah: he or she must hear the call of the ram's horn. Not surprisingly, there were lots of videos of shofar playing on YouTube.

Elijah woke up at 8:15. There was no school that day because of "teacher training," which was good, because the kids needed a break after nearly two weeks of rigorous study. He came down into my basement, where I was sampling shofar videos. I decided this was a perfect time for a little low-level Jewish education.

"Good morning," I said.

"Good morning," he said. "Can I watch a show?"

"Sure," I said. "But first, come over here. I want to play something for you."

"What?" he said, suspiciously. He sensed that I was about to delay his SpongeBob fix for something ostensibly edifying.

"Well, you know how the Jewish calendar is different than the regular calendar?"

"No."

"There are different months and it moves in different cycles. Tonight starts the Jewish New Year, called Rosh Hashanah."

"OK."

"And to ring in the New Year, someone blows a ram's horn at temple."

"Why?"

"For many ancient reasons. Anyway, I have a video of someone blowing a horn here. Do you want to see it?"

"OK."

He came over and snuggled. I called up a video of a cantor at a congregation in Skokie, Illinois. I chose it because the cantor was wearing what Elijah would probably consider a funny hat, and also because it was only two and a half minutes long.

The *tikiyah* call went out, and the first bleat escaped the horn. Elijah smiled at the funny sound. He liked the second blow, too. But by the time we got a minute and a half in, he was looking bored.

"What do you think?" I said. "Do you like it?"

"Good," he said. "It's a little loud."

I turned it down.

"Check it out," I said. "In about a minute, he's going to blow for a really long time."

He blew for a really short time.

"Is that the long blow?" Elijah asked.

"No."

"Is that?"

"No. Be patient."

Finally, the long blow came. Elijah listened patiently, then got out of my lap. He went over to my big blue armchair and sat down.

"So there you go," I said.

"OK," he said.

"I wanted to ask you a question."

He sighed. "What now, Daddy?"

"Do you know what happens to a Jewish boy when he turns thirteen or fourteen?"

"He grows a beard."

"Well, maybe a little, but more importantly, he has something called a Bar Mitzvah, where he leads a service in Hebrew."

"But I don't speak Hebrew."

"I know, but you go to school to learn it."

"I speak English mostly."

"Yes, but you will learn Hebrew, and then we'll have a Bar Mitzvah. We've decided to do it in a country called Israel. Which is the Jewish homeland."

"Why do it there?" he asked.

"Because it will be cool and meaningful."

"I think Jojo and I will go pretty crazy in Israel."

"We're not taking Jojo to Israel for your Bar Mitzvah."

"Why not?"

"For many reasons, most of them financial. We'll take Grandma and Opa and maybe your aunt and uncle and cousins."

"OK," he said. "Can I go watch a show now?"

"Sure," I said. "Happy New Year."

"OK," he said.

With that, I'd pretty much assured myself a spot in the Book of Life for another year.

A father is supposed to teach his kids the difference between right and wrong. But we rarely get to play Atticus Finch. Mostly, our lessons involve making banal statements like "it's wrong to swallow gum" or "that was very nice of you to share your Stormtrooper with Dexter." Like Raymond Carver's baker, we mostly have to deal with small good things, or, conversely, small bad things.

For instance, one summer afternoon, I picked Elijah up from day camp. I took him to the packing store because I had to send something via UPS. Elijah liked going to the packing store, since unlike many such stores, it has a toy aisle. I sat him down there and went about my business a few aisles away; I couldn't see him, but he didn't seem to be making a lot of noise, so I assumed that all was copacetic. When I was done, I went to the aisle. He sat on the floor, surrounded by all manner of plastic balls and rubber dinosaurs.

"What the hell are you doing?" I asked.

He bounced a ball.

"Look, Daddy," he said. "This one lights up!"

"That's great," I said. "Now clean up this mess."

"Why?" he said.

"Because you made it."

"I broke one of the toys and water came out and some stuff got wet."

"You did what?"

I looked around to see if anyone had heard. My voice lowered to a whisper. I moved closer to him to inspect the trouble. He'd taken one of those plastic cannoli-shaped things that slides in and out. I feared that it was full of some sort of horrible liquid poison now infecting the rest of the toy aisle. The cannoli itself sagged, half-deflated, like something that isn't appropriate to metaphorize in this space.

Then I saw the wrapping, indicating that the toy had, in fact, contained water.

Wait. Why was the wrapping open?

"Did you open the wrapping?" I asked.

"Yes."

"You can't do that. If you do that, then you have to buy it."

"But I don't want to buy it," he said.

I looked around. No one had noticed. Elijah had cleaned up his toy mess. We could have walked out of there and no one would ever have known of our guilt.

But I decided to take the moral path. We went to the counter.

"Um," I said. "One of your toys got broken."

I held up the limp plastic inside-out cannoli.

"Oh," said the counter guy. "No big deal."

"We're going to pay for it anyway," I said. "That's the right lesson to teach, isn't it?"

He shrugged. I bent down to Elijah. "If you break something

that's not your property," I said, "you have to buy it." I turned to the counter guy. "How much do I owe you?"

"Two bucks," he said.

"Oh, thank God," I said. I hate it when doing the right thing costs more than five bucks. I gave the counter guy the money and tossed the limp cannoli in the trash can.

"Why'd you do that?" Elijah whined.

"Because it's broken."

"Why'd you buy it if it's broken?"

"Because you broke it."

"But I didn't mean to break it."

"I understand that," I said. "But you have to take responsibility for your actions."

"OK," he said.

When we got home, I told Regina what had happened.

"He only gets to play with one toy at a time at that store," she said.

"Why didn't you tell me that?" I said.

"I don't know."

"It could have saved me a lot of anxiety."

"But what would you do without all your anxiety?" she said.

"Good point."

We briefly discussed making Elijah pay me back for the toy out of his piggy-bank money, but we decided we'd had enough anxiety for one day.

I was listening to ESPN Radio because I needed another reason to despair about the collective intellect of humanity. The host, like most sports-radio guys, had many important things to say about morals and values. This particular rant involved "strong father figures." When a professional football player is acting out and behaving like a prima donna, he said, you can be sure that there's one common denominator: he didn't have a strong father figure when he was a kid. Plaxico Burress, Vince Young, Terrell Owens, naughty Negroes all, had each lacked a father figure. Nothing against moms, the host said, but if you don't have a dad around to lower the hammer and lay down wisdom, then you don't have a chance in the real world.

Putting aside the passive-aggressive racism, there were many things wrong with this argument. Many people raised by single moms grow up with decent values. Also, you don't make it to the NFL without *some* self-discipline. The fact that guys behave like babies once they arrive probably has more to do with their outrageous salaries, infinite opportunities to have sex with gorgeous women, and that everyone always wants to take pictures of them. I've never faced such temptations myself, but I'm sure I'd have moments of weakness.

As the shining opposite example, the host presented Sam McNabb, father of the Philadelphia Eagles quarterback Donovan, who had not only brought his boy up right, but had done it with a motivational-talk-ready parenting philosophy. Ages zero through twelve, according to Sam McNabb via Colin Cowherd on *The Herd*, are the "Intimidation Phase," where you put the fear of God in your boys with your deep voice and imposing presence. The teenage years are the "Motivation Phase," where you encourage them to excel, do their homework, and stay away from drugs. In the subsequent "Counseling Phase," your kid learns how to be a man and to deal with disappointments.

This seemed designed to ameliorate the guilt of guys who give their kids a swat on the ass with a belt once in a while. Mr. McNabb also forgot to mention certain other phases, like the "Stop Trying to Lick Mommy's Boobs" phase, the "Get the Hell out of the Bathroom While I'm Trying to Take a Dump" phase, and the "Don't Smother the Dog with the Sofa Pillow" phase.

Fatherhood is about small victories and small defeats, incremental lessons in absurdity that add up to nothing in particular. Hopefully, in the end, the fact that I have been present nearly all the time while not being abusive will mean that my son can pay his rent on time, hold down an interesting conversation at a cocktail party, and have a freezer empty of human body parts. Whatever small tidbits of wisdom he absorbs along the way are just sauce.

For instance, one night Elijah asked me to teach him to play poker.

"The problem with poker," I said to him, "is that it doesn't work unless you gamble money."

"What does gamble mean?" he asked.

"It means you bet."

"We could bet M&Ms," he said. "Lots of them."

"We could," I said.

"So let's do it."

"Let's learn first."

So I ran down the basic hands. I told him about pairs and two pairs, and full houses, and straights.

"You mean like two three four five six seven eight nine ten eleven jack queen king ace?" he said.

"Yes," I said. "Except there's no eleven card."

"Oh right," he said. "I forgot."

"And then there's the flush."

"Is that when you flush your cards down the toilet?"

"No. It's when you have all the cards in the same suit."

"What's a suit?"

I had to explain that. By then, dinner was nearly ready. But we had time for a few sample hands.

We played a modified version of Texas hold 'em, in that we kept our hole cards visible so I could advise him on whether to fold or stay in; if your cards aren't good, I said, you must fold. Never gamble on a bad hand. At that moment, I realized that I was, essentially, teaching my son by using the chorus from a Kenny Rogers song.

He seemed to get the principle, so we hid our hole cards. I turned over the next three.

"Do you want to drop out, or stay in?" I asked.

"Stay in," he said.

"Let me see your cards," I said.

He had a queen and an ace, off-suit.

"Good choice," I said.

We played through the hand. He didn't win, but that was because of a bad draw for him, not bad decision-making. Then I dealt the next hand. This time, I asked him before the flop, "Stay in or drop out?"

"Drop out," he said.

"Let me see."

He turned over the cards: a nine and a four, off-suit.

"That's a great decision," I said. "I'm proud of you."

Maybe we've already entered the Counseling Phase.

CANDY MAN

RICK BRAGG

We put in at Cotton Bayou, where the dark, brackish waters of the bays and inlets flow into the deep green of the Gulf of Mexico. It is not an idyllic, romantic place—no place dotted with $950,000 condos really is. But if you had a big enough Evinrude, and enough Dr Pepper, it could lead you to one. Still, in the early, early morning, when the only sound is the lap of the water on the docks and the soft click, click of crabs across the chert rocks, you feel like you are on the edge of something fine. And you are glad that you and the boy got up in the pitch black, to make it here in time to see a sunrise, to scramble onto a boat and head out into the Gulf in the general direction of Cuba, even though you know you will run out of Vienna sausages before you ever get so far.

I had always wanted to take the boy fishing in the Gulf, in the deep blue where, I once wrote, we would catch giant fish and talk about life. Instead, he sat in the front of the boat with his buddy, Taco—so called because the only sentence he muttered to me across three days was "I like tacos." There, shoulder to shoulder, the spray whipping them with every bounce of the boat, they talked about whatever it is that thirteen-year-old boys talk about now, iPods or cell phones or whatever brain-rotting video game is en vogue, and I was left to talk to myself. My mother started talking to herself at fifty. I am forty-nine, but I already have long, long talks with myself, and sometimes I even make sense to me.

I never really wanted a son. Or at least, I thought it was better not to have one. I believed that it would be fine if my family line and name ended with me. It wasn't any particular self-loathing, just the simple knowledge that we were prone to be drunks.

Not Faulkner drunks or Hemingway drunks, but mean and hopeless drunks, broken-bottle-fighting, wife-hurting, selfish drunks. My grandfather on my mother's side was a fine man, but even he drank himself to death, smiling. My father drank himself to death on purpose, spinning the lid of a Seagram bottle instead of the cylinder on a .38.

I grew up with the music of empties clinking together as they rolled around in the backseat of a car that always smelled of stale beer, learned to walk with the rank smell of moonshine—a cross between skunk and kerosene—drifting from a can of paint thinner on the kitchen table. It wasn't always that way—we ran from it when the three-day drunks escalated into monthlong drunks—but it still sticks in my mind.

I am not a drunk, but I could be, because the only time my mind has ever really been at ease was when I was pretty well half-lit. But that's no sob story. I would be and could be a drunk, but I always had a lot to do, too much to do, so I chose not to be one. Maybe someday, when I am through with it all, I can finally be a drunk. We'll see.

But I know I carry a gene in me—the drunkard's gene—just as I carry one for blue eyes. It would be selfish and foolish to pass it on. This may not be the exact science of it, what I believe. But that doesn't change my belief in it.

So there would be no sons, could be none, and that seemed fine. I am not one of those scions of the Old South who would have cried over that, grieved over it. "Oh Lawdy, who will we give Great-Great Grandpappy's saber to?" I've noticed that, at least down here, the more money a person has, the more he seems intent on an unbroken line, to pass it on.

But I guessed the liquor stores would just have to get by somehow without one more Bragg.

"You can adopt?" a well-meaning friend once half told, half asked me.

"Lord, what for?" I said.

If you can't have your own boy, then why raise another man's? I know the noble reasons to do it, but they plumb evaded me.

Yet here I stood with the wind and the salt and the water baptizing me halfway to hypothermia, alongside a boy who did not have a damn thing to do with me except that he came with the package when I married his mom.

And I knew that, somehow, I had won. I didn't deserve to win. But I did.

Past the age when most sensible men become a father, when it was almost too late, I got this boy, like a prize in a cereal box. It hits me, now and then, and it hit me hard as I watched that boy cast his bait fish into the blue, as his face shifted from stern concentration to something like pure joy.

He pulled red snapper and Spanish mackerel from the saltwater like they were waiting in line down there to jump on his hook. Taco was catching them, too, but for some reason he was also catching some of the oddest creatures I have seen this side of Animal Planet, so they had to stop and examine them.

"Dude," one would say.

"I know, dude," the other would say.

I think they also discuss world peace and global warming this way.

And I laughed out loud.

"I caught bigger fish," I bragged.

"I caught more," my boy said.

"I caught weirder ones," Taco said, and we allowed as how, yes, that was true.

And later, after the boys had talked about how this was the best fishing day in the whole world, my boy asked me what I thought about it all, because he believes that, because I am a writer, I should always say something profound.

"I think," I said, "that if a frog didn't have legs, he'd bump his ass when he hopped."

The boy snorted and I think some Dr Pepper came back up through his nose, and he laughed for five solid minutes. And though it wasn't exactly what I had in mind, it was a conversation about life, wasn't it, kind of?

"Tell your momma that," I told the boy, "the next time she starts spoutin' on about what she thinks."

He tried to do that, but he is thirteen and has the attention span of a tick on a hot rock.

"I believe . . . ," his mother started one day, not long after.

"You know what I believe?" he piped up.

"What?" she said.

"I believe that if a frog didn't have an ass, he'd bump his . . . no, wait, that wasn't it . . ."

And she looked at me, knowing.

I could lie.

I could say what a hard and thankless and even odious job this is, to help raise another man's child.

I could whine. I could resent his very presence, and complain of the extra weight I am forced to carry through this life, while another man skips childless through his middle years, free, leaving me to explain to the fruit of his loins why it is unwise to run out into traffic, and unacceptable to stick your face all the way into a plate, to suck up a string of spaghetti.

But even though I complain, a lot, about the fact that he sometimes seems subhuman—mostly when he has a fork in his hand—and the fact that his bathroom is a Superfund site and the fact that he likes to adorn the TV room with noxious sweat socks, it all comes down to a simple truth.

I could call him a gift, if I was a prissy man.

I could call him a godsend, if I was a religious one.

What he is, is my great good luck.

Well-meaning people like to tell me that I was a father waiting to happen, that I have a lot to give. But I don't buy it. I am not a good and unselfish man who believes that he has something deep and profound and fine to share with this boy.

No, we just live together, just live, and every damn day some little thing happens that makes me glad we stumbled across each other in the imperfect world of broken marriages, fractured futures, and mislaid plans.

•　　•　　•

I am probably unfit to be a real father.

I was single and childless for so long that I turned danger-ous irresponsibility into art.

I am the man who once heated a can of peas on the stove—not by putting the can into a pan on the stove, but by placing it on the electric eye and turning the knob to H. When the paper began to burn off, when the Jolly Green Giant began to writhe in flames, I figured they were pretty well done.

I am the man who cut his own hair for twenty-five years, looking, at various times, like a sheepdog, a Beatle, a medieval monk, a cockatoo, a scrub brush, Sergeant Carter, a prickly pear, and the lead singer for REO Speedwagon.

I am the man who still believes that a fistfight is a logical and reasonable outcome to any disagreement between people of the same sex, who once lost a stand-up fight to a man about as big as my leg, and who challenged a tow-truck driver to a duel, and then wished he hadn't.

I am the man who patched a leak in a Porsche's fuel line with a Bic pen and a drinking straw and then sold it to a friend, the man who fell overboard in the middle of a pitch-black lake during an alligator hunt, who flipped a convertible at a hun-dred miles an hour in the middle of an illegal drag race, who stole two women from the same man.

And the sad thing is, most of the time I was sober. I have been to church three times, if you don't count funerals; I have driven a million miles without tags, licenses, or brakes; and I believe that cream gravy is a vegetable and that majorettes are a sign God wants us to be happy.

What I had never done is doctor a cold, or meet with a teacher, or do any of the others things—which, truthfully, would have bored me unto death—that real fathers do.

I never wanted to be judge, jury, and executioner to a boy.

I never wanted the moral authority, which, of course, I had no currency to buy, anyway.

But a stepfather, now, a stepfather is no one's judge.

He's more like a paralegal.

He knows some law, and can even quote some law, but nobody really gets nervous when they stand before a paralegal. And besides, everyone knows who the high court is.

She, the mother, not only knows the law, she rewrites it, twists it, spindles and mutilates it, and we best just by God live with that or we boys, stepfather and stepson, will suffer. But worse, she expects me to be like her, solid and thoughtful and mean as a striped snake, but mostly she expects me to be that most hated of all things.

Mature.

The worst it got was last Halloween.

The woman has a sickness for holidays. It takes her three weeks to decorate a Christmas tree, and she leaves it up until Easter. At Halloween, she and the boy covered the yard with ghoulish decorations, fashioning a grave in the shrubbery, a giant spider web in the magnolia tree, and lights everywhere. The worst of it was a gruesome, battery-operated specter that screamed and clicked its teeth together whenever anyone triggered its motion sensor. She hung it from the light fixture in the doorway, so that every child—every child—would set it off.

"You have two choices," she told me the evening of October 31. "You can either take the boy trick-or-treating, or you can stay here and pass out candy."

Passing out candy meant that I was in charge of the candy. That would be like being in charge of majorettes.

"I will be the candy man," I said.

But she could drain the fun out of anything.

"If you are in charge of handing out the candy, you can't do anything else," she said. "You can't be distracted, and most of all . . . LISTEN TO ME . . . you cannot, cannot cook. No cooking."

"OK," I said.

"And watch the dog," she told me. The dog is a big, stinky, neurotic product of the union of a black Lab and a traveling man, and likes to bark and growl menacingly at chipmunks and toddlers, but has never bitten anything except fleas.

"OK," I said.

Now go away, I thought.

She and the boy—at least I think it was the boy, since he was dressed as a grim reaper—left to beg for candy, and I settled in. I had a remote control and a giant pumpkin full of Butterfinger miniatures. I sat down and searched for educational programming, or anything with fangs and cleavage.

It went well. The doorbell rang every five minutes. I handed out gobs of candy, and ate only one candy bar per dispensation. Then I got hungry. A grilled cheese would be nice, I thought.

What happened next was not my fault. I never should have been left unsupervised in the first place.

The grilled cheese was toasting nicely when the doorbell rang. I went to hand out candy, which took only a few minutes, but long enough for the grilled cheese to catch on fire. This alarmed the dog, so she was already pretty well on edge when the doorbell rang again. She began to bark and growl. Then off went the fire alarm, which I tried to disarm, but it was too high to reach. I ran to get a stepladder but it was in hiding, so I grabbed a broom and ran back to the foyer, where the dog was all but running in circles, the smoke was roiling, and the alarm was chirping. The children at the door, knowing that this was a gold mine for candy because of the excessive decorations, jabbed the doorbell every other second, and it was more than I could stand. I beat the hell out of the smoke detector, but they must make those things pretty good, because even as the plastic flew around the room the WHOOP, WHOOP, WHOOP screamed into my skull. As I swung at it, I triggered the motion-activated ghoulie, which began to laugh manically.

Then I snatched open the door. The children took one look—at me, at the big dog with hackles raised, at the swinging ghoulie—and backed away. It would have been a better story if they had screamed and run for it, but I guess the draw of the candy was still strong, even in the din. One little girl's face clouded, and I'm pretty sure she went home and cried.

I told the woman what happened. There was no hiding it, really. The smoke alarm was scattered across three rooms, the house hung with black smoke, the dog still breathing hard.

She lectured me, and gave me the look. We all know the look.

"I told you," she said, and I do not know why, honestly, women believe that will somehow head off a disaster. It has not, since the dawn of time.

I went to my easy chair, to heal.

The boy walked up, patted me, and gave me some candy.

Then, just before bedtime, he gave me some more.

I could have lost this lottery. I could have gotten a pampered snot, which I was certain I would get, since all I saw in the malls and movie theaters and schools seemed to be pampered snots, little princes and princesses who thought a bad day was a day without a latte. But instead I got a boy with a good heart and a sense of humor, and all I can do is hope that I do not ruin him, somehow, by being me. I taught him some bad things, on purpose. I taught him how to throw a punch, because he asked me to. I taught him a few other things, things I hope will help him survive.

But the frightening thing is what I have taught him without meaning to. I had believed that, because he had a real father, there would be no osmosis, no learning from me just by watching me live.

I am prone, when under attack by the woman, to joke that I will "just leave."

"I," I say dramatically, "am the only one holding this family together."

The other day, the boy was under attack for some minor transgression.

"Well, I'll just leave," he said. "And I'm the only one holding this family together."

I hope there is something good, some scrap of something I have dropped that he picks up, something that will make him a good boy and a good man.

But that might be hoping for too much. He is already a good boy, a fine boy. He is the kind of boy who walks over and says hello when a boy at school is being made fun of. Last basketball season, when a boy on his team had been forgotten by the coach, he got up from his place on the bench and walked over to tell the coach that the boy had not played, risking the coach's displeasure. He does things like that, all the time.

Me, I just make him grin every now and then.

I am, after all, just the stepfather. Not evil, not good, just getting by.

I joke, sometimes, that the worst thing about having no blood offspring is that there will be no one to come and see me in the county home when I am old.

I have a fear. I have seen the workers in such places put little party hats on the heads of the old people there. I don't want that. I would hate that.

But with no blood kin to come see me, who would stop them?

"I wouldn't let them put no hats on you, Ricky," the boy said.

NINE TIMES (AMONG COUNTLESS OTHERS) I'VE THOUGHT ABOUT THE PEOPLE WHO CAME BEFORE US IN MY BRIEF CAREER AS A FATHER

ANTHONY DOERR

1.

We're in New Jersey, my wife is pregnant with twins, and I'm walking home from the library on a dark and relentlessly cold afternoon. The row of brick-and-siding apartments we live in comes up on my left, originally built as barracks, old railings and old steps, a capsized tricycle in a snowbank, door after identical door, window after identical window, apartments built with GIs in mind, their cigarettes, their wives, their red-white-and-blue children.

I have spent the morning reading about some

footprints in Tanzania, seventy impressions fossilized across twenty yards, left by three bipedal hominids, trudging barefoot through volcanic ash, three and a half million years ago. Two runty adults and someone smaller.

"It is tempting to see them as a man, a woman, and a child," Mary Leakey, who found the footprints, writes. One of the walkers veers to the left momentarily before continuing on. The spatters of raindrops have been preserved in the mud around the tracks.

A wet day, a volcano erupting nearby, mud pressing up between their toes, and someone—a father?—has a second thought, or stoops to pick up something, or looks back at what has been left behind. Then they're gone.

In New Jersey twenty yards of ice crunch beneath my shoes. I climb our three steps. Through the front window I can see Shauna inside, bearing her huge abdomen from kitchen to couch, her feet swollen bright red, her body stretched to its limits. The two creatures that will be our sons are crammed against the underside of her skin, twisting, she tells me sometimes, like snakes.

I stand in the cold and a flight of geese cruises overhead, honking above the trees, and I think: my sons might see Paris, Cape Town, Saigon; they might get in fights, swim the English Channel, cook banana pancakes, join an army, fix computers. They might kill someone, save someone, make someone. They might leave tracks in the mud to last three and a half million years.

2.

Owen is born with acid reflux and has to be given Zantac every few hours. Henry has to be strapped to an apnea monitor the size of a VCR that squeals like a smoke detector any time his breathing pauses or the adhesive on a diode slips off his chest. The doctor makes us put caffeine in his milk to stimulate his breathing.

They are five pounds, fraternal, wormy-armed, more blankets than flesh, no eyebrows, no kneecaps, and they need to be fed every three hours: three, six, nine, noon, three, six, nine, midnight. Most nights I take the shift from midnight to three a.m. I change diapers, fill bottles, listen to the BBC. The traffic light out the back window makes its mindless revolutions, green, yellow, red, green, yellow, red. No cars pass for hours.

One April night, two in the morning, I come out of a half dream on the sofa. Henry and Owen are in their Moses baskets on the carpet beside me. They're lying on their backs, wearing cotton hats, eyes open, neither making a sound, their gazes trained on some middle distance in the gloom. Henry's monitor flashes green, green, green. Owen shifts his eyes back and forth. In the dimness I can watch expressions flow gently across their faces; they assume enchanted, glassy, mysterious looks, then frowns, then their eyes widen. They are partly me and partly their mother, but they are partly strangers, too, tiny emissaries from forgotten generations, repositories of ancient DNA; there are genes in them from Shauna's great-great-grandfather, from my great-great-grandmother. Who are they? They are entirely new human beings, genetic combinations the universe has never seen before and will never see again. They are little brothers arrived from the mists of genealogy to lie in wicker baskets on the floor of our apartment.

As I lean over them, watching, they blink up at me at the exact same second.

3.

We move to Rome, Italy, for a year. I research stratigraphy, excavations, the accumulation of sediment. Mud, ash, sand, pollutants, and bits of architecture rain down over the city at a rate of something like half an inch per year. Emperor Hadrian would have entered the Pantheon by climbing stairs; now we have to brake the big double stroller as we coast down toward it. Today's Romans cannot dig a subway tunnel, swimming pool, or basement without stopping construction to call in archaeologists. In some sites researchers find ten, fifteen, twenty different layers of human settlements.

Emperor Nero built a three-hundred-room, one-hundred-acre party villa in the first century C.E., and fifteen centuries later it had become a series of underground caverns. Renaissance painters used to rappel into the rooms to study the frescoes by torchlight.

On Thanksgiving morning I take Henry and Owen to a Roman landmark known as the Protestant Cemetery. Inside the walls are umbrella pines, box hedges, headstones in clusters. The pyramid of Cestius, a magistrate's tomb a hundred years older than Nero's party villa, looms half inside the walls, its marble-faced blocks mottled with weather and lichen. Crumpled leaves roll across the paths, and big, dusky cypress trees creak like masts.

John Keats, whose grave we've come to see, is buried near the corner. The stone reads:

This Grave
contains all that was Mortal,
of a
YOUNG ENGLISH POET,

> *Who on his Death Bed,*
> *in the Bitterness of his Heart,*
> *at the Malicious Power of his Enemies,*
> *Desired*
> *these Words to be engraven on his Tomb Stone*
> *Here lies One*
> *Whose Name was writ in Water.*

The tombs sleep heavily in the grass. Henry and Owen squirm against their stroller straps. I gaze down rows of memorials into silent corners. We are hemmed by brickwork, ivy, history; we are the only living people in the cemetery. I begin to feel outnumbered. A breeze drags through the trees, the lawn.

On the bus home I hold Owen at the window, put my thumb in Henry's palm. For every living person on earth, I wonder, how many dead people are in the ground? Do they care that we walk around on top of their heads? Do our ancestors follow us around throughout the day, and do they shake their heads at us when we repeat their mistakes?

We get off the bus in Monteverde; I wheel the boys home. In the old cage elevator they smile into the mirror from beneath their hoods. We rise through the stairwell. Owen reaches for the bakery bag in my fist. Henry fumbles for the keys.

I heap the boys onto their mother. They laugh and laugh. We eat croissants; we drink pineapple juice from a box. Yesterday, Shauna tells me, Owen clapped his hands twice. Henry can now roll halfway across the room.

It is a strange thing to bring five-month-old twins to a city stamped so indelibly with age and ruin. Every street corner rings with decline: decay of republic, disintegration of empire, the ongoing crumble of the church—decay is the river that runs through town, driving along beneath the bridges, roiling in the rapids beside the hospitals on Tiber Island. And yet nearly everyone we pass smiles at the twins. Grown men, in suits, stop and crouch over the stroller and croon. Older men in particular. "Che carini. Che belli." What cuties. What beauties.

In the States, practically every time someone would stop us on the street or in the grocery store, they'd gesture at the stroller and say, "Twins? Bet you have your hands full." They'd mean well, of course, but to be reminded of something you can't forget is debilitating. I prefer the Italian mothers who lean over the stroller and whisper, "So beautiful," the smiles of passing children, the old Roman who stopped us today outside the cemetery and grinned at Henry and Owen before shaking my hand and saying, with a half bow, "Complimenti." My compliments.

4.

We take our sons to Sardinia for a week. Early May is early for tourists and everything is closed and hardly anybody is on the beaches. The big resort hotel below our rented condominium is completely empty, just a lonely bartender named Claudio and a white stretch of beach and the wind blowing our footprints into dunes.

Henry and Owen are fourteen months old; they run laps in the sand, half-drunk with the pleasure of such a forgiving surface, tipping past us and cackling, "Go, go, go." Around and around they go, carrying their Legos or water bottles or balls, wiping out every twenty or thirty seconds. Shauna lifts them, kisses them, brushes them off. In a heartbeat they are running again.

Despite some telephone wires and the little hotel, this still seems like a place the first Sardinians would recognize: the flies, the thorns, the big granite hills crumbling and baking all day, the hours folding over the inlets like fog; the stars and sea, the caps of the rocks that show themselves at low tide before going under again—all of it has been there since before any of this had a name, and all of it will still be here after the names are forgotten.

Gulls soar hundreds of feet above us like confetti. The sun swings over the hills in a low, smooth arch.

Inside, Claudio makes us caffe lattes, hot and foamy and perfect, and he wheels a little round table toward the boys with great ceremony and busies himself filling tiny coffee cups with foamed milk and sprinkling chocolate on top. The boys sit strapped into their backpack carriers and show varying degrees of interest. Mostly Henry just wants the spoon so he can drop it and hear it clink on the tile and then peer down at it and say, "Uh-oh."

In the evening we carry our boys up the hill to their port-a-cribs and the maquis fills with night sounds: the wind, some insects, an owl. A herd of goats tramps along the cape road in the darkness, and their wooden-sounding bells clank softly.

After everyone is asleep, I hike back down to the abandoned hotel for a drink and tell Claudio that his resort is very beautiful. I am his only customer. He shows me a snapshot of his daughters, who live on the other side of the island, in Alghero, an hour and a half away. They are two and four years old, one blond, one dark.

We grapple forward in my sledgehammer Italian. Claudio's father was a fisherman. He does not like George W. Bush. He sees his wife and daughters one day a week.

"Is this common?" I ask.

"It is Sardinia," he says, and then says more, but I don't un-derstand it. I nod anyway. Claudio chews his lip, and folds and refolds his bar towel into a perfect white square.

"Is it difficult?" I ask. "Not seeing your daughters?"

He nods, and I nod, both of us at the limits of our fluencies, and we look up at the TV where two Indian men wrangle a cobra into a basket. When I look back at Claudio, tall and trim in his vest and collar, there are tears on his cheeks.

5.

We move back to the United States. Idaho. Suburbs, exurbs, brown foothills, and long-drawn skies. Welcome to Amer-ica: in our first week back I drive to six ATMs, a bank, and a check-cashing agency; I spend an hour on hold with someone in a magazine-subscription department; I wait two hours on the leather sofa in a car dealership to get a "check engine" light turned off in our car.

We buy a house with a slate stone fireplace. One crystalline, frosty night, when they are not quite two years old, Henry and Owen refuse to go to bed; they sprint laps around the family room singing, "Chasing! Chasing!" and Owen chants, "Jump, jump!" and they grab opposite ends of a dog leash and perform short-lived matches of tug-of-war. It is after eight p.m. when Owen jumps off the sofa, trips, and strikes his forehead hard enough against the fireplace that a piece of stone, the size of a dime, chips off. The sound is that of dropping a small block of wood onto a concrete floor.

Shauna has Owen in her arms in an instant. His screams are loud and edged with fear: a new kind of scream. The fireplace has gouged a hole in his forehead just below his hairline—it is the size of a paperclip and a quarter of an inch deep. There is enough blood that, by the time we have strapped Owen into his car seat, every square inch of a dish towel we've clamped over the wound is wet.

We drop off Henry at his grandmother's. The examination room at the hospital is glaring, fluorescent. Owen is brave. A nurse numbs his forehead. Teletubbies wander across a television mounted in the corner. The doctor says it is good news that Owen did not get knocked out. He checks his eyes, his ears; he says our son is going to be fine.

There is dried blood on Shauna's hands, arms, and T-shirt. I'm thinking how lucky we are; I'm thinking about cholera, dysentery, fevers, oxcarts, and open wells—all of history's child destroyers. If you had a baby in Chicago in 1870, there was a 50 percent chance he'd die before he reached age five. If you had a baby in London in 1750, there was a 66 percent chance he'd die before he reached age five. For the entire history of humanity, except for the past, say, eighty years, parents were losing every other child. You get to keep Henry, but Owen's got to go. That's how things were for Phoenician dads, Babylonian dads, Aztec dads, Cherokee dads, for pioneer dads, and for caveman dads. The earth brims with the bones of children.

Just two days before this trip to the emergency room, Shauna was watching the boys play with ice in the backyard when she turned to me and said, "If we lost them now, after getting them this far . . ."

Instead of a needle and thread, the doctor uses superglue on Owen's forehead. One gloved hand pinches the wound, the other floods it with epoxy. Owen watches the Teletubbies, holding his mother's finger in his fist.

Afterward we drive home in the frozen darkness and pet the dog and scrub the blood off the kitchen floor and put our son to sleep next to his brother.

6.

A brown disk of glue clings to Owen's forehead for months. When it finally peels off, the scar beneath is smooth and forked and pale. He and Henry turn two; they become muscular, long-haired, frighteningly smart. Their enthusiasm for the world astounds. Everything warrants investigation: spiderwebs, thornbushes, potato bugs. They crouch in our driveway, poking strips of sun-softened tar with their fingers.

"Boys," I say, "let's go. I've told you three times." I stand over them, clap my hands. "You guys need to learn how to pay attention."

They don't even bother to look up. Usually I would grab them, wrestle them into the car. But today I pause. Whoever says adults are better than children at paying attention is wrong; we adults are too busy filtering out the world, hurrying to some appointment or another, paying *no* attention. Our kids are the ones discovering new continents all day long. Sometimes, looking at them, I feel as if Henry and Owen live permanently in that resplendent state of awareness that grown-ups reach only when our cars are sliding on ice through a red light, or our airplane is thudding through turbulence.

The boys drive their fingers deeper into the tar, then pull back and laugh as the tar rebounds to its original shape. They try jabbing sticks into it; they take off their shoes and press their toes into it. I try to imagine my great-great-grandfather at age two. Did he also think poking at tar—or squishing palmfuls of mud, or throwing pebbles into a creek—was the greatest pastime imaginable?

Eventually I coax the boys into the car and drive them to a park and release them like hounds into the grass. They sprint toward the playground equipment and yell, "Running!

Running!" As I watch them, the shadows of leaves flicker over the grass and the afternoon seems so precious that I wonder, only partly in jest, if I ought not to spend the rest of the week doing only this: watching my sons, watching the light falling through the trees. As if every minute spent doing something else would be a minute wasted.

7.

Soon Owen and Henry talk in complete sentences, carry backpacks to preschool, and want to know if the Elks Hospital is a hospital for elks or for "big people." And they have passions, hundreds of them: Tinkertoys, Gwen Stefani, puddle stomping, garden tomatoes, floor puzzles, ice cream, Elmer's glue. They find letters of the alphabet everywhere they look: Os in noodles, Ts in bathroom tiles, Xs in the poos our dog drops in the grass.

At work, as a kind of procrastination, I start reading Herodotus's *Histories*. Here he is on the Egyptians:

> *When the rich give a party and the meal is finished, a man carries round amongst the guests a wooden image of a corpse in a coffin, carved and painted to look as much like the real thing as possible, and anything from eighteen inches to three feet long; he shows it to each guest in turn and says: "Look upon this body as you drink and enjoy yourself; for you will be just like it when you are dead."*

An hour after I read that passage, I learn that Henry and Owen's great-great-aunt Dorothy has died. I spend the next few days thinking of Dorothy: who loved to sift through waist-high stacks of mail-order catalogs, who went for long walks inside the mall on winter mornings with her friends, who had a gold Saturn SL2 with six hundred miles on it. Who was child-less but must have had some love stories folded tight inside her heart. What men loved Dorothy Lyskawa? Certainly some: she wore trim dresses and stylish skirts and crimson lipstick and worked as a secretary at Owens Corning and would pile onto the corporate plane and take notes at meetings and then rove New York City with her friends. And yet who stayed unmar-ried, who lived in Toledo, Ohio, all her life, the gray Februar-ies and the big, brown Maumee sliding along beside the glass factories.

Again I wonder: Is there a heaven? Some place where our lost relatives peer down at us from the fleecy rims of clouds and know our hearts? And know each other's?

What's the alternative? That when we die all our stories disappear? Are our private lives so inconsequential?

Maybe consequence is something you have to create. Con-sequence is doing something like Aunt Dorothy did in the first years after my grandfather died, before I was born, when my mother and father lived in Meadowlawn, Ohio, with two ba-bies and one car and no money and Dad wore homemade suits to sales training sessions and Mom rode a bicycle with both kids to get groceries. Dorothy would slip Mom a twenty-dollar bill every time she visited. And twenty dollars, my mother says, "bought a lot of groceries back then."

Dorothy never got to see Henry and Owen.

8.

Shauna signs up our boys for dance camp. The evening after the first day, Henry breaks his arm in two places. Without his twin brother, facing down the enormity of dance camp by himself, Owen spends the entirety of day two with the front of his polo shirt clenched in his teeth. He hides on the outskirts of the activities, trying but failing to follow directions. He tiptoes through the songs, shy, afraid, the front of his little shirt dark with saliva and wrenched into wrinkles. Twice he is sent to the "growing line" for talking when he shouldn't.

Owen and Henry haven't spent a night apart since conception, and as I watch Owen chew his shirt to a pulp I wonder what his life would be like if his brother were permanently removed from it. Doesn't every little twin assume—wrongly!—that the world must naturally contain his twin? And on what awful day do they learn that the truth is the opposite?

"Even lovers," Annie Dillard writes, "even twins, are strangers who will love and die alone."

After snack time, with half an hour to go, the dance-campers take a walk around the block. And though there are probably twenty kids in the class, Jon Jon, one of the instructors, a kind-faced drummer with a beard and ponytail, who already seems to know every child's name, makes a point of finding Owen and holding his hand.

Jon Jon and Owen start off at the back of the column of children, Jon Jon leaning over now and then to hear if Owen has anything to say.

When they come back, Owen hugs my leg. His shirt-front is twisted and wet but it is no longer in his teeth. Jon Jon smiles. "He reminds me of my son," he says. "He notices everything."

9.

It's September. I'm sitting with the boys in loungers at the neighborhood pool. They are three and a half years old. We're eating Wheat Thins. Twenty hours ago their drum-playing dance-camp instructor, Jon Jon, had his whole, unknowable, interesting life abbreviated to two sentences:

Thirty-three-year-old Jon Stravers of Boise, Idaho, was driving the sedan. He and three-year-old Jonah Stravers were both killed.

Henry says, "You always say the pool is warm when it is cold, Daddy."

It's on my mind again, our ancestors, Mary Leakey's footprints, Keats's epitaph, Herodotus's Egyptians, the appalling brevity of our lives. We twist and swim and fold back into the invisible; our names are written in water.

How could the world possibly be better off without Jon Jon? How could anyone ever argue that his was a superfluous life? And what about Jonah's life, and shouldn't a prayer be sent up, too, for the now-ended twenty-six-year-old life of Bryant Hays of Sussex, Wisconsin, who (investigators suspect) had some alcohol or drugs in him and sent his pickup, grille first, across the eastbound lane and into Jon Jon and Jonah's sedan?

There are so many lives that deserve prayers in this: Jonah's mother, Jon Jon's parents, Bryant Hays's parents, the woman who might have poured Bryant Hays his beer that night, who might have delayed his departure four or five seconds by dropping his change: a quarter and a nickel and a penny rolling down the wood floor behind some bar. "Sorry," she might have said. "Wait one second," she might have said, and that one second might have been enough—enough to set Bryant Hays on his ruinous trajectory: father and son, Jon Jon and Jonah, hurtling east along a mountain highway, Bryant Hays climbing into his truck, turning the key, starting west.

All those lives, all those people—each of us operates at a vertex of a vast, three-dimensional, crisscrossing network of relationships. Son, brother, husband, father, friend, teacher. No life is superfluous. And yet thousands go out the door every hour.

Look upon this body as you drink and enjoy yourself; for you will be just like it when you are dead.

There goes Mary Leakey's family of three; there goes John Keats; there goes Aunt Dorothy; there goes Jon Jon Stravers and poor, sweet, three-year-old Jonah. The great network vibrates and swings as lives are plucked out of it, one after another.

When you watch your kids begin to grow up, you cannot help but feel your impermanence more acutely; you cannot help but see how you are one link in a very long chain of parents and children, and that the best thing you have ever done and ever will do is to extend that chain, to be a part of something greater than yourself. That's really what it means to be a father—to be continually reminded that you are taking part in something much larger than your own terrifyingly short life.

A reef of clouds builds in the west, so gray they look almost black. Owen finishes his Wheat Thins and takes the pool key off our lounge chair and walks barefoot across to the gate and stands on his tiptoes while he tries to work the key into the lock.

Henry says, "I love Wheat Thins, Daddy," and crunches another one, spilling crumbs across his towel, and the wind blows into the valley and the sun slinks down into reds and purples and the sky takes on that deep, clarion blue of a September evening and we pack up our towels and swimsuits and walk home as the first cold air of the season slides down from the mountains.

FOR ELLA

MICHAEL THOMAS

Considering that, all hatred driven hence,
The soul recovers radical innocence
And learns at last that it is self-delighting,
Self-appeasing, self-affrighting,
And that its own sweet will is Heaven's will . . .
　　　　　—W. B. Yeats, "A Prayer for My Daughter"

Dear Ella,

You have just turned seven, and over the past
few months—some of the darkest in my life—I
have begun to understand that you trust me, you
have faith in me, you love me.

Darkness: it would seem that this time in
my life would be anything but. I've received the
critical attention that most writers long for; I've
been married to your beautiful mother for more
than fifteen years; I have two healthy, handsome

sons who paint, play piano, run and jump with grace and power; I have you, my daughter, who every day looks at me as though I was the greatest man she has ever seen. But darkness has a knack for eluding, or extinguishing, light, and it comes in many forms. Like my father, and his, I have at different times in my life been lost in it. It is an awful place to be, and when I search inside myself for some resource—a map, a light—I find the same night as the one outside.

My condition is exacerbated by the distance I feel between myself and those I love—the irony being that surviving my childhood has made me into someone who doesn't know how to enjoy what I have now. And perhaps the greater irony is that what I need to survive my adulthood—innocence—is what I, as a child, relinquished.

But this life, now, requires an opposite trait, or at least necessitates that we shield something so fragile as innocence from what we witness daily—foster children subsisting on pancake batter and fiberglass, cities drowned by storm, paddy wagons unloading their cargo of chained brown men onto the sidewalk of the Atlantic Avenue jail—so that the impact upon us is somehow lessened.

I wonder how you remember it—last summer when the cat *disappeared*—how you'll recall it later. She was taken, an alleged case of mistaken identity, from our stoop, where she'd been basking for the last twelve years. You, your brothers, and mom were away, and I was charged with finding her before you got home. I lied to you on the phone, told you I couldn't come to the beach to watch you *"not run from the waves"* that were over your head because I had work to do.

You've been carrying her around since you could toddle. Mini: elegant, lean, and black. She'd see you wobbling over to her—half dozing on the couch—arms out, as though imploring her to jump into them. She wouldn't, but, rather, would stand, stretch, and wait. Grown-up willful cat, the boys never troubled her, but she'd let you scoop her up by the chest and belly, then teeter around the room with her until you were ready to put her down.

I stalked the neighborhood, postering every nonliving surface within thirty square blocks of our house to which packing tape could adhere. I rang doorbells, stopped strangers, and called to her through open windows. "She's my daughter's best friend," I began telling people. I knew I had to find her even if it meant ransacking every home in Brooklyn.

After four days I did—near dusk—that cat you love, who sounds more ducklike than feline when she meows; who now trots to you, purring. And with a strange sense of pride that I haven't felt since I was a boy, I called your mother with the news.

"We knew you'd find her."

"We? You told her?"

"I let it slip."

"So, she's been hysterical all this time?"

"No."

"Really?"

"She was a little sad at first—no tears, though—then she just said, 'Daddy will find her. My daddy can fix anything.' And you did."

I've been trying to write this to you—for you—but I'm of different minds: I'm sorry that I feel the need to reveal any intimate detail that has gone into making me the father you now know, but also that I haven't written it sooner—that

I've withheld that same information. Perhaps it's because I've never been good at speaking intimately to anyone, and at this time, a letter is what I have to offer. And writing seems to have an indelible quality that spoken words do not.

I don't know to whom I'm writing, though. Certainly not the girl I can still easily lift over my head so she can touch the ceiling, but who is so unbearably ticklish she cackles and wriggles dangerously up there; who wraps herself around my leg to hitch a ride down the hall. Although I can see your chocolate eyes, your soft and wild ringlets—umber to gold—to say that I can fully envision the woman who may someday read this limits you to what I can conceive.

A great author wrote, "I saw that even my love for those closest to me had become only an attempt to love," and I worried, last August, that my frantic search for the cat was just such an *attempt*. I have, for most of your life, been hiding from you, moving to empty rooms when I could. And my *attempts to love* come in the form of elaborate meals, prepared to loud music, along with manic dances by the kitchen sink and other *feats of fatherhood*. I'm not saying that what we've done together wasn't, isn't, real. As I said before, I'm beginning to understand that you love me—feel it—and that feeling frightens me, as it yanks me back to a time it wasn't safe to do so.

Your father has had a strange life: some of it I inherited, some of it I made. "Strange": what an imprecise word. I've used it a lot, though, allegedly to protect you from what lies behind it, but the euphemism is really a feeble effort to obscure things I'd rather not review: the different times a police officer left a bruise on me, or drew blood, when I was a boy; or now, on the subway, how sometimes when I'm without some badge of distinction—a tie, a child, or a white person—women of all age and hue pull their bags to them when I pass by.

It seems reasonable—not to trust your innocence to another. And practical, wise even, not to possess any at all. Early in his autobiography, W. E. B. DuBois recounts the time when his valentine note was spurned. And I can crush most of my young life into a metaphor for unrequited affections. And not only for me; it seemed that the confessional missives of everyone I knew had been returned to sender.

The world I grew up in was oddly similar to the one you see now. I remember long lines at the gas station and the unemployment office. There were junkies in the park and pedophiles in the bushes. There was a war on TV. I was a dreamy boy who, like my father, was oblivious and ill-equipped to negotiate the perils of the world. There are old photos of me—you wouldn't recognize your dad—in which I look unreasonably happy. Most of the time I was. I listened to birds sing, and their melodies, in my head, attached to words that I couldn't quite pick out, but I felt confident that if I just sang, it would all make sense—"it" being the junked car, the weedy hedgerow, the lonely mother, the missing father, and the uncertain future. But the song never worked: things stayed as they were—grew worse. The car remained in the driveway, up on blocks. And my father's domestic and professional failure—his hideous emasculation—was completed. And I could begin to clearly see my future—the grim one that had already been enacted by many poor, black men whose one asset was the "radical innocence" of which Yeats spoke.

I watched my mother—your nana, who is the bravest, toughest person I have ever known—struggle alone to

raise your uncle, your aunt, and me. She'd left her home
in Virginia when she wasn't much more than a girl herself.
(Now, when I see the young women at the college where
I teach, or in line at the movies down the street, I think,
my mother: how could this be?) She endured the multiple
humiliations of being a poor, single, black woman among
people who had little use for her except as a domestic, or as a
convenient receptacle for their pieties and their pity.

But your nana paid them no mind. And I would secretly
think, *Why do you do that? Why keep exposing yourself?* And
as for me, my concerns weren't even *practical*. I wanted to
tell everyone about the secrets in the language of the birds.
In later photos of me, I'm a little stoic—near dead-eyed,
probably more familiar to you. I was only a little older than
you are now (*how can this be?*) when I realized that I had to be
hard. I went from being a dreamy boy to being, outwardly, a
reasonable one, and eventually, that reason migrated into me,
until that area of me which housed those secret languages, the
answers to the world's problems, was overrun, and I couldn't
access it anymore, even if I wanted to.

This letter isn't a cautionary litany for you—brown girl,
brown woman. What you will face—racism, sexism,
objectification, fascistic beauty *standards*, which in the simple
mind render you ugly or even invisible—I cannot protect you
from. The TVs are on, the hot irons are fired, the billboards
sit high, and the newspaper rattles our door every morning.
The conditions they advertise, report on, and even celebrate
have preceded you and, regrettably, will outlast you, but that
doesn't mean that they will, while you live, defeat you. The
only antidotes against these afflictions are faith and love.

I'm sorry I have to use these words; myriad individuals

bandy them about in common, tired ways. That, however, doesn't make the words common, or strip them of their power. You will hear people twist them for their own purposes. I have. Regardless: faith is the "belief in, devotion to, or trust in somebody or something, especially without logical proof." And love, "an intense feeling of tender affection and compassion." Rather than cling to definitions or popular notions, think of them as callings. We do not choose who or what calls, but rather whether or not we'll listen, answer, and go—enter conditions that can, beautifully, dovetail into one.

Love: I've always been terrified of revealing those parts of me that need it—emotionally limping through the world, favoring the damaged, overburdening the well. I have always felt myself too broken to be loved, an identity formed long before I met you. "Hearts are not had as a gift but hearts are earned / By those that are not entirely beautiful." And I've believed my only chance of earning any heart was through Herculean labors and Olympian distance, protecting my beloved simultaneously from a world of hurt and loss and from my own jagged edges, my rages, my mourning the parts in me I thought long dead.

I don't remember, clearly, the things one would expect a father to—first teeth, steps, and words—the milestones we use to somehow identify our offspring's qualities, their peculiarities, their charms. I remember when you cut your hair, and when you set it on fire—that acrid smell on a cool afternoon. I remember, will remember, your quiet laugh, the patter of your sparkly shoes on the secret bluestone path through the church garden that led to your kindergarten.

I also remember the top floor of the old house in the

early afternoon, ambient light about to warm the window
at the top of the landing. I was coming up the stairs and
your mother had just hung up the phone. She was standing
in the hallway, on the other side of the shaky rail. I stopped
three steps from the landing. "There's a real chance of Down
syndrome," she said, paused, and leaned against the wall.
"That's what the screening seems to say."

What I wanted to do was sit and rock and weep and
moan, not because you might have Down syndrome, but
because there was nothing I could do. It's a shattering
moment, when you realize how stiff and empty you may
be, and find yourself stranded in a storm. I remember your
mother, watching me try to be strong, but perhaps I should've
done something else—shake or cry—that would have told
her that I trusted her, and knew how much she loved me. But
I recited some statistics—numbers as a balm—as I walked to
her, slowly, up the stairs. She asked, "We're having this baby,
no matter what?"

"Yes," I said, at the top.

We waited twenty-four days to find out—ten until the
amniocentesis date, and then two weeks for the results—
twenty-four days of not knowing, of trying to calculate,
manipulate, do anything but feel. I used to prepare, in school,
for my father's Sunday visit. All week long I'd practice not
hoping, snuff out expectation. Marking time. I'd try to
outlast the clock's second hand—stare down its spasmodic
ticks—get so close to it that I'd forget I wanted the day to be
over. All so my Sundays by the window wouldn't end with
heartbreak. And if he did come, he'd get the same deadeye
every cop or teacher got.

You never miss your water . . . Ella, those three-odd weeks I
was a desert of reason. I should be clearer: I felt for you. I felt

for your mother. I can *feel for* another, but that's relatively easy. I don't know how to be *felt for* by another, to expose myself to their scrutiny, *truly*, without bracing beforehand for the slap of their judgment. I lost this quality because I ignored it and let other parts of me—what I mistook for reason or wisdom or maturity—inform my decisions: how to be; how much of myself to expose and invest in moments with those I claimed to love. But what is love when it isn't informed by innocence? What is faithless love?

One of the last acts of desperate men is prayer. So I prayed, not for some conventional *wellness* or *health*—my child would be my child, regardless—but for strength. What a paradox: alone, on my knees, asking for the strength to change things, the strength to endure, the power not to bend. *I pray so I won't need to pray*—hardly humble. In supplication one should experience one's greatest vulnerability, be open to faith. Only a cynic makes requests for power while kneeling.

The test results discounted the screening. And although I was present for your mother—through her hypertension, your early arrival, your early lungs, and the umbilical cord knot—I was frightened, but also hardened to the wish that for a time I could be wrapped in your mother's arms. But you were the tiniest of things, less than half the size of your beloved cat. You couldn't get enough air. All you did in the ICU was sleep among the tubes and wires. I rubbed your belly—only two fingers—thought for a moment about how good it felt. And for that moment, I was the boy with the birds again—"all hatred driven hence." Then he had to disappear.

I pride myself on being someone who rejects our culture's stifling conventions, but I'm so typically male. This trait would simply be boring if it wasn't so dangerous to me and to those I love. I have wrestled with your brothers too much, tried to make them what I thought they needed to be, as though they'd been born *ill-equipped*. Frightened, faithless, I've never trusted that my love and presence would be enough. Ugh, my manhood; my insistence on being hard, on believing that being so, and making my boys hard, could profit us anything worthwhile. But this hardness stokes whatever spark of resentment they may have for me, forces them to move secretly under my cold scrutiny, fuels their desire to escape it; wounded boys with matches in their father's tinderbox house. When they have left, and that house is burned, this hardness I have taught will serve them only in their ability not to feel for me—not to rue the distance between us. I'm a fool, because I know: my father helped make me hard, but I still miss him every day.

Your grandfather wasn't innocent, but he was an ignorant man—a lonely man, and not just in the end, but most of his life. He spent much of it, at least the part I'm aware of, clutching that ignorance. He had neither the humility to ask for help nor the strength to help himself. When he was dying, I didn't bring you with us for that last visit, although you wanted to see the man you'd met once as an infant, a second time as a toddler. I didn't want you to be haunted by visions of the gaunt man—cleft chest, toothless—by his desperate rooms with oxygen tanks and cigarettes, or by the face I'd have to wear to greet him: the one with the dead eyes. Insane: my punishing him with a more pernicious strain of his original sin of absence; the one stoic son and *his* poor sons, lost as to how to emulate such blank cruelty.

But he was already there, roaming through your head. You mourned a man you didn't know. You made me that book: *I Didn't Want Him to Die*—held it up, crying for him, for me. Looking with sad wonder at why I didn't do the same. Radical innocence, I have grown to understand, is not willful ignorance. It exists in spite of what we come to know. It perseveres "while the storm wind howls." It's what allows us to have faith beyond reason, when such faith seems to profit us naught.

O Ella, sometimes my mind is barren and dry. And in the narrow cracks strange weeds grow, which, in time, will strangle the host. I long to recover that radical innocence, the part that believes. I feel myself too much of a burden for a child of any age, but there's something in you that makes me believe and want more than mean survival. Like your maternal grandmother—your namesake—you possess rare grace, fierce intelligence, a resolve that belies your small frame. You have her heart face. You both have those delicate, sloped noses, which make you look wise and young. Like my mother—soul-brown eyes—you will not quit, no matter what. You have a voice that turns a simple word to song. And you have that glow of the recognizable yet unfamiliar. Perhaps it's the influence of so many lines of different folk—African, Celt, Anglo, American Indian—converging, becoming reconciled in one. I should just say I think you are beautiful.

It's taken me seven years to fully feel your love. *Seven years*—a long time for a man, a lifetime for you, waiting for your father. I don't know how much of this letter will resonate with you, or when, but it's as honest as I can be, it's, humbly, what I have. In order to be honest, one must *express or embody the truth.* But I don't know *the* truth. I can only begin, somehow, to move roughly toward my own—what I have tried to keep hidden. When you call I will always answer yes, and come. Perhaps now I have the faith that you will answer mine.

This past winter, just after New Year's, I was sitting in a room in the growing dark when I realized that you were kneeling on the floor. I could see only a few soft coils of your hair. I don't know whether you were trying to hide, but you must have sneaked in, like one of those elegant cats that are always padding through your imagination. I wonder if you remember it, or how you will. You pressed into the small space between the armrest and my side, lay back, and tried to see what I'd been searching for in that gloom. I wanted to send you away—I've grown used to living in the dark, hiding, enduring, hoping you'll never see anything more than the strong man with the funny dances. But you climbed into my lap and stayed with me.

Ella Sweet, I've watched you from the beach as you sprang to the water: a bronze, bright, lissome girl. Not fearless, not ignorant. You know about the crab, the jellyfish, the great white that prowled the waters of Naushon, and the riptide—but you don't yield. First you run, then paddle out beyond your depth, turn and ride the high swells, and coast in on the foam. If I believe I can fix anything and everything for you, that belief is just the edge of a great expanse of love. The farther shore can be gained only through the willingness to be made well by another, to recover that radical innocence so I can love and be loved by you.

Love,
Your father

ZEKE

DAVY ROTHBART

The story of my strange, unexpected foray into fatherhood starts with a girl named Cassandra. Cassandra was a childhood friend of mine who moved away when she was thirteen—to Chicago, then to California, followed by a few brief stints in other places before landing for high school in Pensacola, Florida. She always had a tough go of things growing up—she never really knew her dad, and she and her mom and brother moved around so much that a couple of times she called me crying when she had to pull up stakes again. For the most part, though, she was incredibly upbeat and resilient, a good listener with the kind of sweet laugh that made any troubles in my own life seem to evaporate in an instant.

All through high school we wrote letters back and forth, and when we were twenty we traveled around eastern Europe together, not as romantic partners, just as friends. Every couple of years since, she'll surface in my life by way of a middle-of-the-night phone call. She'll be in the midst of a crisis, and desperate for advice about problems at her work, or with school, or with a boyfriend, or worried about her little brother and his scrapes with the law. She'll say to me, "You're so sensible. You understand how things work. You're so smart about things—not just smart, but wise."

When she calls me with a problem, for a week or so we talk every day, just going through it all, and by then we've figured out an approach. If she's got a manager at work who's overly flirtatious and making her uncomfortable, I'll ask her a bunch of questions: What's he doing exactly? How often? Have other people witnessed his behavior? Who's his supervisor? After all of our discussions, she inevitably feels a whole lot better. We make a plan for some kind of decisive action and I always end up feeling sensible, knowledgeable, and smart—not just smart, but wise.

A few years ago, Cassandra called me all freaked out. She had a new kind of crisis that wasn't like anything I'd ever dealt with before. She was pregnant—almost three months pregnant. The dad was her sometime boyfriend, a hippie wanderer type who went by the name Rainbow Bear, though his California state ID said Paul Danielewski.

She was living in Santa Barbara without any close friends around. She had no one to turn to, she told me, and she sounded upset and confused, torn up about whether she should have this baby or not. "Davy," she said, "tell me what to do and I'll do it."

"Holy shit," I thought.

I ended up doing pretty much what any sensible and smart

(not just smart, but wise) person would do in that situation: I told her I couldn't make the decision for her, but that I would do everything I could to equip her with as much information as possible so that she'd feel better suited to decide on her own what to do.

I knew of one friend of mine who'd had an abortion and had always been haunted by it, and another friend who'd had an abortion and, while sad about it of course, really believed it had been the right thing to do. I also found a woman who'd given her baby up for adoption and another who'd kept her baby and was a single mom. I wanted Cassandra to talk directly to all these women, but she was really shy, and too upset to reach out to strangers. "Those are your friends, not mine," she said. "I'd feel weird calling 'em."

Instead, I talked at great length to each of these women myself, then relayed their stories to Cassandra, careful to present the stories in a balanced way, so that it wouldn't seem like I was favoring one option over another. I told her how one of the women who'd had an abortion still had horrible dreams about it, and how she still—miserably—celebrated the child's birthday each year on the day her baby would have been born. Cassandra gasped. "But the other woman who had an abortion," I told her, "she ended up having a wonderful family many years later." My friend who was a single mom had given up her promising music career to work as an attendant in a parking garage, and even though her little son was dear to her, she was consumed with disappointment that she'd never been able to follow her dream of being a singer. The woman who'd given up her baby girl for adoption felt like it had been the right thing to do, but still had bouts of loneliness and wondered if her life might be richer if she'd raised her daughter herself. Cassandra listened to all these stories very quietly. I told her I'd even gone so far as to talk to a couple of friends in medical school to gauge the risks of an abortion late in the first term. (Relatively safe, it turns out.)

At the end of all this, Cassandra was only more confused. She seemed frustrated and anguished and utterly overwhelmed about her decision. "Please," she begged me. "Tell me what you think I should do."

Now that's where I should have said, "Look. Nobody can tell you what to do in this situation. This is a decision you have to make by yourself. Spend a day in the woods. Meditate. Pray. Of course this is agonizing. But only you can know what path to take. And whatever you choose, that will be the right decision."

But that's not what I said.

Cassandra was barely getting by on her own as a cashier at a health food store. No medical insurance. Shady roommates. A shaky lease. A boyfriend named Rainbow Bear. "Umm, Cassandra," I said. "I know being a mother appeals to you, but you're still so young. Maybe this isn't the right time. Down the road, you'll have the chance to have a baby with a guy who's gonna be there to raise the child with you. It's just gonna be so hard on your own. I think you should wait."

I Think You Should Wait. Sort of a pleasant euphemism for Kill the Fetus.

Cassandra seemed to understand and quickly come to terms with what I'd said. We talked maybe once more the next day, and then she disappeared again. For months afterward, I felt weird about what I'd done. I did think it was probably for the best, but what if something went wrong and she was never able to have children again? Or what if she never found the right guy and this had been her one chance to be a mother? I think I would have felt equally weird if I'd told her to have the baby, too. I just felt like I shouldn't have been the one to decide.

Three years later I was living in Chicago and I got a call from Cassandra. She was in the Chicago suburbs, staying with her grandfather. She invited me out to visit her, and we agreed to meet the next day at the playground across from her grandfather's house. I pulled up, hopped out of my car, and there was Cassandra, waving to me from beside the swing set. Then I saw, tearing through the grass toward me, a little blond two-year-old boy. It was Cassandra's son, of course—she'd had the baby after all. And he had the same name as my favorite basketball player in the world—Isaiah. Like Isiah Thomas. "Davy," she said, "meet Isaiah Bear."

I felt overjoyed, completely shocked, knocked off balance—a whole bundle of emotions all at once. My eyes got watery.

Isaiah, I quickly discovered, was the most incredible, joyous, dazzlingly intelligent two-year-old boy I'd ever met in my life. I swear this is true: that night we brought him to my friend Nicole's house—I was couch-surfing at her place at the time—and when we introduced him to twelve people in a circle, he went right back around and knew every single person's name. A truly incredible kid.

At the same time, as amazing as Isaiah was, Cassandra was struggling. Rainbow Bear had rumbled off, and she'd been bouncing from town to town, first staying with his parents, then with an old boyfriend or two, and now with her grandfather. But that was a bad situation, too—her grandfather was a drunk and his place was in shambles; he needed as much care as Isaiah did. She had to get out of there.

I felt pretty guilty for having pressed Cassandra to have an abortion. Now that I'd seen how ill that advice had been and what a beautiful boy she'd had, I felt all the more responsible for Isaiah's happiness and well-being. Somehow, I thought, if I could help his path toward a good life, I could make up for that little part where I'd suggested he be exterminated. So I jumped back in again. I took over. Because, you know, I was smart. Not just smart, but wise. And I came up with a plan: I'd move back home to my folks' house in Ann Arbor, Michigan, for a little while, and bring Cassandra and Isaiah to live with us for a couple of months. A chance to make a new start. My folks had lived in town for thirty years and I'd lived there most of my life. Helping Cassandra to find a job, a place to live, friends, a support network—it all seemed feasible. Those are the kinds of things that can be really difficult if you're entirely on your own, but with me as advocate they could be accomplished quite easily. Cassandra was up for it all—stay with my folks, get a job, work and save money, then move into her own place and raise her son. She had no drug problems or anything. It seemed like a reasonable plan.

I was excited by it all. Cassandra had been a lifelong friend and I truly wanted to help her, and I also liked the idea of feeling altruistic—and the idea that this other girl I was chasing after at the time might see me as altruistic.

There's also something kind of gangsta about having a little kid when you're young yourself, and it occurred to me that living with Cassandra and Isaiah would be like having my own kid. At the basketball court where I'd played a lot of ball in Chicago, there was a guy who always brought his two kids with him, two and four years old. He'd play ball with us, and his kids would shoot around on the sad little eight-foot rim that faced the grass, or just watch us and roll in the dirt. Between games, he'd mess around with them lovingly for a couple of minutes or shout at them for wandering too far away.

I liked the idea of showing up at the court in Ann Arbor with Isaiah, and being able to cuff him, scold him, roughhouse with him, love him and teach him how to shoot. Fatherhood makes you seem a little more tough and rugged, like getting a tattoo on your face. And being a dad—or acting as a dad—makes you feel more like a man.

So we did it. We drove from Chicago to Ann Arbor and installed Cassandra and Isaiah at my parents' house. My parents loved Isaiah. They'd clearly begun to crave grandchildren, and their grandparental instincts swelled instantly. They pulled all of my and my brother's old favorite books from the attic and scooped the boy onto their laps and read to him; they finger-painted with him; they played Tangrams; they took him for walks in the woods. My mom got a little kiddie pool for the backyard, and Cassandra and Isaiah would spend all afternoon and evening back there. Cassandra made soup and all kinds of complicated vegan foods in the kitchen and washed her clothes with a hose and hung them up to dry on the old rusty playground equipment in the back.

We had a basketball hoop in our driveway, and my friends and I started showing young Isaiah how to shoot. We called him "Zeke"—Isiah Thomas's nickname. The kid—Zeke—had the sunniest disposition, and he was a natural athlete. I'd make a hoop with my arms and let him dunk the ball through.

I also started in pretty quickly trying to find Cassandra a job. Between me, my friends, and my parents, we found a few solid leads, solid enough that all she would have to do was show up for an interview and the job would be hers. These weren't dream jobs, but they were decent-paying jobs that a young single mother might be happy to have, like working the register at a Birkenstock store, or hostessing at a vegetarian restaurant, or taking phone orders at Bell's Pizza. But every time we had an interview set up for Cassandra, she managed to miss it. She got lost on her way there, or Isaiah was nursing and she couldn't leave him right then, and on and on.

Finally, one day I drove her to an interview, though she had her own car—I just wanted to make sure she actually went to it. She got the job, receptionist at a yoga center. They asked her to start work the next morning. I drew a careful map with clear directions so she'd have no trouble finding the place, and even set her alarm clock to wake her in plenty of time to get to work. The plan was for my dad and me to split the day looking after Zeke, and then on days we weren't around, Zeke could go to day care. But the next morning, I woke up and Cassandra was just lying in bed playing with Zeke. I charged into the room, a bit indignant. "Oh my God, you're two hours late for work and it's your first day!" And she just said, "Oh, I decided not to go."

If you knew Cassandra, you'd be surprised if I told you that she never smoked pot. She just had this total glassy, dreamy air to her. She was completely unperturbed by real-world situations. In a lot of ways, she was like a child.

I was so frustrated—with her, with myself, with the situation. Cassandra kept putting all of her decisions in my hands, but then she wasn't actually doing any of the things I was telling her to do. I realized that things that were easy for me, like showing up for work on time—or showing up at all—were not easy for her. It became clear that she wasn't going to get a job.

It wasn't that Cassandra was lazy—it's just that she didn't want to do anything but hang out with her two-year-old son, which I guess was pretty understandable. She was also exhausted all the time, and really, I began to understand just how difficult it would be to raise a kid on your own. That shit is relentless when you have two parents, but all alone, it's brutal. For me, the allure of playing dad began to wane. I was stuck babysitting a lot. When I tried to take Zeke with me to the basketball court, he didn't understand that he couldn't come on the court when the grown-ups were playing, and I had to take him home. I'd be changing diapers while my friends were all out playing disc golf. Every night, I'd be on the phone with one of them: "Man, forget the bar—bars are too smoky—why don't you grab some beers and come by my folks' house and chill with me and Zeke." Most days I'd be trying to get some kind of important work done on the computer and play Hungry Hungry Hippos at the same time. The hippos always won.

Suddenly I felt a desperate need for an out. My parents recognized that Cassandra had no intention of finding her own housing—and they were ready to have their house back, and I was ready to have my life back. My generosity, my "wisdom," my stab at playing dad revealed itself for what it was all along: a theme-park ride, a novelty, a selfish gift.

So, naturally, I hatched a new, even more ill-conceived plan, and tried to hook Cassandra up with my friend Brande, so he could take her off my hands.

I knew Brande was into Cassandra, and he was great with Isaiah, so I kept making plans for all of us to hang out together, then ducking out at the last minute. This worked excellently at first—Brande took over all of the dad responsibilities I'd felt saddled with, and Cassandra enjoyed Brande's kindness and attention. There was actually a momentary romantic spark, and I saw everything unspooling beautifully. I even started calling Brande "Big Daddy" because Zeke adored him so much, and because Brande had this lovable roly-poly quality to him. But Brande was living at home with his own mom, and they were barely making ends meet as it was. Brande's mom quashed everything quickly. "There's no way they're moving in here with us!" she said. Besides, I don't think Brande was interested in taking over as dad for good, and I don't think Cassandra was into him as a long-term boyfriend. One of the lowest moments of this whole strange saga was when Cassandra said to me one day, not angrily, just plainly, "If you want me to leave, I'll leave. You don't have to try and peddle me off on your friends." I felt horrible; I'd had no idea that my crappy, diabolical machinations had been so transparent. But that's how Cassandra was—seemingly out of it but actually extremely sensitive and aware.

There's a TV show from the 1980s that I saw only a handful of times but always really loved called *Quantum Leap*. Remember that show? Each week's episode would revolve around a different person caught up in a difficult and complicated situation that he or she couldn't fix. The star of the show, Scott Bakula, would actually be zapped into that person's body—become that person—and he would make things right, and then once he'd done his job, this lightning bolt would envelop him and he'd be beamed away into the next person's body, the next tricky mess. I know I like to see myself in that light, making one Quantum Leap after another after another. That's why *Quantum Leap* always appealed to me so much: it's one thing to be down with O.P.P.—you know, Other People's Problems—and do your best to help them, but it would be another thing entirely if you could actually inhabit someone else's body and fix everything up yourself. Then you could really help some people. I'm sure, in the end, it's not the best way to handle things; at the very least it's kind of a bullying way to look at other people's problems. But I guess that's me—wanting the ball in my hands, wanting to run the show, like Isiah Thomas.

Not long after Cassandra told me that I didn't need to

peddle her off on my friends, she decided that she and Zeke would pack up and leave town. She'd been talking to Zeke's dad, Rainbow Bear, on the phone, and they were going to try to get back together. Rainbow had moved to Hawaii, naturally, and Cassandra and Isaiah were headed there to meet up with him. It was one of those things where it seemed clearly sad and hopeless, and at the same time I didn't want to talk her out of it, because it meant that they'd be gone and I could resume my own directionless life. Cassandra, in telling me this, was nothing but sweet and kind and totally appreciative of what my family and I had done for her, but I felt miserable.

I worked with Zeke one last afternoon on his perimeter shooting. That evening when Cassandra and Isaiah left, I watched them pull out of the driveway with all their possessions piled into the backseat, and saw them wave out the window, smiling but with scared eyes. They drove off down the dirt road, bound for I-94, completely on their own, not even sure where they'd sleep that night. Their taillights disappeared out of sight over the crest of a hill, and for twenty minutes or so I stood at the end of the driveway and cried. Then, once night had fallen, I turned and went inside.

FAULT

RICHARD BAUSCH

There are six people who either are now or have been in my care as child to father. The sixth is Lila, from my second marriage, the only one I'll name, since she's two years and four months old and is not yet fully formed as a mind and a set of passions, though she is possessed of a very sharp and obvious intelligence—and like any proud parent, I can point out all those places where it shows. For instance, if you'll indulge me with allowing one: very early—and she's the only one of my offspring to have done this—she grasped the word "yes," and took to using it correctly, in context, before she was much past one year old. With my other children, those years ago, I realized that any inflection of a question led to the answer "No," mostly, of course, because one has to say it so often in those first years. ("No, that's hot." Or, "No, don't hit your brother.") So, knowing this, I took to using that knowledge, both for the entertainment of friends and, as they grew, for the delight of the older children. I would put the most complex matters into a question for the baby, within hearing of others—in a grocery store line, or at a restaurant, or in someone's living room.

"You believe in the ineluctable modality of the visible, right?"

"No."

"You believe in the inevitable triumph of the proletariat, right?"

"No."

It was a stunt that worked every time. People would turn and look—this toddler apparently discussing philosophy, aesthetics, politics. Even religion. "You believe in an all-powerful God who will reward the Republicans, right?"

"No."

With Lila, for some reason, this never took hold. She started letting me know very early that she had the concept. I'd ask a question having to do with something practical. "You want more milk?"

"Es," she'd say, with an emphatic nodding of her head.

The first time it happened, I couldn't quite believe it. The normal infant response, I had come to believe from experience, would be a reaching of the hands, or maybe a smile. She actually nodded her head twice, and said the word, without pronouncing the "y."

"Es."

I marveled at this, and started looking for other contexts. Watching a movie has always been a big thing with my children and me, and we did a lot of it through the years when they were small. For instance, I have seen *The Wizard of Oz* at least a hundred and fifty times, and quite probably many more times than that. One bright winter morning, when it was too cold and windy to go out and the drafty house we lived in then made it necessary to stay close to each other, I sat Lila under her blanket on the little sofa across from the TV and asked her, "Do you want to watch a movie?"

She nodded vigorously.

"Es."

I said, "How about *Aladdin*? Want to watch that?"

"Es."

So, laughing, feeling the delight of communicating in this direct way with this eleven-month-old baby, I put the movie in. The word "Aladdin" came to the screen, in gold script, and because I simply believed that she must be able to do it, I said, "Can you say 'Aladdin'?"

She looked directly at me, bald and clear-eyed and fat-cheeked, with almond eyes so green they seemed, in that light, black, and with a perfectly serious and straightforward expressive little shake of her head she said, "No."

I laughed very hard, and I couldn't wait to tell her mother about it.

Like every father I know, my pride in the abilities and accomplishments of my children is deep; it is also, of course, quite ordinary. One of them is a very good motorcycle mechanic who can play guitar beautifully, and, like his father, remembers every joke he's ever heard, even the bad ones. He is also unfailingly kind, direct, and shrewd about people—though, also like his father, he can be fooled by his own best hopes for others, and tends in an argument to lean toward the doctrinaire. Two others of the grown children also play music; one of them is seriously writing songs, and the other is pursuing a career as an actor, though this one, too, writes songs and is also writing poems and a novel. Another has taken an MFA degree in fiction, and is a story writer. They are wonderfully talented and very smart. Still another of the grown children lives and works in Manhattan as a manager of a ticket-sales firm, has been interested in making movies, and possesses demonstrated talent at that, along with a marvelous and unbeatably quick wit.

That one also does not speak to me anymore.

Over the years, I have had, like most men, good days and bad ones. I have failed probably more often than I have succeeded. Each time, I hoped to fix the perceived failure. Someone once said that every child born is nature's attempt to make a perfect human being. I think that's a dangerously false vision, since a perfect being by definition cannot ever be human. I once heard a character of mine say, in a story I was writing, "It is a terrible fate to have to be raised by a human being."

"Human it is," Boccaccio tells us so tolerantly, and with the gentle smile of his prose, at the beginning of his great book.

But I did want to correct things, fix things, be better with each child. I feel it now, with Lila. I want to be better than I ever was—more patient, more involved, more loving.

I remember my father, trying to help me, more than thirty years ago now, telling me to take a switch to my oldest child when that child was acting up; he told me that he had done that with me when I was small, and that I'd scream, and he'd say, "I can't hear you." And I'd scream louder. He told me that I had run out into the road, after he'd repeatedly told me not to do so. And this switching was to impress upon me that I was not to run out into the road. He wanted me to think of the switch every time I came to the edge of the road. As he talked about this, his eyes glittered with pride; it was clearly something he was certain he had done right.

I was appalled; I stood there quite quiet—speechless, really—understanding with an inward jolt that he was sincere, and did not know how I truly felt about it. But I did not say anything to him about it. What would have been the point? His job was done; he was advising me about mine. I just said, "Well, next time I will," or words to that effect—something to get us beyond the subject of discipline.

It was then that I began to see what kinds of things people visit upon each other out of love. But as that boy with the switch marks on the backs of his legs, I did apparently stop going out in the road. And perhaps a year after that conversation with my father, I met my dear friend Roland Flint, a fine poet, whose life's dividing line was the day his little lost boy, Ethan, ran out into the road in front of his house.

Now comes the part where I cleverly change names and disguise myself in fictional gestures. You will not recognize me, nor will you be able to identify any of the principal characters.

Beckworth, at fifty-five years old, believed in the life he had led, and thought of himself as more blessed than most. This was in the winter, a little more than two years after his youngest son, Sean, now twenty-three, was diagnosed with a rare form of melanoma. The whole family had gone through the terrors of that two months—three operations: the one that led to the diagnosis in the first place, the sentinel lymph-node test (one lymph node showed microscopic cancer), and then the surgery to remove a large number of lymph nodes from the neck. That last operation showed that none of those lymph nodes and no tissue around the original incision contained any cancerous cells. Sean had come through it all with bravery and intelligence, and was making a good life for himself in New York. But there was a kind of frenetic quality to family get-togethers now that no one quite noticed, or Beckworth didn't, anyway. It was as if all of the members of his household were fighting to keep this darkness that had so recently threatened them at a remove. Sean was fine; he was visiting with his fiancée, a young bright woman everyone in the family loved. Everyone had gathered for a day's celebration, the week before Christmas. As had become the custom, Sean and his older brother, Tom, had made a bonfire in the two-acre field that was the backyard. The light from the fire went up into the misty chill of the night, and the brothers and sisters—three of them, Carol and Jeanne, and Charlotte, the youngest—were gathered in the light, with Sean and his fiancée, Mary. Everyone was drinking beer or wine except the two youngest girls.

Beckworth saw Sean make a leap through the fire, across the edge of the pit where it burned, and said, in alarm, "Hey, that's too close. Don't do that again." Tom, who, after a two-month stay with Sean and Mary in New York, had recently come back to the house to live, said something about Sean's drinking too much, and walked away from the fire. "I'm going to bed," he muttered.

Beckworth did not see Sean and Mary follow him. The others were still enjoying the heat of the fire, and watching the sparks of it lift into the increasing mist. There were several friends of the grown children present, and Beckworth had that feeling he had often enjoyed of being at the warm center of a light that he had brought forth. This was a pride in having his family around him, and he supposed—if he thought about it at all—that it was a fairly common sensation. Hearth and home. He might've made some joke about it. He was entertaining, talking, being funny for the people standing around in the dimness, some of whom he did not even know.

He had lost track of Sean and Mary and Tom, and was

surprised by the fact that Charlotte was suddenly far across the yard, standing on the back deck of the house, shouting, "They're fighting!"

Sean's a very deeply smart person, with an unbeatable wit, but like his brother and his father, he has also always shown that old inherited tendency to be doctrinaire whenever discussion of cultural matters and history and politics goes around the family table. In this instance, Tom had begun to notice that Sean was becoming especially contentious whenever he had anything at all to drink.

On this night, Sean was drinking and being funny, and he had started an argument with one of Carol's friends who had come to visit; he had said things to his soon-to-be brother-in-law, Carol's Edgar, making fun of his English accent, and he took offense when Tom called him out for having too much. What happened, Beckworth found out later, was that when Tom walked away from the fire, Sean followed him, and tried to confront him about the remark, bringing up that he had given Tom a place to stay in New York. It was all the pathology of too much wine, and when Tom refused to be drawn into the altercation, Sean began swinging at him. He was too drunk to do much damage, and Tom wrestled him quickly to the floor.

By the time Beckworth reached them, they were in the little foyer at the front of the house, Tom holding Sean down on the floor, Sean kicking and cursing. "Let me up, let me up." Mary was there, too, and they were both trying to calm the young man down. Beckworth's wife, Ann, had tried to separate the two boys earlier, and was now standing there, helpless, also crying, but trying to calm everyone, talking to the boy and repeating the phrase, "We love you. We all love you."

And so Beckworth stepped in: he took the boy by the arms,

helped him rise, and then held him as he pulled and strained to free himself. Now it was just Beckworth and his son, faltering and pulling at each other, moving to the side door of the house and out onto the porch, Sean yelling, "Let me go. I'm leaving. I'm going back to New York. Just let me go."

"You can't leave, son. You're in no condition to drive."

"Let me *go!*"

Beckworth held him, was being pulled by him to the end of the porch, where, with all his remaining strength, he got the boy in a forced embrace, using the corner post as an anchor. "I'm not letting you go, son," Beckworth told him. "I love you. You might as well stop this."

The boy kicked three slats out of the porch, struggling to free himself, and now Ann was holding him, too.

There were people off in the dim yard, beyond the circle of dying light where the fire had burned so brightly only a few minutes earlier.

The struggle went on, and Mary and Tom stepped in, too, holding Sean there on the porch.

Beckworth had let go, had walked to the other end of the porch. But all the boy's rage was still aimed at him. "I'm sorry I'm not a big sports figure, Dad! I'm sorry I'm not a baseball player!" They were holding him, keeping him from going off to his car, and he was still trying to free himself, but also looking at his father, shouting at him while the others held him. "Go ahead, walk away, Dad—like you always did."

None of it made any real sense. Beckworth had never pushed sports; he had never been distant. Yet he felt the hurled accusations as elements of some truth, something he could not explain away.

"Go ahead, Dad. You were never there anyway. I'm sorry I'm not a famous baseball player, Dad."

Beckworth went into the house and stood at the kitchen sink and wept.

Later, talking with Tom, he wondered if his failure as a father was in not paying enough attention to the boy's feelings about the very wit everyone appreciated. All of the children were talented, and Beckworth had encouraged them about their gifts—but the girls had music, as Tom did, and Sean had not gone that way. Sean wanted to make movies; his best gift was his wit. By disagreeing with him, or taking contrary positions in talk—remember the father's and the son's tendency toward the dogmatic in discussions—Beckworth was unwittingly denying this gift. "He may be a genius," Tom said. "But that doesn't make him right all the goddamn time, either."

Beckworth stood there admiring this oldest of his children. Twenty-seven years old and wise.

"Did I ever push you guys about sports—or anything?"

"I think he just remembered all the movies about bad fathers he's seen and he just threw it all at you because he wanted to hurt you and he knew it would hurt."

Sean spoke to others about that night. He questioned how he could've said those things to his father. "Why would I say that stuff to Dad? I love Dad."

Those things were reported to Beckworth. He never heard them from the boy, directly. Sean returned to New York, and went on with things. He and Mary broke up, and he came to the house to visit with another young woman. And then still another. He stopped drinking; he had come to the acknowledgment that he had a problem with it. But the slats in the porch remained broken. Years passed. Beckworth remembered the pathology of that night, and it was all tied up in the terrors of the earlier time—that period of days and weeks when the news kept getting worse, and the whole family was in the grip of awful possibility.

He doesn't live in that house anymore. The marriage ended. He moved to another state. The children are all grown and when he sees them now there is always the complication of the divorce—the sorrow of it. Sean has done well in New York, is married, and is happy by all accounts. He has no communication with Beckworth, who keeps up with him through the others, through Tom, who in the heartbreak of seeing the end of his parents' marriage still kept all lines open.

Beckworth thinks of Sean's continuing rage at him, and then remembers the porch, and the broken slats. Always now, his memory of Sean is tied up with fault: those many times when he could have done better—could have paid more attention, or paid the right attention, or said something encouraging, or kept quiet at some crucial moment. But there is also the simple truth that sometimes, when the particulars are counted up, and one allows for the fact that the actors in the drama are all human—sometimes a son can get it wrong, too.

Now there is another child. Two and a half years old. A girl. A bright, wonderful little girl. Beckworth is trying again to be the best father a child can have, and again, of course, he is, as always, faltering and failing. The days pass, the years.

HERE COMES THE SUN

NICK FLYNN

[A TELEGRAM MADE OF SHADOWS]

(2007) This black and white photograph in my hand is an image of my unborn daughter—this is what I'm told. It's actually a series of photographs, folded one upon the other, like a tiny accordion. I was there when the doctor or the technician or whoever he was made it with his little wand of sound. I sat beside him, looked into the screen as he pointed into the shadows—"Can you see her nose, can you see her hand? Can you see her foot, right here, next to her ear?" I was there when each shot was taken, yet in some ways, still, it is all deeply unreal. It's as if I were holding a photograph of a dream, a dream sleeping inside the body of the woman I love, a woman now walking through the world with two hearts beating inside her.

* * *

Here's a secret: all of us, if we live long enough, will lose our way at some point. You will lose your way, you will wake up one morning and find yourself lost. This is a hard, simple truth. If it hasn't happened to you yet consider yourself lucky. When it does, when one day you look around and nothing is recognizable, when you find yourself alone in a dark wood having lost the way, you may find it easier to blame it on someone else—an errant lover, a missing father, a bad childhood. Or it may be easier to blame the map you were given—folded too many times, out of date, tiny print. But if you are honest, you will be able to blame only yourself. If you are lucky, you will remember a story you heard as a child, the trick of leaving a trail of bread crumbs through the woods, the idea being that after whatever it is that is going to happen in those woods has happened, you can then retrace your steps and find your way back out.

One day I hope to tell my daughter a story about a dark time, the dark days before she was born, and how her coming was a ray of light. We got lost for a while, the story will begin, but then we found our way.

This, at least, is the version I hope to be able to tell her.

[PROTEUS]

Proteus lives at the bottom of a steep cliff, down a treacherous path, at the edge of the sea. You can see him from the top of the cliff, lolling on a flat rock, staring into the endless nothing of the sea, but to reach him is difficult. You've been told that he has the answer to your question, and you are a little desperate to have this question answered. As you make your way down, you must be careful not to dislodge any loose gravel, careful not to cry out when the thorns pierce your feet. You must approach him as quietly as you can, get right up on him, get your hands on him, around his neck. You've been told that you have to hold on while you ask him your question, you've been told that you can't let go. As you hold on he will transform into the shape and form of that which most terrifies you, in order to get you to release your grip. But if you can hold on through your fear, he will return to his real form, and answer your question.

My mother told me a story, just once, of how as a girl she'd been tied to a chair, the chair teetering at the top of the attic stairs, her captors threatening to send her end over end, tumbling down. I don't know if they did this more than once, and I don't know what they wanted—a question answered, a promise made—beyond the usual childhood cruelties, or if they ever got it.

And then there's my father, and the stories he tells. The two are nearly inseparable, my father and his stories—the same handful over and over, his repertoire. A liar always tells his story the same way, I've heard said, except that some—most—of my father's stories have, improbably, turned out to be true. The story of his father inventing the life raft, the story of the novel he's spent his whole life writing, the story of robbing a few banks—all true.

This morning, in my inbox, I find this note from Julia, a friend in Berlin:

I was standing on the Teufelberg (The Devil's Mountain) with a friend last night, listening to Patti Smith playing in the stadium below, and

I thought of you. The Teufelberg is made from all the junk of the war, the broken houses and so on. It is a big mountain, and we stood there looking out over my strange and terrible and beautiful city. Where are you?

Teufelberg. Devil's Mountain. All the junk of the war.

Here I am, I think, writing about my mother (again), and here I am, writing about my father (again), writing about my shadow. If asked, I'll sometimes say that I'm writing about the way photographs are a type of dream, about how shadows can end up resembling us. Sometimes I'll say I'm writing about my unborn daughter, and sometimes I'll say I'm writing a memoir of bewilderment, and just leave it at that. What I don't say, what I should say, is that what I'm really writing about is Proteus, the mythological creature who changes shape as you hold on to him, who changes into the shape of that which most terrifies you, as you ask him your question, as you refuse to let go. The question is, often, simply a variation of, "How do I get home?"

[A BOX OF DOLLS]

Two months before our daughter is born we go to an infant CPR class. I have taken CPR classes before, but never specifically to save an infant. The woman leading the class is passionate about safety, pumping us with gruesome details of what could happen if we fail to put our child in a secured car seat, if she swallows a penny, if we spill hot coffee on her. "One day you will come upon your baby and she will be blue," this woman says. "What will you do?" At her feet sits a box of dolls with removable rubber faces and chests that can be compressed only if the air passage, the "windpipe," is opened. As she speaks she wraps a face around each skull, assuring us that each has been sterilized since the last class. "I take them home and boil them," she says, as she places a doll face-up on the table in front of each of us, along with a packet of alcohol, so we can give the doll's mouth one last wipe before we attempt to revive her. By the looks on the faces of the others in the class, we are all a little freaked out. "Take two fingers," the teacher says, "place them just below your baby's nipples, in the center of her chest, and push."

[SELF-PORTRAIT AS AN INFANT IN MY FATHER'S ARMS]

In the photograph he is sitting in a chair, and I am the infant in his arms. We are both looking into the camera, or at least at whoever it is that is taking the photograph. My mother, I imagine, since I found it with her things. The look on his face is heavy, as if I were a burden, as if he were burdened, though perhaps I am simply reading into it, knowing that he will be gone in a few months. Impossible not to read into it. How old am I? He was gone by the time I was six months old, or I was gone, my mother taking me, us, away. Choose a version, choose a victim. The look on his face is a tunnel, leading out. No one would call him happy.

And now I have a picture of me with my daughter in my arms, almost the same picture, all these years later. Now I am older than any of them, older than my mother made it to, older than my father before he walked into that bank with his forged check, smiling into the camera. I have her in my arms, and I am smiling so broadly that I barely recognize myself. It's a form of ecstasy, my face. I thought it would break me, before she came, and it did, but not in the way I feared. First Lili cried her

Electra cry, then Maeve cried her first breath cry, then I cried, with a newfound joy. And at that moment I thought of my own father—it surprised me to think of him at that moment. And it surprised me that I felt sad for him, having denied himself this, this simple moment, having given it away. "I had car trouble," is how he explains his absence now, but we both know it was the vodka.

[HERE COMES THE SUN]

Every Christmas, for a few years, which seemed and still seems forever, the new Beatles album waited beneath the tree. Some years there were even two—1968, the Year of the Monkey, there were two—two perfect squares wrapped in red and green tissue paper. We already half knew most of the songs, but we didn't know all the words, we didn't know which followed which, we didn't have the pictures. One opened up like a kid's picture book, John Paul Ringo and George looking out at us in the uniforms of some psychedelic army; John Paul Ringo and George walking across a street in white suits and black suits and barefoot and in jeans. Before that day we'd had to sit in the car and wait for "Here Comes the Sun" or "Hey Jude" to end— no one until that moment, nowhere on earth, had ever heard "Hey Jude," but from that moment on it would always be here, from then on it would never not be here.

A few years after the Beatles broke up I was delivering newspapers before the sun came up. Sometimes my mother would drive me, if it had snowed in the night, if I was late for school, her car warm and waiting after I trudged back between houses, the radio playing low. Most mornings I was alone, on my bike or walking, and I would pause under a certain streetlight to see what was happening in the world. I would follow a story for the days or weeks it would appear, first as a headline, then as it moved further and further into the body of the paper. Watergate. Patty Hearst. Vietnam. One morning the photograph on the front page was of a plane that had crashed at Logan Airport, thirty miles to the north. The plane had tried to take off but something had held it down—maybe there was ice on the wings, maybe one of the wings was broken, maybe a screw was loose. I can't remember now, I'm sorry. All I know for certain is that it crashed, the photograph of the wreckage there on the cover of the *Boston Globe*—plane parts and body parts, or at least word of body parts. Logan is on the sea, there is a breakwater around it, huge blocks of granite for the waves to break themselves on—as I write this I now think it was trying to land, I think it went down too soon, I think it slammed into the breakwater and flipped over. Too far or not far enough, too fast or too slow, something happened, everyone died, that is, everyone except one man, and this one man, this survivor, was the reason I read the paper every day, searching for news of the wreck, which soon became news of this man, whose name I remembered for years but cannot locate now in the vault of my mind. A Latino name, I think—Humberto, Eugenio, Emmanuel—I thought it was a funny name. Wait—Manuel Tavares, maybe that's it. Tavares sounds right. Let's call him Manuel— Manuel stayed alive for days, and then weeks, horribly burned, 80 percent of his body, wrapped in gauze and immobile but alive. I searched the paper every day for word of him. Something inside me wanted him to live, something inside me was desperate for him to make it, to pull through, for one person to walk away or be dragged away from this impossible disaster—if he died on me then no one would have survived.

[DISSOLVE]

I wake up early, carry Maeve from the bed to the living room, let Lili sleep in. Maeve smiles at the daylight, at the shadows crossing the brick wall outside the kitchen window. She seems happy that the sun came back. It's so simple. At dusk she looks in terror out the windows, seemingly confused by the darkness, by where everything goes. In this she is like me—I smile in the morning, and as the day progresses I get more and more confused by everything coming at me. Overstimulated, they call us. At sundown she cries, simple as that. "Nothing you can do that isn't done," I sing to her, swaying slowly around the kitchen with her in my arms—"nothing you can sing that isn't sung."

For a long time after my mother's suicide—ten years or so, off and on—I lived on a boat. When my father got himself evicted and ended up homeless I was still on that boat, I still hadn't made my way to shore. My twenties, you could say, were water, you could say I was more of the ocean than of the earth, you could say that whatever was solid in me was slowly dissolving. I had read somewhere that nothing should change after a "serious trauma," in the face of "such a loss." I was away at school when I got the call, but when I came home it was no longer my home. I dropped out of school but I never spent another night in that house. If I tried I'd wake up, hungover, slouched in the front seat of my car, the car itself sideways in the driveway. The boat was on land in a friend's yard, and I'd often go to it in the middle of the night, crawl aboard. We put her back in the water that spring.

Ten years—why did it take so long, you might wonder, to get my feet back on the ground, why did it take so long to lose my sea legs? The book on how to deal with trauma had failed to say when change could resume, when one could go on, and so, year after year, I continued to row my body out, to scan the shoreline, to wait.

The boat was built the same year my mother was born (1939, the same year *The Wizard of Oz* was released, the one film we waited for every year to come on TV) and therefore contained something of her, or so it seemed. We'd scattered her ashes in the Atlantic—you could say that living on the boat was as close as I could get to her, to something of her. You could say I felt held by the water. You could say I was, like Dorothy, only trying to find my way back home. It worked, for a while, to dissolve myself into something larger than myself, until by the end not even the ocean was big enough to contain it all. Until in the end I had to quit everything.

Last night there was a lunar eclipse. I held Maeve up to the window to see it. I told her about the sun, about the earth, about the moon, about the eclipse. I said, "You are the sun, I am the moon, I am circling around you, and sometimes a shadow falls across your face, sometimes a darkness rises up inside us, but it isn't real, we cannot believe it's real." I held her head like a sun, and we moved around the room, singing, "Little darlin', it's been a long cold lonely winter," until she stopped crying and fell asleep.

[PROTEUS REDUX]

I have been on this train, heading south along this river, the river off to my right, forever it seems. I can't complain, I got on early, I got a window, and if I want I can look up and see the river and whatever is washed up along its banks and the little fallen houses that I still imagine I will one day wander through—like that one, its door left open, as if someone went out for a look at the river on a day like this, a warm fall day, and simply never came back.

Let's just accept that Proteus knows your innermost fears, and that he plays on these fears, hoping you will let go, hoping you will give up, hoping you will stop asking your question, hoping you will lose hope. This, then, is a vision of Proteus as both torturer and tortured. He plays on your fears, he wants you to lose hope, but at the same time, you are the one with your hands around his neck, asking the questions.

My terror with being a father, with having a child, was never the threat of some abstract maniac snatching her. It was always that I would look at her and it wouldn't mean a thing. That she would appear and nothing would change. That I wouldn't be able to feel, that I could simply get in my car and drive away, that I wouldn't remember. My fear has always been with me—it has always been the fear of my own shadow.

But it didn't happen that way—minute by minute, day by day. Life is long, they say, and then it isn't. The shadows will always be there, there will always be flying monkeys and a scared fat fraud behind a curtain telling you he is in charge. And you will always be able to tell him that he should be ashamed.

And now some weeks have passed, some sleepless weeks, and I am less certain. That photograph of me in my father's arms: maybe he is simply tired, maybe he's been up all night, trying to get me to sleep, and what I see in his face is only that—exhaustion. Not unhappiness at this burden, but simply tired, bone tired. If you took a photograph of me one of these sleepless nights, pacing the apartment and singing "All you need is love" softly to Maeve, desperate for us both to return to the land of sleep, you might say that I, too, don't look especially thrilled at this miracle I am holding in my hands. But you would be wrong. And so maybe I've been wrong, all these years, about my father.

[THE POND]

Hungry, Maeve cries her small cry with the first light ("cell by cell the baby made herself"). A few minutes before this she let out a coo ("the cells / Made cells"), a coo that became the texture of the dream I was having ("That is to say / The baby is made largely of milk"), a coo that to me meant that everything was going to be all right. I get out of bed, step into the cold of the barn, and make my way over to her room, which we insulated and now heat with an oil-filled electric radiator, like our room will be one day, once—if—we get around to hanging the doors. The rest of the barn, which I pass through quickly, is essentially the same weather as the outside world, and this morning the outside world is thick with fog, and cool. Since we've been living in the barn there have been nights when I've woken up to take a piss and been stopped on the way to the toilet, the darkness around me filled with fireflies. Or if there was lightning outside, then inside the barn would be bright with lightning as well. But those were summer nights, when we slept with the big sliding doors open, so the night and its weather and creatures could just wander in.

After I change and feed Maeve we play together quietly for a while on the carpet, the same carpet we roll up each night so the shrew doesn't leave its droppings on it. Then we make our way down to the pond, to let Lili sleep in a little longer, Maeve's little body strapped to my chest like a parachute.

We moved into the barn last May so that we could rent out the house. Money got tight after the baby came, so in the spring I offered to fix the barn up, since I knew how to do it, or at least knew enough friends I could call on to help, especially if I let them hold Maeve when I asked. For the last ten years or so, before I was here, before Lili and I even knew each other, the barn had become simply a place to gather junk: a lawn mower that doesn't start; a hundred mismatched windows; another entire barn, dismantled and neatly stacked; a padlocked refrigerator, said to belong to Ronnie, though I've never met Ronnie.

When I first got here, four years ago now, I'd wash the dishes in the house kitchen and look out at the barn—enormous, a cathedral. I couldn't help but imagine what one might do in it. The barn is a hundred and fifty years old, held together by sixty-foot-long hickory beams, a quality of tree that hasn't grown here, maybe anywhere, for nearly a hundred years now. The roof is slate, kestrels live in the cupola—anything could happen in that barn. It could be a theater, it could hold an airplane. You could build a room inside it, a hidey-hole for when things got bad, when things went south, as they say, as they do. You could set up a desk in a corner and write a book about it.

By the time we make it to the pond my boots are wet with dew. Steam rises from the surface, the surface utterly still. The pond was never like the barn. When I first got here it didn't even exist, not really, not as anything other than an idea. The land had overgrown it so much through the years that you could only glimpse it as you walked along the narrow path connecting one meadow to the next. At night you could hear the bullfrogs, but at night it's hard to locate where sound is coming from. It seemed to come from the low point in the land, the place a pond would be, if there was a pond. I asked Lili about it, but all she'd heard was that in the winter one couldn't skate on it because it wouldn't freeze, and in the summer you couldn't swim in it because it wasn't big enough. This seemed contradictory, but not being able to see it, I couldn't verify either claim. Every year the wild roses grew thicker, sending out their long tendrils of thorns, which tore at your arms if you tried to pull them back to see a little more. From what I could see, it was possible that the pond was no bigger than a bucket, which would mean it wasn't a pond at all. In all likelihood it was simply vernal, evaporating in the summer and leaving only a muddy patch. When I first got here my mind was unsettled, and I'd have to drive off every day to find a pool or a lake where I could swim, which was the only thing I'd found to calm it.

The land hadn't been bushhogged for eight years or so, which is why the wild roses and the locusts and the sycamore had taken over. I found someone who had the machine and could do the job. He promised to clear away what he could, along with the rest of the overgrown land. By the end of the day he'd gouged a path to the pond's edge, and I was able to walk up to it and look across to the other side. Hundreds of frogs splashed the surface as I approached, the water tea-colored, a few trees draping their branches into it, their leaves floating on the surface. The pond wasn't large, but it wasn't small, either. One could swim the length of it in about ten strokes, I estimated, once a little more was cleared away.

I spent the next several weeks doing just that, whenever I had an hour or so, usually when Maeve was napping. I had just finished a draft of a book that had consumed me for the past four years, and so I had time. It was now August, and a friend was renting the house. Later he'd tell me that he'd look out at me, hacking away at the undergrowth, and wonder if working on the book hadn't driven me a little mad. From his window the pond was still invisible. All he could see was that after an hour or so I would come back up the hill, shirtless, sweat dripping off my nose, my legs muddy, my arms bleeding from the thorns. At night we'd all have dinner together and I'd talk about it, how beautiful it was, how at dawn lately I'd been seeing a heron, or perhaps it was a bittern, sitting on a branch, watching over it all. I didn't know if the heron had always been there, no one knew, because until that moment no one had even seen the pond, not for many years. In the weeks I worked on it I didn't write a word, and it is very possible that I didn't have a thought in my head, beyond the thought of Maeve and that pond.

[A BETTER PLACE]

I need to write something about returning the key to my father's apartment to his management company, about the end of something. About him being in a better place. Not dead, which I don't necessarily think of as "a better place," but a "long-term-care facility," a nursing home. The first time I met him as an adult, twenty years ago now, he was in the middle of a five-year homeless odyssey, and then, for the past sixteen years, he lived on his own in an apartment near the Fenway. That apartment, by the end, was a disaster, and so was he. Now he has a bed by a window, his clothes are always clean, he eats three meals a day. He's on a little Atavan, which seems to dissolve his anxiety. And he doesn't drink—this is the first time I have ever known him outside of alcohol. His stories are different, he no longer tells the same handful, over and over. But his mind, sadly, is shot—he knows who I am, dimly, but he cannot remember when he last saw me, or anything about my life. I could tell him a hundred times that he is now a grandfather, and it simply will not sink in. "I have to talk to you," he says, "they're treating me like I'm a millionaire here, and I got no money. I don't know what I'll do when they find out." "I'm working on it," I assure him, and pass a few folded dollar bills into his hand.

The next time I visit him is to introduce him to Maeve. By now he has met Lili a dozen times, and yet he is still uncertain who exactly she is. His daughter? His sister? His ex-wife? Even without the vodka his short-term memory is frazzled. "This is a beautiful woman," he says to me. "Look at those legs," and he begins to stand over her, but Lili orders him to sit back down, which he seems to get a kick out of. "You say her name is Lili? And this is my granddaughter? My son, Nicholas, should meet you two." I'm Nicholas, I remind him. Lili takes a few pictures of us sitting together on a couch against a window looking out onto a hallway, each of us looking happy and bewildered in our own ways. After an hour or so, as we stand to leave, he takes me aside, asks sotto voce, "Are you leaving the woman with me?"

[WIZARD OF OZ, WIZARD OF ID]

At dawn I sit on the couch and slide *The Wizard of Oz* into my computer, Maeve asleep in my arms. Almost immediately, for some reason, tears well up in my eyes. Dorothy, right from the start, is trying to get back home—mythic, yet simple as a fairy tale, like following a trail of bread crumbs through a dark forest.

Maeve stirs, smiles up at me, reaches for my nose, then gets distracted by the leafy plant behind my head. I shut the computer, a pure simple joy filling the room. The leaves she is staring at now, she can't even see them, not the green, not the shapes, she's simply staring into this world—everything hazy but slowly coming into focus. Soon she will have her Wizard of Oz moment, the rods and cones in her eyes will develop and the world will transform from black and white to color. I missed it as a child, because the only television we had was black and white. When I first saw the movie in color, when Dorothy opened the door on Oz, I gasped.

COMPARATIVE HISTORY

BRANDON R. SCHRAND

It is July of 2000 and my wife, Kelli, is seven months pregnant. We've rented a guesthouse overlooking the Strait of Juan de Fuca, in the woods of Port Townsend, Washington, where I am enrolled in the weeklong Port Townsend Writers' Conference. The drive from our home in northern Utah was long—thirteen hours—but I have it in my head that I want to be a writer. It is a crackpot notion, perhaps, especially for an expectant father whose dreams are often besieged by certain realities on the ground: seven frat-boy years in college, some time in jail, and an unhingedness that lurks within. At this conference I've been dreaming of the things I have dreamt of for so long: my future son, and what I imagine to be my future career. But fears compete with dreams, as fears are wont to do, and I begin to worry that my career is fantasy, and that my son will inherit too much of me—a bloodline from my own absent father and his genealogy of dirt-floor poverty and alcoholic unrest. At the time, I don't know much about my hotheaded, dead-in-the-grave, felonious father. But I intuit a lot from what I have heard, and worry about genetic prophecies that might reveal both who I am and who might be growing in my wife's stomach.

I am at this conference not just because I want to be a writer, but also because I see writing as a way of recasting my future. If I am indentured to some genetic script, my reasoning goes, then I can write a new ending, and that ending begins with my not-yet-born son. I can upend what needs upending. It's faulty, if not fatuous, thinking, I know now. You can't write away your past or script your future any more than you can reorder the stars.

In the evenings Kelli and I leave the guesthouse behind and walk down a path cut through the tall grass to a bench with a view of the Strait. I bring a glass of wine and a book—Robert Pirsig's *Zen and the Art of Motorcycle Maintenance*. Kelli brings a book, too, and some lemon water. Foghorns moan in the distance. Orcas break the water's surface. And I peer out into the Strait and daydream about one day taking my son on a motorcycle trip through the switchgrass plains and showing him the great system of systems we call the world.

As an only child who grew up in the sagebrush town of Soda Springs, Idaho, I often thought of the absent fathers in my family, and would continue to be troubled by these broken linkages in the system of fathers and sons all my life. I never met or knew my biological father, Jerry Imeson. I knew only my stepfather, Bud Schrand, who married my mother when I was four. He has been Dad ever since, and so I took his name. The specifics of my ex-con, biological father are these: he died when he was forty-four. Heart failure, hepatitis C. He was a drug addict. He had served several prison sentences; one, for robbing a pharmacy. The drugstore cowboy and all-around ne'er-do-well. He was too much boy in a man's body and he lived his life in accordance with a reckless streak, drag-racing straight to an early grave.

Clearly not the model father.

Perhaps because of this conspicuous absence in my life, or perhaps because Bud, too, had grown up without his father, my stepdad felt compelled to overcompensate—not in the touchy-feely ways of love and compassion, but in the pragmatic ways of discipline, work, and instruction. To my dad, an electrician, life was a complex system of circuitry. There wasn't a problem that couldn't be diagrammed with a mechanical pencil and a notepad. His was a world of positives and negatives. Diverge from the diagram, and you will know the consequences. To me, electricity was something dangerous (an idea reinforced by my dad's stories), and he brought absolute order to that chaos. He bent it to his will. In a sense, I was impressed by the power he wielded, but I also found his occupation unremarkable and small-townish.

Like so many young people who hunger to leave the trappings of their small towns and small houses and small expectations, I felt a bone-deep itch to create a life in diametric opposition to my parents'. They had little means and even less education. They were lower-middle-class, middle-aged folks living in the middle of nowhere. It sounds haughty to me now, if not downright arrogant, but I suffered from an unnamed need to shuck off my blue-collar background. If accused of social-climbing, of trying to find meaning in the world through books, through writing, I would have happily pled guilty on all counts. The story I started writing in my head—the story of the future me—became the most urgent when I dreamed of having children, when I cast myself in the lead role of Father. Like a lot of people, I resolved to do things differently when it came time to take the fatherly reins.

I wanted most of all for my children to know their father, to know the story of how they came to be. I wanted to give them a traceable, discernible lineage. The trouble was this: I didn't want that traceable, discernible genetic map to be their actual lineage. I wanted to take someone else's bloodline—a clean family history devoid of the drugstore cowboy and the romping, falling-down ways of my sagebrush kin—and over-lay my children's lives with it. I feared a pattern stirring within me, viral and inevitable, a kind of genetic foregone conclusion. We are judged by the fathers we keep, and I didn't want my children to be judged as the progeny of trouble.

Back in Utah, these final weeks of Kelli's pregnancy haven't been as smooth as we hoped for. She has preeclampsia. "It's like high blood pressure," the doctor tells us. "And it can affect both you and the baby."

My heart goes wonky in my chest, my body cold and inert like channel iron. "But it will be OK, right?"

Kelli is the strong one here, back straight, inquisitive. While my questions tend toward the abstract, hers are calculated. She wants numbers, specifics, as if she has come prepared for this report.

It's a fairly common condition, the doctor tells us, and as long as we monitor it, everything should be fine. There can be cases, however, when it is more serious.

Ever since we received this news upon our return from Port Townsend, Kelli has been on bed rest, and I have been frantic to clean the house and fetch her meals and drinks and extra pillows and movies and books and anything she needs. The constant bustle keeps me busy and that is what I need, what we both need. Even though I am an agnostic, nights find me issuing crazy, desperate prayers to gods unknown. "Please," I beg while wringing my pillow. "Please—let the baby and Kelli be OK and I will be the model father. I will."

Mason was born without incident in the small hours of September 11, 2000. I remember cutting the umbilical cord (which I hadn't expected to do). I remember weighing him. I remember wanting to sleep. I also took pains to remember the data because that seemed like an important thing to do. His weight, length, time of birth. Memorizing the data seemed like something a model father would do, and I wanted to start out right.

In those early days, when I wasn't reading *What to Expect the First Year*, I was reading John Irving's *The World According to Garp*. For all its quirky, frightening, and hilarious moments, for all the high jinks and madness, *Garp* laid bare many of my insecurities as both a wannabe writer and a wannabe father. It was alarming, in fact, just how easily I recognized myself in Garp. Yes, like me, he was a wrestler in school and a writer. But more than that, he was fatherless and this absence in his life explained much of his panicked and bumbling attempts at fatherhood. He had a fever-pitched paranoia that the world, as Irving put it, was simply too dangerous for children. When Garp ran after and cursed at the cars that sped through his neighborhood, I felt the sheer inevitability of disaster not just in his life but in my own. Dangers lurked everywhere. In our family history. In our blood. In our neighborhoods. Our home abutted the property of the local high school, and daily a league of pimply hotheads gunned their junkers down our street. I would stand on my lawn and watch in jaw-set anger as they roasted their tires in front of my house, forcing me to tuck Mason's head into my jacket as the foul black smoke swirled around us. "Sons-a-bitches," I'd mutter. I was angry at the very presence of these feckless boys, and I was angry, too, because I still had a lot of their drag-racing ways roiling inside me. There was much boy yet inside this man I was now supposed to be.

Three weeks after Mason was born, I applied to graduate school at Utah State University. Every day after work, I would come home, put Mason in his crib, and check the mail and phone messages. For weeks, I heard nothing. And for weeks, I drank myself to sleep. Finally, after nearly two months of hand-wringing, my worst fears were confirmed: my application had been denied. The abysmal grades, my iffy letters of recommendation, my murky letter of intent, and my noodling paper on Edmund Spenser's *Faerie Queene* all amounted to an apologetic nay. Sort of. "Take some upper-division courses," they said, "and we might reevaluate your application." Here was a glimmer, a backdoor in. I was by turns dejected and hopeful, and so I would drink nightly to the gloom and hope in equal measure.

That spring, I enrolled in two classes and quickly became the embarrassing nontraditional, nonmatriculated student with too much to lose, and too much to prove in every class. My arm ached from raising it all too often: "Call on me! I know the answer!" My arm stretched toward the ceiling as if my son's life depended on my answering every question correctly. Here was my chance to reorder the circuitry of genetics, to rechart the future, to rewrite the story of who I had come to be.

Which was who, exactly? Consider this brief comparative history:

CRIMINAL HISTORY OF BRANDON'S FATHER

- One count burglary, January 1974.
- Felony burglary, January 1974. (This was the pharmacy job, executed when I was not yet two years old.)
- Drug possession.
- Drug-trafficking charges.
- Various moving violations.

CRIMINAL HISTORY OF MASON'S FATHER

- Felony drug possession (charges dropped to a Class B misdemeanor).
- DUI.
- Drunken disorderly conduct (arrested two weeks before my wedding day).
- Various moving violations.

The trouble with criminal histories is they are not read in the past tense. They never purport to explain who a person *was*; they mean to explain who a person *is*. They are read less as static documents recording time-swallowed events, and more as clues telegraphing the future.

So, to take a thoroughly dour view, I wasn't merely becoming my father. I had already become him. And, following this line of thinking to its logical conclusion, my son would become me. The blood circuitry fulfilling its genetic promise of hardwired danger.

That's the dour view.

The hopeful view said that I was nothing like my father. He never graduated high school, but here I was finally admitted into graduate school, after all my hand-raising and showmanship during the spring semester. The hopeful view said that there are ways to outrun your blood, that nurture trumps nature. The hopeful view said that the hotheaded boy inside me would die out and the model father (or some semblance of him) would grow in his stead.

Sometimes the hopeful and dour views collide in unexpected ways. Consider the morning of Mason's first birthday. It comes to me in snapshots. I was brushing my teeth in the hallway, where I could keep an eye on Mason, who was in his high chair in the dining room, and still talk to Kelli, who was in the bathroom. We had been discussing his birthday plans for later that day. Kelli was blow-drying her hair. Then someone on NPR said something about a plane or maybe two planes having hit the World Trade Center. "Can you turn that off?" I asked, motioning to her hair dryer.

"What?"

I pointed to the radio. Mason's birthday cake sat on the dining room table. "Something's happened," I said.

It is nothing new to say that the country moved into an uncertain time, but it was, and had been for a while, an uncertain time for me personally. On the one hand, the father in me took seriously my new station as a graduate student. I was teaching freshman composition and reading truckloads of books. I was distinguishing myself in my seminars and doing good work. On the other hand, the boy in me found a crowd of beer-drinking grad students in whose company I could fully express that unhingedness lurking within. We would pass every Friday at a bar downtown. It seemed like a grad-student thing to do. We met for lunch and left two or three hours later, drunk and sedate. Then it became five hours later. Then we took both lunch and dinner at the bar, and I would stagger home stupid-drunk and broke, pulling crumpled bar receipts from my pockets, these verdicts of excess. I'd stumble into the nursery and sway over the crib with a big dumb smile on my face. One night I woke to take a leak but never made it to the bathroom. Instead, I mistook the bed for the toilet, and pissed all over the covers and the hardwood floor. On another night, I fell down a friend's staircase, ripping the handrail out of the wall on my way down. Everything was coming unhinged, and suddenly I was both absent and present. During the semesters when my teaching schedule included Fridays, I would frequently call my office mate from the bar, and have him walk to my class to announce that I was home with a sick baby, or that I had to take my infant son to the doctor and that class was canceled.

Every staggering and red-faced minute I spent in that bar, every wasted moment I spent swaying over the urinal in the stinking bathroom, with my hand flattened on the wall to steady myself, was time I wasn't spending with my wife, my son. But what to make of this misbehavior? I was not the man or father I had hoped and promised to be. I was still the frat boy who had been hauled into the drunk tank, who had been cuffed roadside, who had stood before a judge like my father so many times before me. What, really, was the root of this trouble? It wasn't the buildings crashing to the earth in New York on my son's birthday. It wasn't that fatherhood was simply too much to bear, and so I sought escape at the bar around the corner. I loved my son in that kill-anyone-who-harms-him kind of way. But I also loved knocking back beer after beer at the bar. If I am troubled by the version of me in those days, I am even more troubled to think that my misbehavior then was an improvement on my misbehavior in my college years. In my mind, the two Brandons didn't compare. At least I wasn't failing out of school. At least my criminal history ended before I married. Or so I reasoned at the time.

Unconvinced, Kelli grew tired of my marathon binge drinking, and, with Mason in tow, she started to spend the weekends at her mother's house, two hours south. We hadn't been married three years, and already she was spending time at her mother's, which, in our unspoken way, was a euphemism for trouble at home. What's worse, I didn't seem to give a shit. The danger in our small delicate circle didn't entail planes falling from cloudless skies, or circuitry gone haywire. It entailed me. I had become the danger.

What saved us, I think—what saved me, really—was the decision to move twelve hours north from Logan, Utah, to Moscow, Idaho. Having graduated in May of 2003, I had been accepted into the MFA creative writing program at the University of Idaho, another second chance to prove myself. Kelli got a good job with the university but she had to relocate immediately. This meant that I had to stay in Utah and sell our house (we were lucky in that, unlike most grad students, we owned our home), while she and Mason moved into unknown country. Two months and hundreds of miles separated us. At night, I would walk around our empty home listening to the haunting echoes of my footfalls on hardwood, and I started to imagine in gut-rending detail what life might look like or feel like without Kelli, without Mason. I would drag my camping mattress into the nursery, slump to the floor with a beer in hand, and try to smell some hint of his skin or his shampooed hair. It sounds sentimental to me now, but maybe I was in a sentimental place, and maybe that was what I needed.

At the end of the summer, I joined them. I left behind the empty house and let my ghostly echoes die there. I couldn't get to Idaho fast enough. I raced the entire way, leaning into the steering wheel for twelve hours straight. We had rented a two-story Victorian home in a tiny logging town eleven miles east of town. The air smelled like ripsawed lumber and you could hear the continual whine of the mill working day and night. Our house had a wood-burning stove and I ordered two cords of tamarack and would spend the cool autumn afternoons splitting and stacking wood. We canned tomatoes and green beans and Kelli made bread and I would play with Mason on our spacious living room floor. I wrote in the mornings to the hiss and pop of the stove and prepared for class in the evenings. We were alone, which is another way of saying we were together for the first time since Mason was born. I was learning how to be a father and husband again. Our small town huddled in a wooded gorge with steep streets, and from our porch we could see wood smoke in the air, and the rooftops of houses farther down below us.

It was our routine that I would pull Mason in his wagon to the post office, where I would mail essays to magazines and pick up rejection slips. I would then pull him to the market for an ice-cream cone and then on to the park, where I would read the mail and watch him play. Or I would stand at the bottom of the slide urging him to let go, assuring him I would catch him, that it wasn't dangerous. Or I would chase him across the baseball diamond and we would crash in the outfield. There was no epiphany in those days. No lightning strike, no sudden moment of clarity. But there was the slow and inevitable accumulation of days beneath the sky and the rhythms of activity you might call life. The dour view, in other words, was losing ground to the hopeful view.

I recall from that period taking a class, from the writer Kim Barnes, called "Finding the Father." The seminar called for an impressive list of works. Adam Hochschild's *Half the Way Home*,

Christopher Dickey's *Summer of Deliverance*, Susan Cheever's *Home Before Dark*, Nick Flynn's *Another Bullshit Night in Suck City*, and others. For years I had been trying to find my own father, and during those falling-down years in Utah, I found him in the mirror every morning throwing a bloodshot gaze back at me.

I was now in the process of finding the father within.

I recall that class, too, because halfway through the semester, Kelli took a pregnancy test and it was positive, a result that, because we had been trying, left us elated.

On December 1, 2005, our daughter, Madeline, arrived in the midst of a horrendous Idaho blizzard. When we brought her home from the hospital, winter was barreling down on us. Snow drifted against the house, punctuating our new togetherness. We were socked in. I split kindling in the snow and loaded the stove and tried to keep the large house warm. The woodstove wasn't the only source of heat (we had a furnace), but it was the most cost-effective. Mason helped me feed the fire, and I taught him about draft and fuel. This was another of our routines. Lighting fires. "It's important," I told him, "to know how to start every fire with only one match."

"How come?"

"Because," I said. "One day you may find yourself having only one match." It was one way of teaching him how to guard against the unexpected.

At five years of age, Mason was excited to be a big brother. But he was also nervous to hold his sister, nervous that he would do something wrong. I recall holding her out to him while he danced from one foot to another. "What if I drop her?"

"You won't drop her," I said.

"But what if I do?"

He gets his nervousness from me. When he is a father, I imagine, he will chase speeding cars down his street, waving his arms in the air, cursing their feckless ways.

But if he is nervous, he is also curious. He asked questions about his sister, about childbirth, about breast feeding. And I talked with him. I told him the story of his birth and Kelli's preeclampsia and bed rest. Each story prodded more questions. As with most five-year-olds, his world was made up of questions, which became more complicated over time.

"Dad," he said one morning over breakfast. "Did the big buildings fall on my birthday?"

It was a subject that came up infrequently, but one that he had keyed in on whenever someone asked when his birthday was.

I paused, considered my response, and set my coffee cup down. "Yes, they did," I said, taking the less-is-more approach.

The question came almost as a non sequitur, catching me off guard. One day, I knew, we'd have to have the talk about how those buildings crashed to the earth. We'd have to talk about outward, unforeseen dangers.

It is a Saturday morning not long after the New Year, Madeline just beyond a month old. I am in my office writing, Madeline cooing on a blanket near the bookcase. Kelli is cooking breakfast. The thick scents of bacon, coffee, baked bread, and tamarack hang in the air. Outside, the skies are clear but with the kind of cold that waters your eyes. From the living room, where Mason is playing with his action figures, the stove radiates waves of dry heat. I slip into the kitchen to refresh my coffee and talk with Kelli.

"Dad?" we hear Mason call from the living room.

I sip from my coffee and turn.

"Dad, something's wrong."

He is standing in front of the woodstove, pointing up. The white sting of fear strikes fast and electric. The black stovepipe that runs from the stove top to the ceiling has popped its seam and come loose from the ceiling plate. The pipe leans slightly and spews foul black smoke and soot, and sparks shower the carpet and couches. I tell Kelli to get the baby out of the house. "Mason, get outside." He starts to cry. "We're fine, buddy," I say, softening the tone. "Just go outside."

The smoke detector begins chirruping steadily. After I shut down the damper, I put my leather gloves on, stand on a chair, and grab the stovepipe. But the gloves are too thin, the pipe too hot. In one fluid motion, I leap off the chair, dash to the kitchen, and return with four hot pads. Back on the chair, I try with no success to reconnect the pipe to the ceiling plate. Sparks are singeing my hair and the house is filling with black smoke, and even with the hot pads and gloves, the pipe is burning my hands. Desperate, I cock the stove pipe at an angle so that the upper sleeve binds against the lower shank, preventing it—I hope—from crashing down, and begin pulling burning wood from the belly of the stove and dropping the chunks in threes into a scuttle. It takes three trips to convey the burning wood from the house. I have dumped each load into a backyard snowdrift. Kelli and the kids are standing in the front yard. Are they silent? Are they crying? Are the neighbors watching this whole thing unfold? I have no idea. I cannot see them nor can I hear them for the quick rush of blood in my ears.

A half hour later, the fire is dead, the smoke mostly cleared, and Kelli has brought the kids back inside. We're fine, if shaken. That night or maybe a few nights later, I have a nightmare that the house is burning to the ground and I can't get to my children. They aren't screaming, but I can hear Mason's searching voice, hauntingly calm. He just keeps saying, "Dad? Dad? Dad?" The dream rattles me so much that I get up, grab Mason from his bed, and pull him into ours. Madeline is fast asleep on Kelli's chest and I lie awake looking at all of them and thank those gods I have cursed and thanked before for this—for this very moment right here in the long quiet of night.

Those years in that hamlet seem marked by improvement. I was less idiot, and more writer. Less boy, and more man. Less barfly, and more husband. Less son, and more father. Eventually, though, we had to leave. Rising gas prices, the quality of schools, and a range of other variables made our move into Moscow inevitable. Two weeks before we moved, though, the grain elevators caught fire and nearly took the town with them. A black cloud hung over us. The mood was grim. The silos had been packed with wheat and dry peas when they burned. The entire yield was gone, and the fire meant not only crop loss, but job loss.

"Wow," Mason said, looking over the twisted, smoldering metal. "They're just gone."

"Yeah," I said. "Fire does that."

He pointed at the charred wreckage and debris and said, "Is this what the buildings that fell on my birthday looked like?"

"Sorta, buddy. Sorta."

What I wanted to say is that they didn't compare. Or that they compared only in their unexpectedness, and, in that way, compared with any other unforeseen, outward danger. In a more insightful moment I might have said that a lot of things don't compare even if they look the same or share the same histories. Or blood. I might have said you can go crazy living a life by comparison. In a more insightful moment I might have said there can be dangers within and dangers without, and you can control only so much.

Buildings go up in smoke. Cars speed through neighborhoods. Planes fall from the sky. Fathers stagger home drunk. You can't chase away all the dangerous things with flailing arms and curses. This much I know. The dangers I can chase away, however, the ones that stare back from the mirror, the ones that seem wired into the genetic map, those I can, and have, chased away, more or less. I still fall down, just differently. I erupt over small things. I am impatient with my children on mornings when we're running late. I am preoccupied with work, with tasks that dog me. My attentions are divided. In these regards, I am not that much different from other fathers. The pressures and fears and worries are always there, for most of us, I would guess. And like so many fathers, I am always trying to slow down and stop the clock. I am trying to pay attention.

And when I am not paying attention, I can count on my children to call me on it. A month or so ago, I was lying in bed reading when Madeline—who was not yet three—crawled up on my chest and grabbed my face with both hands. "Look at me, *boy*," she said. It was one of those comments that was by turns hilarious for its Katharine Hepburn–like coolness, and arresting for how it undivided my attention and pulled me into the present.

In *The Gift of Fatherhood: How Men's Lives Are Transformed by Their Children*, Dr. Aaron Hass argues that fathers need to find their way to the "Zen of Fatherhood" and work to secure an "orientation of the present." I'm not entirely sure I will ever find the "Zen of Fatherhood" (or the art of motorcycle maintenance, for that matter), nor am I convinced that books like Dr. Hass's fine volume will show me the way. I picked it up because I have been thinking about fatherhood lately and about my failures and blunders and my ongoing mission to root out the ne'er-do-well that lurks within. Little in the book surprises me. Hass articulates what most of us already know about fatherhood. It's difficult and rewarding. It is important to be present, to foster a loving marriage, to "discipline with love," and so on. There is much that is implied, too. Don't spend your nights at the bar. Don't piss on your bed. Don't fall down the stairs. It is a clean and orderly book that seems written for a clean and orderly reader. After all, the kind of father who would buy this book and who would read it straight through (I did not) probably doesn't need any of the advice contained its pages. And the fathers who would benefit most by reading its pages—fathers like my own, for instance—never will.

The book did articulate the importance of tuning in to those Zen moments, and for that I am grateful to have thumbed through its pages. Zen moments abound. Consider the Sunday afternoon I stepped into my children's bedroom and spied Madeline sitting on Mason's lap. He had been reading her a book. Now they were chatting. He was talking about how he would go to Harvard when he graduated. I froze and thought, "Maybe all my hand-raising might pay off." Maybe you can script the future in some small way. Maybe you can reorder the stars, after all.

NOTES FROM ADOLESCENCE

RICK BASS

Another August has gone by, and another year without getting my young daughters in to meet their country music idol—who, truth be told, is really a long-haired handsome rock star who happens to wear blue jeans and have a banjo player in his band. It relieves me hugely that if the girls are going to listen occasionally to country stations, they admire this star's music, rather than the flag-draped commerce of stay-at-home crooners who wax and wail with alternating doses of self-pity and passive-aggressive "bring it on" jingoism; and the girls have learned, as well, to recognize the repulsive misogyny too often prevalent on the country radio stations, an altered misogyny, even slightly more dangerous than the purer form, in that it masquerades as a nod-and-wink parody of misogyny, as in, "We're just singing this to be funny," or "We're just singing this to make money, we don't really believe this stuff in real life." Misogyny for Fun and Profit.

The country rock star, however, is not simply the lesser of the many evils available on these stations. Instead, seemingly miraculously, he makes art and rhythm out of some of the things my wife and I try to stress to the girls regularly in our dry-as-dust lectures about a culture that is too often predicated upon an ability to race downward toward the bottom. It pleases me, as a citizen and a parent, to hear the positive values espoused in the star's songs, which possess their fair share of heartache, disappointment, setback, and longing—the stuff of life—as opposed, perhaps, to the stuff of the country rock star who has it all. The songs are about celebrating the specificity of each moment, about taking nothing for granted. Songs about how incredibly quickly the days go by.

This last idea carries particular resonance for me. When each of the girls was born, everyone told me how fast it would pass by. Often, these were the first words out of people's mouths. And I understood and believed them, and lingered as long as possible. But then despite my foreknowledge, the girls started growing up and pulling away.

"Oh, they'll come back," everyone said. (There were even more people telling us this than had told us that the days would go by quickly.) It's hard to imagine that they'll come back, though, and the fear that they won't is further magnified by the fact that with savage acuity my oldest daughter has zeroed in on, and identifies daily, the multitude of flaws within me, which are intensifying, like some dreaded curse, as youth and strength and focus and everything else exfoliates from me, leaving only rubble and clumsiness. The bifocals, the diminished hearing, the pause for a deeper breath when going up a flight of stairs, the absentmindedness that was always present but which is becoming amplified: how can she bear to be seen with me?

"Dad, stop treating me like I'm twelve," says the fourteen-year-old, Mary Katherine. And she's right: but I can't keep up. "Dad, you're so protective," says Lowry, the eleven-year-old. And again I plead *guilty*: slow, and guilty.

"They'll be back," everyone keeps saying. As if you get a second chance at love. Many days it is a leap of faith to believe this truism, whereas I believed the earlier one intuitively. And what none of those earlier advice-givers ever mentioned was how god-awful much it would hurt, once the pulling away started. As if this revelation possessed so much density and pain that not even the most callous or insensitive among them had the heart to reveal that forthcoming leave-taking.

Which returns me, indirectly, to the country rock star. Back in the early days of Mary Katherine's pulling away, I had gotten into my mind that one way to inoculate myself against any pending wave of scorn might be to show her that I could still possess some worth in her world.

"Maybe I'll see if I can interview him," I told her one evening when she was being distant. Where had my chum gone, the girl of only a year ago, only six months ago? "Maybe we can interview him together," I said. "Maybe all three of us will," I amended—for how could one daughter get preferential treatment when the star was the idol of both?

Mary Katherine turned to see if I was joking. "Yeah, well, that might be cool," she said. "Sure, OK. I guess." She was washing a dish and it seemed to me she lingered there at the sink for a moment or two after the plate was finished: as if wanting more conversation, more connection. Or so I chose to hope. I have no idea what she was thinking, but I imagined it was one of two things: either her teen heart was leaping with a wild joy that would never do for her father to witness, or— more likely—she was thinking, "Oh yeah, right, another big idea he won't be able to deliver." The rock clubhouse I've been working on for ten years now, with more yet to go. The vacation to Australia for which we've been saving. Etc. Less than perfect, so far.

Thus began the year in which I set about trying to arrange a simple meeting with an entertainer who was, unfortunately (from my perspective), having the biggest year of his career, to the point where things might have been easier had the girls decided they wanted to meet one of the Stones, or a Beatle.

I read all the trade magazines and began pitching the story idea to editors of those magazines, as well as to larger, general-interest magazines with which I had worked on other stories. I contacted friends in the public relations industry, who put me in touch with friends of friends in the recording industry.

As with most things, the first five or six degrees of separation were shed quickly—within the first day or two, we had closed the distance between utter anonymity and near access almost completely, and were visiting with people who knew people who worked with him; and not long after that, I was trading cell-phone messages with his road manager.

I had high hopes, but, in order to keep from jinxing it, mentioned none of it to the girls, instead allowing them to go about their lives harboring the thought that maybe such a thing might work out someday, but more likely than not, it wouldn't; that I was probably just being old dreaming dad again, well-intentioned and sweet but in the end ineffectual, unpossessed of the power to shape the world in such fashion as to fit their dreams.

But after closing those first five or six degrees, I hit the wall:

rejection everywhere I turned. "No, no," came the expected answers. "No, he doesn't do that kind of thing anymore." The responses from the star's camp were understandable, but oddly, even the editors and magazines I was counting on to help give me entrée were suddenly incommunicado: as if some great Murdochian invisible e-mail had gone out into their blood saying, "Do not do this story, protect our property . . ."

It was the damnedest thing. Did they not see what a great story it was? Even magazines that had been asking me to pitch them various story suggestions didn't respond. I had written before for these magazines—about firefighters and dictators and bird dog trainers and Olympic athletes—but now they thought I either was unsuited to writing about country music or was instead, again, simply a fan gone a-stalking.

Which I guess I was.

We began to go to concerts. Not stalking. Just going to see him, and to listen to the music. Or one concert at first, anyway, at which—in a bolt of grand luck at least partly inspired, I like to think, by the residue of my efforts, the hundreds of pages of letters and queries, and the hundreds of futile phone calls—the star's road manager saw our daughters sitting in the distant balcony of the Paramount Theatre in Seattle—the cheap seats— and invited them down to the front row, where, in the midst of his thunderous, enthusiastic show, the star held his guitar down into the crowd and let them play a few chords.

So goes childhood; and so it should be.

I wrote a little essay about that experience, published in the *Los Angeles Times Magazine*. The morning after the essay appeared there was an e-mail from some Hollywood person— the first time in my twenty years of writing that someone from that neighborhood had gotten in touch with me—saying that he had a deal to make a movie in which the country rock star would be featured, and wanted to know if I had an agent, and if I would be interested in writing the screenplay.

It was August, summer in Montana. I stood outside by the garden talking on the portable phone and said yes. This Hollywood person stated that just the previous week he had eaten lunch with the star. Then the Hollywood person, whom I did not know from boo, said he was going to put his boss on the line.

We chatted amiably. The boss had just started a new company, and he, too, had just had lunch with the star, and indicated he was best friends with the president of the star's management company. They flew everywhere together, the boss and the star's manager—had just come back from a vacation in Europe, in fact, flying on the manager's private jet, and the three of them would be meeting up again to go mountain biking somewhere in Idaho. Somewhere posh. "He really likes nature," said Film Guy. "We think you'd be the perfect writer."

I remember the sun's heat, as I stood out there in my garden. I remember thinking, "Wow, how am I going to keep this secret from the girls?"

There wasn't any money available yet—they needed to see two pages first, then another page, then thirty or so, they said—so I went straight to work. I dropped the big novel I'd been working on—the one I still intend to get back to; the Big Novel, as I think of it, as I suppose all forty- and then fifty-something novelists must, at that point in their lives, begin to think of things, as in, "Am I ever going to do this or not?"—and I set about dreaming, structuring, writing a full treatment and synopsis, with scenes and beats, all that stuff.

My benefactors and I corresponded daily—I kept pouring in the ideas, really fleshing the screenplay out, developing it, until I had what I thought was the perfect vehicle for this sensitive, handsome star, who by this time had begun dating a true Hollywood starlet, a grand actress.

In some of our e-mail and phone conversations, my benefactors kept asking me to float my script work past certain other screenwriters, famous and established ones, for ideas, and so I did. I called up my friend B—— in Texas, who laughed and told me they were trying to scam me for a free story—"throwing something against the wall and seeing if it sticks" is how he put it—and that these very folks had called him, too. My agent said, "Look, Rick . . ."

"I'm going to play it out," I told myself: not really caring so much about the money, but instead holding fast to a vision of the girls, at some near point, buzzing out to the set to watch their star go through his lines. I could always get back to the novel. I still had plenty of time to be a writer. Or at least more of that than there was time to do fun things with my girls before they grew up.

Sure, there was a part of me that whispered daily, "Put it down, walk away; go back to the solitude of your novel; choose literature over family scrapbooks and dream stuff, choose cold art over the long-shot chances at making a fine family memory."

And every day—moving deeper into the ethereal land of the dream, and of hope—I put aside those whisperings and instead moved forward, as if into the wind and without a map. Is there any foolishness, any craziness, as severe as that of middle age?

It would be interesting to tally the resources spent in the pursuit—the miles of carbon embedded in the script of letters mailed to New York and Nashville, to L.A. and Texas, and the stacks of envelopes, the rolls of stamps, the blizzards of faxes, the triple-figure long-distance bills—and more interesting still to tally that rarer and more precious commodity, time: the days, weeks, and then months accumulating in both the crafting and then the execution of the dream.

But even more costly and precious, I think, would be a tally of the balance sheet of the most valuable thing yet, *hope.*

I hadn't given the girls the specifics of the dream—was still planning it as a surprise—but I did let them know that I was working on something, on a Big Idea. A special project.

"How's it going?" they would ask every few months— those first many months, when the idea was still new—to which I would give the predictable answer of adulthood, and of life—"Well, I'm working on it."

And sometimes, in their quiet nods, I could see hope, though other times I would see the other thing—the suspicion, or even belief, that it wouldn't work out.

I suppose I should have been surprised by that call from out of the blue, and to some extent I was; but there was also a part of me that wasn't: the part that has never been interested in *not* dreaming big—isn't that why it's called dreaming, after all? This was precisely the kind of thing that I wanted the girls to believe in. Some might call it magic; I tend to think of it as just niceness, or sweetness.

Certainly magic was still in play. The star, it turns out, was coming to Montana, to play in Missoula; we got tickets, and that same day a country-music trade magazine called and said they wanted to reprint the story about the Seattle concert, and the publisher of that magazine—who was good friends, he said, with the president of the record company for which the star recorded—would try his best to set up a meeting between us and the star, to get a photo for the magazine.

Feverish calls, frenzied e-mails; I suggested to the publisher a place where the girls and the star and I could meet for lunch and dinner, in Missoula, and make that photograph, and visit, in the most abstract way, about what kind of script might hold the most interest for the star. An environmental theme, a romance, a small-town mill preserved, wild country protected.

Such things seemed very close now, very real. I could imagine my girls sitting at the table grinning, and forgetting to order. I could see them being clumsy with shyness, clumsy with childhood. I could see them later, as adults, laughing at the audacity of youth and dreams and at the splendid way improbably good things could still happen, then and now, on any given day.

We didn't connect with the star—the calls to the publisher, and to the star's management company, were not returned—but they did hold some tickets for us at will-call, and we headed south anyway, on a fine fall day, full of hope and excitement and a strange intoxicating elixir of sweetness. An early snow high in the mountains already. And luck was still with us. We got there early, and when I took the girls over to stand by the chain-link fence that separated the star's idling bus from the real world, the bass player came out, visited a bit, signed a scrap of paper. A nice lady appeared and distributed photos of the star, as well as some of the star's trademark guitar picks, to the dozen or so young people standing around in the September evening, and it was enough. It was life, and it was good.

And at that show, the kindly floor manager—the same one who had come and gotten the girls in Seattle—told the girls he'd see what he could do at this show.

True to his word, once the concert began he did indeed find them, and brought them up to the front row, made a place for these two girls, eleven and fourteen years old, rather than for

the less chastely dressed twenty-somethings who were screaming and clamoring for those same places. And the country rock
star at one point wandered over to my girls and leaned down,
took each of their hands, and gave each hand a princely kiss,
before continuing on; and despite my belief, my understanding, that magic, sweetness, goodness, can exist in the world, it
did seem like over-the-top luck.

It occurred to me, driving back home, that early autumn
night—four hours back up into the mountains—how strange
and wonderful it was, that the girls should be able to continue
to access such magic: *of course their goals, their dreams, should be
met; they were my girls, did I not want everything in the world for
them?* And this even though the object of their dream, the
country rock star (or at least his management committee),
had screened and deflected our ridiculous efforts for an actual
meeting.

The world simply would not have that. And yet was there
not plenty of magic already, for such things to be happening
despite the deflections? And the most wonderful part of all—
experiencing not the completion of the desire, but instead, the
desire itself, unending.

And best of all, I knew these things—that we were traf-
ficking in magic, despite our failure—even as the girls were
unaware of it: unaware of this distance, in so many of our
lives, between the sleepwalking world above and that magic
vein, like a wild river, just below. The magic vein was still all
they knew—where not only was almost nothing impossible,
but better, where almost any noble dream was still attainable,
or at least probable.

It's been nine months since our last concert. The movie deal
fell apart, as is, I am told, the natural order of such things—the

contact who claimed to have the inside track was just bullshit-ting, stringing me along the way my agent and screenwriter friends said he was. I've come to a bit of a dead end, creatively, on this venture. The star got married, moved on to a new phase in his life, and in the meantime, our lives are moving on. Some days it seems that the ticking clock is becoming more noticeable—or as if certain other things around that clock are becoming quieter. It's hard to explain—hard to pin down the absences of things that never really were.

Lowry, at eleven, is still a firm and full believer in miracles, but—and I knew this day would come—Mary Katherine is be-coming increasingly a citizen of this world, in which there are other things to look at instead of, or in addition to, that strange bright river beneath us, which informs, or once informed, so many of our dreams.

I would still very much like to put it—a meeting, an inter-view, a story—together, not so much before the country rock star passes on to the relative oblivion and larger irrelevance that awaits all of us, but even more quickly than that—before a girl totally grows up. That part will be wonderful, too, but I still cannot help wanting a little more time.

There is an element of foolishness, and audacity, in any magic. You have to keep hoping and believing, and yet you also have to live a life. The desire for some magical thing can and will drift on. You can't spend your life waiting for those strange little windows of magic, or near magic—moments made up of the curious and invisible fermentation of that sustained desire and belief, moments when the dreamer stands beside that river, moments when all the conditions for a miracle are ripe.

Instead, you go on with your life. You live your life, you

wander the world. Hopefully, though, you don't turn your back on that magic.

I think I want the girls to be great dreamers. I know that there are sometimes liabilities associated with such a thing, but I think I want them to retain access to that river, and to have the faith and belief that if they want to cross it, they can; that the world will occasionally accommodate, even support, such crossings.

The other evening at the house in town, where we stay during the school week, from out of the blue Mary Katherine—complete in her fourteen-year-oldness—surprised me at dusk by asking if I would go out on the lawn and play catch with her. It's been ages since she has been willing to be so associated with me, and I fairly leaped from my chair when she asked. She had a new glove she wanted to break in, it turns out, but so what? *Use me*, please. More astonishing, she was in her pajamas: another decidedly uncool circumstance, with the full potential for spectacle, were one of her friends to pass by.

And yet there we were, in the spring twilight, on the new-mown lawn, an easy silence between us, tossing and catching, alternating high pop-ups with delicious leather-smacking zingers, and the snap of our gloves echoing smartly through the neighborhood.

We played on into true dusk, with the bright yellow ball somehow becoming more luminous, not less, as the light of the spring day faded, and as even the roosting calls and chirps of the birds in the trees around us grew quieter and then silent. We played on until it was absolutely dark, and then went back inside to get ready for bed.

My fear is no longer so much that the girls won't ever get

to meet the country rock star, but worse: that one day, and far too soon, it might no longer matter to them.

Did I really expend all that energy, trying to help them secure a little dream? Who was that man whose focus wavered a bit, whose eyes shifted slightly away from his novel for a moment? And yet: in these last years before they leave home, it is clearly the novel that should be at the perimeter of vision, not the center.

Slowly, I turn back to the idea of that novel, if not to the thing itself. Maybe this summer, maybe this fall, I will start making some new notes: checking in on it, as if taking care of an animal in a corral. Making sure it is still waiting there— perhaps patiently, perhaps not—at the corner of my vision.

I will continue to encourage the girls to believe in their dreams. It's the trying that matters. I don't mind holding on to this quality myself in middle age, and I certainly do not want them to lose it, when they leave the dream-filled territory of adolescence.

A YEAR IN THE LIFE OF
A HOMEBOUND WANDERER,
MASTER AVERY IN ATTENDANCE

SEBASTIAN MATTHEWS

For my wife and me, having a kid was never a make-or-break issue. We married relatively young—Ali twenty-four, I about to turn twenty-nine. We'd always entertained the idea, even toying with adoption; at the same time, we could also see ourselves living happily without children. There were enough kids in both of our families for us to interact with and love. We figured we had ample time to decide.

What we didn't count on was for the juvenile rheumatoid arthritis that Ali had been dealing with since her teens to move gradually into a more serious stage. Gone were the long mountain hikes, the late nights, the all-day road trips. Well, we could still do all this, but for the following few days (sometimes weeks) Ali paid the price physically. Slowly we changed our lifestyle to accommodate her condition.

When we looked into it further, we learned that having a baby would initially bring about positive effects for Ali; something about the whole process placed most women into temporary remission. But her doctor warned Ali of an intense, possibly yearlong postpartum episode. Ali wasn't sure she could go through with such a pregnancy, and I wasn't sure I could carry the extra load required of me. Since we both had relatives who had been adopted, and I had been mentoring a boy as a Big Brother, it wasn't hard for us to return to the idea of adopting.

It wasn't until Ali's cousins and our closest friends, Marc and Ellen, adopted their lovely girl, Kira, that we realized that we wanted to do it ourselves. Our first thought was to go overseas, as Marc and Ellen had. But on a Barbara Walters special one night, an interviewee said, "People go all over the world to find babies to adopt when there are babies in our own communities who need good families." It made perfect sense for us to do just that.

We adopted our son, Avery, in August 2003, when he was only seven weeks old. The whole thing took, from start to finish, eighteen months. Because we spent the last nine of those months waiting on a list, we didn't feel all that different from our friends who were on their own journeys conceiving and having babies. And like a couple whose newborn arrives prematurely, we received our phone call earlier than expected. In fact, the agency told us that we had two days to come and get him. And we hadn't even cleared out the room. *His* room! The next day we spent so much money at Sears and Babies "R" Us (car seat, stroller, digital camera, diapers, wipes, diaper pail) that the credit card company called to warn us that someone had stolen our card and gone on a spending spree.

We live in Asheville, North Carolina, where the Blue Ridge meets the Great Smoky Mountains—as the brochures like to say—so we had to drive the three hours down the mountain to Greensboro to pick up our boy. I remember being scared to change lanes on the drive back lest I disturb the newly beating heart in our midst. That first night, sleepless and awestruck, we peered into his crib, afraid our boy might stop breathing in his sleep. Those first few sweltering days were spent floating on swiftly moving water astride a bare futon raft. A revolving door of visitors cooking for us, checking in. Then came the run of whitewater rapids through those first weeks. All that parenting on the fly, with its slew of ragged, on-the-spot saves—little improvisations laced with love and fear and the hope that allows us to make it through all the turns, the changes.

About halfway through this eye-opening first year with Avery, I began to write morning lines—a paragraph or two jotted down for a three-way e-mail exchange with two of my writer buddies. Quickly I saw the lines as a way to hold on to a fast-receding creative life. If I couldn't get to any of my larger projects, at least I could write a few poems, attend to my morning lines.

After more than a year of this back and forth, I found there were quite a few pages on daily life with Avery. In the pages that follow, Avery jumps over the hurdle of his second year, firmly stepping into toddlerhood. Ali and I trail behind, ready to pick him up when he falls. As I write this now, Avery strides deep into his fifth year, moving lithely in his newly sinewy body as he dribbles the soccer ball around the house. I can hardly believe he was ever so small, so young, so in need of our unconditional love.

OCTOBER

The morning dance with Avery can be graceful and easy. I feed him breakfast and make coffee while he sorts his food by color, shape, texture. (He insists on eating the yogurt with his hands.) When the local radio station follows the arts calendar with Old Crow Medicine Show's "Wagon Wheel," I dance around to amuse my boy. Even Ursula, ever the Lab, joins in. The rain starts in, seasoned jazz drummer. Ali is up, the showerhead adding its percussion to the day's banal playlist.

But this dance breaks down, too, its precarious balance toppling into a jumble. I drop an egg, whack my hand on the kitchen door; Avery throws his spoon on the floor and refuses his food. Inattention at every turn. After half an hour, I give up and bring the boy to his mother, retreat to the shower. Soon a gleeful Avery tosses all his tub toys at my soapy feet. Before I know it, the little monkey has roped me into his room to play blocks. There goes the morning.

A good friend laughingly dismisses the notion of a child's first years as "magical." She quips: "More like the *relentless* years." I think, "relentless and magical both." On my morning walk, two hawks hover above, tipping their wings back and forth in an elaborate dance. I head back to a day of writing, grading papers, housework, Master Avery in attendance.

Hurricane Katrina hit the coast two months before, sending heavy rains and evacuees our way. Ali and I keep trying to imagine what it would be like to be trapped down in New Orleans—no car, no money, no way out. We'd try to walk out, we agree, knowing nothing. Hating that we know nothing. We'd put Avery on our back and just start walking out. We're being naive, we know it, but can't stop imagining the endless hours in huge lines waiting for help to arrive that keeps not arriving. We'd need to move, find high ground, some sort of sanctuary. Trapped, no way out—this scenario is repeated up and down the coast for miles.

Which makes me worry for Avery, now tottering toward the river. I lift him on my shoulders and bring him up close to the flood damage. Trees piled along the ruined trail. Sand and sludge jammed into the bushes. Everything dead-brown and sad. All except for the old cold mud pit at the bend, which has somehow sprung to life, as if spring-fed, water saturating the mossy earth, lapping at tree roots. Avery passes, blissful, ignorant, into our very own miniature Eden!

DECEMBER

Ali's off for the weekend, so it's just me and Avery moving through the day—and a restless dog wondering where the walks will come from. The weekend opens up as a great expanse. We walk out into it, alone, together. Fittingly, Garrison Keillor celebrates Rilke's birthday on his morning radio *Writer's Almanac*, quoting: "It is good to be solitary, for solitude is difficult; that something is difficult must be a reason the more for us to do it. To love is good, too: love being difficult."

I dread weekends like this, alone with Avery. I know I am being selfish, but what'd you expect, I'm a writer! I need time to get my work done, turn to my daily lines, pick up a book. Does it sound like I am blaming Avery, bemoaning being a parent? Maybe I am. But also the phone is on the fritz, the whole house a mess. It takes half the day to bring some small semblance of order to the familial chaos. And the only reason I do it is that if I don't, I'll start to scream or shout or run out the front door. "Breathe, man. Breathe!"

Tonight we'll eat the rest of the leftover pasta. Maybe a basketball game will be on. I have papers to grade. Anyway, Ali will be home in the morning. I fill a tub for Avery, pick out pajamas, three books to read. Check, check, check. "Oh yeah, brush your teeth, Avery. Where's your toothbrush?"

When he falls asleep, I'll return to my writing. Solitude is difficult. Love is difficult. Gradually, piece by rooted piece, I work to transform routine into the charged attention of ritual.

Picture the snow falling softly, no wind, not too cold. Picture the sky a cool curtain of gray. Cars in the driveway dusted with a layer of wet snow. Now a winter-jacketed man comes out and begins changing a tire. A dog, let out to romp in the snow, runs off to relieve herself under a tree. Another man comes out, hat on his head, to throw sticks for the dog. A hooded little girl joins the scene, wandering around the yard happily, tasting snow off the tip of her gloves. Inside, a mother dresses her boy who has been at the window, mouth to cold glass, watching the girl and dog. The first man has now jacked up the car, two tires in a pile. The other man has retrieved his son, decked out in snow pants and bright red gloves. The dog is running in mad circles, kicking up snow. A woman comes out to help with the tires. The mother stays inside and makes herself an omelet to go with the bacon on the sideboard. Coffee brewing. Someone has put on Chopin. Outside, the snow has turned to sleet.

When the dog grabs one of the boy's gloves and tears around the yard, one of the men stalks after her, mock growling. The boy climbs along the fence imagining a great fall below, arms out like a high-wire walker. The second tire on. The snow converting to its first falling. And, as these things go, the boy's hands get cold and the whole group decides to go back in.

Someone turns off the Chopin and puts in a video for the

children. One of the men has brought in the paper, the dogs two clumps by the fire. Picture this scene. Underneath it, place a caption in your mind that reads "Happiness."

JANUARY

Ali and I argued last night, the open bottle of wine between us acting as interpreter. We wondered aloud how to create a consistent response to the testing of a willful child, but we sit on opposite ends of a philosophical seesaw. How to punish misbehavior, reinforce positive acts? The books all say something different. Ali says we should stop Avery at each small crossroads and tell him which way to go. Teeter. I want to let things slide, attend to the problems as they arise. Totter.

Another hour of hard talk, and around about midnight we forge a middle way: we'll use Ali's method for a while but combine it with a reward system that we dole out together. We go to bed still disconnected, each a little hurt by the tussle. No kiss before bed, only a light touch on a turned shoulder. So of course I wake up dry-mouthed, wounded, weary.

Master Avery rambles around the bedroom, as is his wont: picking up books, exploring the closet, manhandling Ursula, who has sneaked onto the front edge of the bed and is slowly pushing my feet out into the chill.

Maybe it will help to think of the morning's task list as farm chores. Empty the diaper trash in with the bathroom garbage and bring the smelly bag downstairs (trailed by the boy, curious). Set the boy up in his booster seat with banana and cheese, put on his new favorite video ("Head, shoulders, knees and toes, knees and toes"), then drag the garbage to the curb.

The bed sure is warm. I could be downstairs opening a new

box of freezer bags, dumping coffee beans into the grinder, chopping Avery's tofu into bite-size pieces, or pouring food for the dog (making sure she gets a little wet food so she'll eat it straight off and Avery won't come later and send the dry food in a shower across the floor).

I think about writing these lines and how, behind them, three student poems and two stories await my response. I have been resisting them again. The spare poem bereft of visual detail needs to be dressed by the class; the poem decked out in all manner of fanciful language redressed.

Soon I will go about the day's work, step by step.

Soon. But not just yet.

FEBRUARY

I'm finally getting the hang of this fathering thing. I don't wake up in a panic so often now on the days when I change the first morning diaper, strap Avery in his car seat, drive him to day care. I guess I've relaxed a little, gotten used to the four-hour blocks of solo child care. Avery is at an age now where the ratio of need to self-reliance, demand to openness, is well balanced. Most of the time.

I awake to a quiet house. Little Avery kicks at my kidneys, slippery bottle dancing in his hands. When I raise my palm up by his face, he takes one hand off the bottle and gives me a rhythmic high five. That is, until he discovers my wedding band. He keeps mouthing sounds inside his bottle, "ring" or "daddy" or "ball," and turns his head to make sure Mommy still lies beside us.

I remember my dream. In it, the truck is edging toward a small cliff. I'm braking but it's not helping. Even the emergency brake proves useless. The whole show is going over. I reach for the driver's door, start pushing it open with my shoulder, but we're going down. It's not until I am up pissing in the toilet that I think to question. Was Avery in the backseat of the car, strapped in the car seat?

MARCH

I just tried to put Avery's shirt on while he was in Ali's lap. The maneuver took him by surprise and he resisted. When Ali tried to soothe his screaming, Avery threw a soft jab toward her face. "Time out!" I said authoritatively, and took him to his room. "No hitting Mommy!"

"Not!" Avery answered, somehow managing to sound weak and belligerent at the same time. Ali followed us in to remind me, "It was your move that surprised him." I promised Avery I would not pull the shirt over his head. Avery relaxed and relented. "Ha," he said. "Hum."

It took a while for Avery to warm back up to me; you could see his worry slowly dissipate. But as soon as we were all hanging out on the bed, Avery began to scream and holler. He didn't seem distressed, more like he was trying on Daddy's anger, throwing his voice into the charged air.

Eventually Avery kissed his mom's nose by way of apology and accepted his stuffed cat. We headed back downstairs. "My cat!" he said, thumb out of his mouth. And I agreed. Most definitely his cat.

When Avery cries, something in my gut churns; when he spies something new, my heart leaps with his. I remember just a few months ago joining a friend and his son for a Saturday morning canoe ride. The fog came off the bathtub-warm water in little riding waves, splatters of mist lifted up by the breeze in a swirling white spray that splashed Avery softly across the face. Avery pointed out a heron in the trees. Our two canoes glided through the fog silently—the only sound, two fathers chatting quietly. Then Avery cried "bird," thrusting out his hand, his little extended finger following the line of a crow to the tippy-top of the tallest pine.

APRIL

Though my father has been dead now for seven years, there are times late at night, alone in my study, when I pick up the phone and start dialing. It takes a moment to realize that he is no longer at the other end of the late-night phone line. It takes a while to comprehend that, though I am still his son, he is not around to be my father. How important it is to be there for Avery as long as I can and in every way possible. Our daily conversation *is* the way we love each other. Silence is a river we cross at flood tide.

In the last years before my father died, our relationship as father and son transformed dramatically. We'd both found partners with whom we hoped to settle. Each planned to stay in one place for more than a few years. None of this is new. Both of us in a state of serial-monogyny recovery.

But somehow the roles had reversed. All of a sudden my father was looking to me, to my marriage with Ali in particular, and seeing the stability I'd found with her as something to strive for. I mean really hope for. That maybe I had become, in some small way, his role model for a new way of life. But I'm unsure he was really going to make it that way. (How could he? It had never worked before.) At the funeral, one of his best friends told me that my father had already had one foot out the door. "He kept making promises he couldn't keep."

I don't know. I always thought a promise was a sailor looking for wind, angling his boat toward its best chance at speed. All I know is how happy his grandson would have made my father. How happy I'd be to watch them play together.

In this morning's *Writer's Almanac*, Paul Bowles is quoted as saying: "Everything happens only a certain number of times, and a very small number, really. How many more times will you remember a certain afternoon of your childhood, some afternoon that's so deeply a part of your being that you can't even conceive of your life without it?"

I am not sure if this quote depresses me or lifts my spirits; affirms something I've always felt but never before articulated, or quietly strips me of hope. Maybe a little of both? Perhaps this is why having a kid is so rewarding: That, besides everything else, through Avery I am able to return more often to the mysterious well of the past. That I live vicariously in his journey. On an outing to a neighborhood park, I share the adventure with my son while reconnecting to that "certain afternoon." I get to be a boy again.

MAY

I've come to see raising a child as hands-on training for death and dying. The lack of control you finally recognize and then succumb to, the grip (already an illusion) slackening from firm to grasping to loose. Your sense of the future altering under the demands of the ever-pressing moment. Where's your head when the boy falls into the lake with a Pooh-like plop? But, too, the joys—the flashes of insight Ali and I have witnessed and celebrated. Avery, our wonder-filled prince. The day an escapade. In fathering Avery, I am humbled and exalted. With him, I stand at the altar of my life, disheveled, utterly unready for the next thing.

The winter chill has made its last appearance, cloaked in the ghostly robes of fog and mist. When I let Ursula off the leash at the edge of the thirteenth green, the landscape before us has been whitewashed into a coliseum of topless trees, a roofed stage of gray-green pathways. She advances into the scene, low to the ground, radar already attuned to the squirrels running for the stage-set columns. Avery, in his stroller, wakes up from his drift, raising his head out of the blankets to watch Ursula hunt. Two large crows stand like valets on a lawn across the road. I follow the dog down into the white-out holler, hoping no mad morning golfer tees off from the top of the hill. On the road back, Avery hunkers down in his blankets, cold, teetering on the cliff edge of nap.

JUNE

I know Avery is my boy when he stops at the park entrance, spies the pickup basketball game, and calls out "B-ball!" When he looks up to catch the trajectory of a crow's flight from tree to tree and calls out "caw caw" in camaraderie. He runs ahead to the swings and I lag behind to watch the four out-of-shape white guys shoot hoop. I can't help figure out what I'd need to do to beat them. That one guy in the jeans would give me trouble with his quick first step. Avery comes back to the bench, mouthing "B-ball" over and over.

The other half court is free, so Avery and I run around for twenty minutes, dribbling and kicking the ball. Avery picks up the huge sphere and throws it over to me, crying, "Me shoot!"

He even turns to me after I hit a baseline jumper and says "Nice shot, Daddy." I pick him up and let him try his boy best to associate the round ball with the round rim high above. "Dunk," he says, and drops the ball on my head.

Yesterday, on one of our typical neighborhood rambles, a fully built house stood in the spot where, just the day before, I swear, a foundation squatted. The house stood tall in its two-story height, windows in, a freshly painted front door. Even a porch. The branches of two rain-saturated oaks brushed its top gable. For a moment, it was as if summer had fast-forwarded and the light rain we were tromping in had become a fall rain. As if the house was built time-lapse.

Ursula is oblivious, nose tuned to the fine frequency of cat. Avery doesn't seem to notice, either. I ask him if anything about the street or the yard seems different to him. He smiles, enjoying the premise. He looks around. After a minute or so of this concentrated, cartoon silence, I think he's faking. But just then his eyes light up, as if the house suddenly blipped onto his radar screen. "The house," he says, laughing. "Wasn't there before." He starts walking on. Then he stops and turns around.

"How did it get there?"

"My guess is they trucked it here in two or three pieces and set them down with a crane." I start walking and he hurries to stay in front of me. He nods when I point out the red-clay tracks on the road. Evidence of the haul.

AUGUST

Two years ago yesterday, Avery came into our life. Adoption Day. Family Day. We lit a candle, sang family songs. Avery got some new books and an old record player from Ali's parents,

Nana and Poppy. It came with a stash of old LPs—musicals, Disney records, a few folk recordings. Avery stayed up an extra hour learning how to put the records on the turntable, drop the needle on the outer edge, and then push the lever to 33. He loves how the record seems to wake from sleep, the music rising up out of a blurred growl.

So do I. I love how Avery falls asleep in degrees, finally hunkering down in his blankets with Cat, a rainbow of cloth books draped around him. Love his bright blue eyes, the Harry Potter-esque checkmark vein on his forehead. The funny, lovely way he sounds on the phone when I call from Vermont or Los Angeles, or from whatever makeshift reading tour I'm on. How "Vermont" stands for travel, both an act of leaving and a destination. "How was Vermont, Daddy?" I love how Avery has insinuated himself so deeply into our lives and how, in kind, we have grown our life around him. Hard to imagine what life was like even a few years ago.

We take Avery to the aquarium on a drizzling late morning at the end of a long weekend. We are among a horde of parents trying to give their children the freedom to imagine them- selves into a wider world. To take a breather, maybe catch up on some talk as the toddlers get entertained by that wider world. There's so much I hate about these places—the lines of bored people, the trapped animals, the deluge of blah. Despite my desire not to, I become this little airy, acid aristocrat afraid to get dirty. I hate the conveyor belt of canned experience so much.

But it doesn't take long for Avery to open all that up. He's running from display to display, getting high off all the kid energy whizzing around the building. I follow after him like a shadow, like a bodyguard, freed by the duty of keeping him safe. Avery keeps making ill-timed runs at the escalator. Gradually, small moments start to slip in. The tiny mad propulsion of the seahorse's back fin; the way the owl's face turns as if on a hinge, its night mask wheeling into view, mute and old. The heron disguises itself in plain sight, lost from view inside the marshland replica on the roof. Its stick legs doing their best imitation of grass stalks. That sad, soulful look that actually says nothing.

SEPTEMBER

It is the Jewish New Year. Rosh Hashanah. Our favorite time of year! It has always felt like the true New Year to me, with the weather changing over, the fall equinox just passed. A time of repentance and transformation. Time to reconnect with friends and family. To take a pause in the hectic day-to-day, look up and look in. The Green Man in me loves it all; ritual and prayer a kind of moving solace. A charged being walking through a charged landscape.

One way Ali and I have marked our lives (besides the academic calendar) has been to see this block of time as sacred. My birthday one bookend, end of summer; Ali's birthday another, late November, the full turn toward winter. The days between are a landing strip of change, a walking bridge above a burgeoning river.

Now with Avery in our life, we want this time to take on deeper significance. Not sure how, but I want us to pass on a certain sense of things to Avery, a quality of attention and care. For Halloween, we joke, we will dress Avery as the Green Man. He likes getting his face painted green. We want him tuned into the turning of the seasons; he wants to follow the jack-o'-lanterns up the hill and knock on all the doors.

OCTOBER

One morning this week, I find a wasp edging the mirror in the downstairs bathroom. Avery likes to run into this room, shut the door behind, and get lost in the dark for a moment before I "rescue" him. It's easy to imagine the wasp at his ear, waking from a drowse, so I trap the wasp in a cup and bring it outside carefully.

Avery started at a new day care today. He clenched my hand tight as we let the controlled chaos of the class ebb and flow around us. Kids were paired at various stations. Teachers smiled and went back to their projects with the kids. Eventually, Avery released my grip and drifted over to one of the teachers who had waved him over to the watercolor table. Not even looking back, he floated a quiet "bye" over his shoulder.

Picture me driving home from the day care. Imagine with me what it will be like for us in a few years. Avery is turning five, starting kindergarten. He stands at the opening of our street in the half dark, his new school shoes flashing orange as he kicks the soccer ball to me across the street. It's Picture Day and Master Avery has required his new collarless shirt for the occasion. He wants to send cards to Nana and Poppy, Mimi and Charter, his cousin Kira. He's written them each a little note, has spelled out the words all by himself. And he wants to include one of his watercolor drawings. And, and, and . . .

And the bus is coming down the hill, its brights on, brakes hissing. I run my hands through Avery's hair but he knocks them away. "Daaad!" When he climbs the vibrating steps, my boy doesn't even use the rail for balance. His driver, Miss Rita, watches attentively, waving to me before letting the door close. As the big yellow bus pulls off, I wave at the blank windows, catching only a glimpse of Avery framed in the glass. He's waving back but I can't tell if he's smiling or frowning. And then he's gone.

THE SLEEPWALKER

JENNIFER FINNEY BOYLAN

In the last year of his life, my father unexpectedly started to sleepwalk again. In the middle of the night I'd hear his heavy footsteps on the creaking stairs, coming up to the third floor, where I lived in a room sealed most of the time with a heavy deadbolt. I heard him creep through the hallway and open the door to the spare room, diagonally across the hall from mine, and lay himself down in the guest bed. After a while he'd start to snore, and I'd know he was OK, at least until morning.

When the dawn slanted through the small dormer window in the spare room, though, he'd sit up, confused and angry. "Goddamn it," he'd say. "Where am I? What is this? What the hell am I doing here?"

He didn't know I was transsexual, or if he did, he never said anything about it. I'm not even sure he knew the word "transsexual" or the word "transgender," and almost surely he could not have explained the difference between the two. But that's all right. For a long time I couldn't figure it all out, either.

Once, though, when I was in high school, Dad and my mother were watching television, clicking through the channels, and for a moment they rested on a movie-of-the-week presentation of the *Rocky Horror Picture Show*. It was the scene in which Frank N. Furter waltzes around in fishnets singing, "Well you got caught with a flat. Well how about that?"

My father raised an eyebrow and said, "There he is, Jim. Your biggest fan."

For a single, terrified second, I feared that he knew exactly what was going on in my room, up on the third floor, when the deadbolt was drawn. Was it possible, I wondered as Frank N. Furter danced before us, that from the very beginning my father had understood the thing that had lain in my heart, and that I had apparently so completely failed to conceal?

My mother picked up the remote and we moved on to another movie. Kirk Douglas was standing in a sea of men in gladiator costumes. "I'm Spartacus!" the men shouted, one after the other. "I'm Spartacus!"

My mother put the remote down. They loved movies about the ancient world, and I could understand why. My mother was Spartacus. My father was Spartacus. My drunken grandmother was Spartacus. Even Sausage, our gelatinous, overweight Dalmatian, was Spartacus.

In our house, sometimes, it seemed like just about everybody was Spartacus. Except me.

On his fiftieth birthday, we gave my father an inflatable rubber boat. He spent the rest of that day in it, floating around the pool, with a cigarette in one hand and a martini in the other. I'd spent the morning in my third-floor room with the door locked, wearing my hippie girl clothes and reading *The Feminine Mystique*. Then, when it was time for the party, I changed back into boy clothes and helped carry the Hibachi grill and the beef patties and the charcoal and the cheese out to the pool, and I made my father a cheeseburger.

He'd gotten his first melonoma in 1973, but the doctors had removed the mole in surgery. By the time he turned fifty, he'd been clear for five years, but a year later, in 1979, he had a second mole removed, beet in color. Then he was healthy for another six years, until the last mole. That time, they had to follow through with radiation, and interferon, and cisplatin. Too late, though.

After his funeral, on Easter Sunday, 1986, as we followed the hearse through the rain, I thought back to the happy, sun-soaked occasion of his fiftieth birthday, just eight years before. We'd set up a stereo outside and played his favorite music for him. A couple of Beethoven symphonies and the Toccata and Fugue in D Minor by Bach. It was the first time in his life that my father seemed to understand the joys of a kick-ass stereo. He lay back in his boat with a look of complete peace as he listened to the Bach.

You could see a place on his leg where they'd taken off the mole, and another on his back where they'd taken the skin to do the graft.

When the fugue was over, Dad opened his eyes and said, sweetly, "Can we play it again? Louder?"

Twenty-three years after that party, my children and my wife and I were sitting around the kitchen table, the four of us, eating dinner. I was mid-transition. My older son, Luke, gave me a look.

"What," I said. He was seven years old.

"We can't keep calling you 'Daddy,' " he said, shaking his head. "If you're going to be a girl. It's too weird."

The whole bait and switch was nearly over by this time. It seemed like it had been going on for years, and in a sense it had: since the days of my father's sleepwalking, since the days I'd walked through the woods as a child in Pennsylvania, hoping that "I could be cured by love," praying to God to make me whole. In the end, the prayer was answered, although not in the way that I had expected. Because of the love of my spouse, Grace, not to mention that of my boys, I found the courage, somehow, to traverse the weird ocean between men and women, to make the voyage not only from one sex to another, but from a place where my life was defined by the secrets that I kept to a new place, a place where almost everything I'd ever had in my heart could finally be spoken out loud.

But by then, my father had been dead for fourteen years.

"Well," I said to my sons. "My new name is Jenny. You could call me Jenny if you want."

Luke laughed derisively. "Jenny? That's the name you'd give a lady mule."

I tried not to be hurt. "OK, fine," I said. "What do you want to call me?"

"The important thing, boys," said their mother, Grace, "is that you pick something you're comfortable with."

Luke thought this over. He was pretty good at naming things. For a while we'd had a hermit crab named Grabber. Later on, we'd briefly owned a snake named Biter.

"I know," he said. "Let's call you 'Maddy.' That's like, half Mommy, and half Daddy. And anyhow, I know a girl at school named Maddy. She's pretty nice."

His younger brother, Paddy, who was five, thought this over. "Or 'Dommy,' " he added.

Then we all laughed at "Dommy." Even Paddy laughed. "Dommy"! What a dumb name for a transsexual parent! After the hilarity died down, I nodded.

"'Maddy' might work," I said.

By the time my boys were in middle school—six years after Luke had decided to name me Maddy—our family had begun to seem normal to us again. I was in charge of waking everyone up and making breakfast and straightening the house and getting the boys to practice their instruments: Paddy on French horn, Luke on the three-quarter-size tuba. Grace was in charge of dinner and shepherding the boys through their homework and coaching Paddy's traveling soccer team. After a time, Grace and I even began to seem familiar to each other again, and the things that had changed in me seemed, incredibly, less important to Grace than the things that had remained the same.

Was she crazy to stay with me, after I'd come out with the truth and announced my intention to go from regular Coke to diet? Maybe. But that's another story, isn't it. For now let's just agree that she decided, at great length, that her life was better with me in it than not, and if this makes her nuts, well, fine, have it your way, she's nuts. Sweet though.

In the fall we picked apples. In the winter we skied, and sat around the fireplace in our living room afterward, drinking hot chocolate. In summer we fished on Long Pond, and Luke landed one giant largemouth bass after another. Most of the time we forgot that there was anything extraordinary about our family, and—who knows?—perhaps there isn't.

But even though we had now crossed that wide, strange

ocean of gender together, and come to rest at last, a nagging, unsettling question still occasionally returned to me, usually at night when I found myself awake in the wee hours. What kind of men would my boys become, I wondered, having been raised by a father who became a woman? How could I possibly show them, in the years to come, the lessons that I myself had apparently failed to learn?

I'd hear the sound of the grandmother's clock ticking downstairs as I lay there in the dark, awake. I'd think about my own precarious boyhood, with its hidden panels and its deadbolts, and wonder how I was going to help my sons become themselves. At times, I'd even hear a voice in my heart demanding an answer to the same question that my harshest critics had asked of me. "What about the children?" the voice said. "What about the boys?"

This is a question I sometimes wonder if my grandmother ever asked herself. My father's mother was a colorful woman who liked to dance on top of pianos and sing and tell obscene stories and drink vodka on the rocks. Her nickname was "Stardust."

She was married four times, we think, although her first marriage—to the gentleman whom, later, she called only "the Jew"—seemed not to be in the tally. My father was her only child, but she appeared to lose interest in him after her second husband, my grandfather, dropped dead of a brain hemorrhage, just after my father's ninth birthday. By the time my father was sixteen, he was living virtually all the time at a friend's house, on a cot out in the hallway. Now and again he'd show up at his mother's house to find smashed bottles on the floor, dishes in the sink. Apparently a wild party had begun at Stardust's house sometime in 1938 and didn't really finish until 1946.

My grandfather had left her a fair amount of money, but by the time my father hit high school, the cash was gone. What happened to it? As my mother politely put it, years later, "Stardust drank the money."

My father's hobbies, in childhood, had been collecting baseball cards and playing marbles. So it was a surprise when he introduced me to model rockets on my twelfth birthday, with the gift of a kit from Estes. The name of the rocket was BIG DADDY.

Our launch pad was an abandoned horse-racing track on an abandoned farm a few miles from our house. The grass had grown thick and snarly in the center oval of the track, and in the distance we could see the burned-out remains of what had once been the farmhouse. The farmer's windmill had survived the fire, somehow, and it spun in the breeze not far from the ruins. I set up the launch pad, unwound the wires with the alligator clips that connected the rocket's igniter fuses to a battery-powered launch controller. After checking the wind, I adjusted the angle of the launch rod so that the rocket would fly in the windward direction at first, because I knew that once the parachute opened, and the breeze filled it, BIG DADDY would begin to drift.

My father stood at some remove, watching as I ran through my prelaunch checklist. I was very thorough, applying the proper amount of chute wadding into the fuselage (so that the detonator charge that caused the nose cone to eject, thus activating the parachute at apogee, would not cause the chute's plastic to melt). I secured the igniter fuses with masking tape. I double-checked the wind speed and the angle of the launch rod. Then I looked at my father.

"Are we go for launch?" I asked, dramatically.

He replied, with as little enthusiasm as it is possible to imagine, "We are go."

Then I started counting down. "Ten . . . nine . . . eight . . . seven . . . —Ignition sequence start!—six . . . five . . . four . . . three . . . two . . . one! LIFTOFF!"

For a moment BIG DADDY sat there on the pad. There was a sizzling sound. I was afraid that the launch was a dud— that, as they say at Mission Control, we'd have to "scrub the launch." Then, all at once, there was a vast, silvery swooshing sound, and BIG DADDY raced into the sky, leaving only a vaporous trail behind.

We stood there watching the rocket rise out of sight. It neared the sun, and I shaded my eyes with my hand, like I was saluting. A moment later, I felt a hand on my shoulder, and when I looked over, it was my father, who'd placed his hand on my back, probably without even thinking about it. I remember that his other hand was shielding his eyes from the sun as well. I saw the look on his face, a look of surprise and wonder, not only at the miracle of space flight—which was wondrous enough—but also, I imagined, at me. I was a boy of whom nothing might be expected, at times a strange creature delicate and frail. But I'd done this: I'd made this homely creation fly.

I looked back up at the sky. The far-off speck of the rocket passed directly in front of the sun. For a moment I lost sight of it.

Then we saw a bright flash. A moment later there was a fiery, popping sound. I felt my father's hand grip my shoulder blade a little harder. Then there was smoke, and the pieces of the rocket fell to earth. We stood there in silence as the ruins rained down around us, some of them still smoking.

I looked down at the ground. "I'm sorry, son," my father said. Then he got out a cigarette—an L&M King—and lit it with a butane lighter. As he blew the smoke into the air, he gave me a weary look that suggested that this was exactly what the world was like, that in the years that lay before us both, it should be expected that all sorts of things would explode and scatter.

"Stupid thing," I said, angrily. "Stupid BIG DADDY."

Luke got off the bus one afternoon at the beginning of his eighth-grade year, came through the door, and told Grace and me that he "needed to talk about something serious" with us. He said he'd reached two very important personal decisions in his life, and that, as a family, we needed to sit down and talk.

Grace and I exchanged glances. We'd been expecting something like this since the time my transition began, seven years before. And even though both of my boys had reached middle-school age without any apparent psychological trauma—as a result of having me as a parent—we never stopped worrying about them, never reached a point where I didn't wake up, now and again, pondering the same question that had haunted me from the beginning. "What about the children? What about the boys?"

"OK," said Luke, as we gathered in the living room. (His brother wanted no part of whatever this was about, and headed downstairs toward the Xbox.) "First off, I've decided—" He looked down.

Grace and I looked at each other uneasily. What, son? What have you decided?

"I've decided that I want to become—"

What? What does he want to become?

"A pacifist."

Grace and I exchanged glances again, relieved. "A pacifist," I said.

"Yes," said Luke. "I want to work for peace."

There was a moment of silence as we thought this over. Then Grace spoke for us both. "Good for you, Luke," said Grace. "We're proud of you. We'll go online, see if we can find, like, some peace marches we can all go to. If you want."

"Yeah," I said, cautiously. "But you said you'd made—two decisions? What was the other one? Do you want to share that with us as well?"

"Yeah, OK." He blushed. "This is the hard one." He looked at me and said, "Maddy, I really don't want to disappoint you . . ."

"It's all right, son," I said, and shot him a look. I wondered, briefly, if the look I was giving him was similar to the look my father had given me, years earlier, when we'd shared a fleeting glimpse of Frank N. Furter together, dancing in his fishnets.

"All right," he said. "I think I want—to stop playing tuba? And instead to start playing—the Irish fiddle."

He let this sink in. Luke knew how much I loved his tuba playing. I'd even bought him, a few months earlier, a sweatshirt into which was stitched his name as well as the words TUBA KING.

Apparently Luke was afraid that if he switched from tuba to fiddle, somehow I might love him less.

"That's it?" said Grace.

I went over and hugged him. "It's OK, Luke," I said. "You were great on tuba. I know you'll be great on fiddle."

He heaved a sigh. "Whew," he said. "That was really hard."

A month later, he had to write an essay for school about "an experience that changed me." He told me early on that his topic was going to be his own variation on *Stupid BIG DADDY.*

He wrote this:

An experience that changed me is that my dad is transgendered, and became my "Maddy." A person who is transgendered has a lifelong sense of being born into the wrong body.

I was about four when Maddy began the "transition." I don't really remember the experience well because it was over nine years ago. Once the transition had taken place, I was comfortable with it. But I was worried what my friends would think. I kept it secret for a little bit, but eventually they found out on their own. They all accepted it a lot better than I thought they would.

Maddy is funny and wise. We go fishing and biking. We talk a lot, about anything that is on our minds.

One night this spring, Maddy and I had a fancy dinner at a restaurant called A—— in Waterville. It was a special night. I wore a jacket and a tie. I had a steak. It made me feel like Maddy and I were really close. Maddy said that she thought I was growing up and that she was proud of me.

Sometimes it's true that I wish I had a regular father, but only because I don't remember what it was like to have a normal family. Sometimes it's hard to have a family that is different. But most of the time I think I am the luckiest kid on earth. Even though my family is different, I can't think of any way that life could be better.

From this I learned that everybody is different. No matter how different people are, you should treat them all with respect and kindness.

I hope to help support the rights for everybody, no matter how different they are.

I know people from lots of different kinds of families. Some families are divorced, so some of my friends only live with one parent at a time. Other families have someone who is mentally challenged in their family. But no matter how different they are, they are all people. My goal is that some day everybody will be treated with love.

This summer, on my fiftieth birthday, my children and my wife gave me a rubber chair that floats in the water. Since my birthday was rainy, though, I didn't get to repeat the ritual of my father, thirty years earlier, listening to Bach at top volume.

But we had a bottle of dandelion wine that a cartoonist friend had made on his porch, and I drank it, and it instantly made me nuts, in the most pleasant way imaginable. I put the rubber chair on the wooden floor of our house, and put *Peter and the Wolf* on the stereo, and as I listened to the Prokofiev I happily floated around the room as my family waved from the couch. "And if one would listen very carefully, he could hear the duck quacking inside the wolf; because the wolf in his hurry, had swallowed her alive."

One night back in 1973, I was up late in my room with the deadbolt drawn. I was wearing the green paisley skirt and a halter top filled with grapefruits, and I was reading *Tonio Kröger* in German. Your typical Friday night. From a long way off, I heard a glass break, down in the kitchen.

That was weird.

So I took off my girl clothes, stuck them back in the secret panel that swung out from my wall, then put on my boy pajamas and a bathrobe and went downstairs. It was almost midnight.

There in the kitchen was my father. He was sweeping glass off the floor. "What happened?" I asked. "Are you OK?"

"Gotta clean up after Mom," he said, in a sleepy, mumbly voice.

"Dad?" I said. "What's happening?"

"Daddy died," he said, sadly.

This is when I realized that my father was sleepwalking, and that he was playing out some crazy scene from his childhood, from the days after the death of his own father, when Stardust, along with her many suitors, was drinking the money at the endless party. I could see my father's boyhood self, trying to straighten up the house while his mother lay passed out on the sofa.

He was being very methodical, putting the shards of glass in the dustpan. I held the pan still for him as he swept, again and again and again. Then I poured the glass pieces into the trash, and I said, "All done." He stood there with the broom, deep in his trance.

"Do you—," he said, his soft voice sounding as if it were coming right out of the grave. "Do you live near here?"

I wasn't sure what the proper answer was, but I told him no, I was just visiting. Then I suggested it was maybe time to go back to sleep.

"OK," said my father. "We have to make sure—not to wake—my mom."

"We'll be quiet," I said, and I moved him toward the back stairs.

"Who—?" said my father. "Who are you?"

I had never told anyone my real name before. "I'm— Jenny—," I said.

"You should," he said, in his soft, unconscious voice, "come over again."

I looked at my father's face—and even though he was forty-five, and asleep, it struck me that, perhaps for the only time in my life, I was seeing what he'd looked like when he was a boy.

"Maybe," I said.

"Maybe," said my father.

Then I led him up the creaking stairs, tucked him in his bed, and kissed the boy good night.

EVERYONE INTO THE BUNKER!

How Obsessive Parenting Became the New
Counterculture

STEVE ALMOND

When I was about four years old, our parents called
a strange family meeting, just before bedtime. They
sat us three boys down and told us that my father
might be away for a couple of days. I can't remember the exact language they used, but I remember
them explaining that Dad was going to be protesting the war. Meaning Vietnam.

My older brother Dave (he was six) wanted to
know how. Our dad explained that he and some
other people were going to link arms—like in the
playground game Red Rover—across the road
leading into Moffett Field, the local military base,
so that vehicles couldn't go in or out. They would
probably be put in jail for this.

I'm sure I felt frightened and probably confused
by this announcement. But I remember that my

parents were very matter-of-fact about all this. They didn't want us to react to their own fears, though they both were scared. My father later told me that he was shaking involuntarily as he stood there, the next morning, defying the police.

What I remember most vividly about this episode was that next day. My twin brother Mike and I were out in front of our house on Frenchman's Hill, near Stanford University. We were pretending to make pancakes by pouring some ghastly red concoction onto the sidewalk, which we imagined as a griddle. This was an homage to our father, in fact, because he made us buckwheat pancakes on weekend mornings.

A figure appeared in the distance. It took me a few moments to recognize our dad because he was wearing a dark suit (we had never seen him in a suit) and because, as an anxious child, I had immediately assumed he would be going to jail for a long time. If and when he did return he would be dressed in prison stripes. I remember my dad smiling as he came closer and I'm pretty sure we ran to hug him. Ours was not a family prone to such Kodak moments, but this was a special occasion.

I think about this episode a lot now that I have my own child, and with considerable amazement. Partly it's the physical risk my father was taking. This was just a few years after the bloody riots at the 1968 Democratic National Convention, so the notion that you could get hurt—either by the police or in jail—was quite real.

Partly it was the psychological impact of his absence. He had three kids at home, none of whom was old enough to understand fully what he was doing. In other words, he had a ready-made excuse for not protesting the war in such a dramatic fashion. He could have found a safer way of taking action—registering voters, passing out leaflets.

And then there's the sheer logistics of the thing. My wife

Erin and I, with our lone daughter, Josie (one year old), rarely get our shit together enough to make it out to something as low-key as a literary reading. And yet my folks—young doctors with professional ambitions, little money, and three rambunctious boys—were willing to see my father hauled off to the hoosegow to protest the war.

Most of all, when I think about this episode now, it makes me see how dramatically the culture of parenting has changed in a single generation. How many of today's parents—and I include myself in the tally—would take the same action to oppose the unconscionable war of our era?

Consider, for instance, how the current crop of parenting magazines would judge my father's action.

Actually, that's a bit of a MacGuffin. Because as anyone who reads parenting magazines knows, they don't discuss politics. They don't discuss anything that extends beyond the duties of parenting and the products thereof.

But I imagine that if these magazines did discuss my father's decision to protest the Vietnam War, the discussion would show a certain measure of disapproval, because, after all, he was leaving his little boys in the lurch, choosing to place his moral duties as a citizen above his paternal duties.

And herein lies the false dichotomy: the notion that you can separate these two duties. Because my father wasn't just leaving us in the lurch. He was also acting on our behalf, trying to effect a change that might, eventually, diminish the chance that his sons would be drafted to fight in a foolish war. Without quite meaning to, he was also setting an example for us. He was saying: "Boys, this is what it means to follow your principles."

It bears mentioning that my father's arrest was not the largest sacrifice he made. During this era he taught at Stanford Medical

School. He was a popular instructor with impeccable credentials. But he also worked at organizing student groups that opposed the war. He has long suspected that his antiwar activities played a role in the school's decision not to renew his teaching contract.

I want to be careful not to idealize the way my father and mother raised us. They would be the first ones to admit that they spread themselves too thin as parents. A pointed example: in the summer of 1971, they were convinced to buy into and live on a commune a few hours north of San Francisco. The idea was to research and write a book about the back-to-the-land movement.

My memories of that summer are surreal and episodic, as befits a suburban four-year-old plunked into the middle of a rural picaresque. A cow stepped on my toe. The milk on my Corn Flakes had chunks of cream in it. Most memorably, a man nicknamed Big John joined Mike and me in our evening bath, fully clothed. We would learn, years later, that he was crackling on acid at the time.

The Land—as the commune came to be called—was a failed experiment within the smaller community of our family, as well. Mike and I felt out of place. The other kids ran around naked, which totally freaked us out. We worried about getting enough to eat. Our older brother Dave, sent back east to stay with my grandparents for the summer, felt exiled.

And our parents wound up having to pick up the slack for folks like Big John. My mother, for instance, made a point of rising early each morning to grab eggs from the chicken coop—before the other adults could. She was worried about Mike and me getting enough to eat.

So I'm not arguing that today's parents should drop everything and head for the hills, in pursuit of some solar-powered utopia. My concern is that parenthood—as defined by our generation—is becoming the opposite experience: a sort of comfy bunker of apolitical consumerism.

I see this among my own friends, in the endless discussions about our babies, and our babies' products, and our babies' anticipated needs for day care and schooling. It's like some default setting we slip in to the moment we encounter another parent. The world outside the Babysphere recedes.

And what a relief to see it go! Based on the news reports, that world is in awful shape: awash in violence, poverty, political corruption, senseless suffering, and looming environmental disasters. Focusing on our babies—sweet-smelling and innocent—has become a form of rescue that feels attainable. We may not be able to save the world, but we can save *them*.

This dream is unattainable, of course. You can't baby-proof the world, and the effort to do so causes children more harm than good, I suspect. They need to know that the world is going to deal them some blows, which they will survive. More to the point, children aren't vessels of goodness. They contain the same destructive impulses that the rest of us do. An essential part of parenting resides in recognizing and curbing these impulses, not indulging them.*

What I'm talking about, more broadly, is the drift toward what is often called "child-centered" parenting. I recently spent a long weekend with a couple who personifies this approach.

---

* I don't want to sound like a crank who longs for the days when children were "seen, not heard." But I've observed plenty of households in which the parents refuse to discipline their kids, and the kids always strike me as incredibly anxious. What they need to be rescued from is the horror of their own aggression. That's often what makes them act out in the first place—the secret wish for a parent who will rein them in.

Their three-year-old—let's call him Max—controlled everything in that house: the scheduling, the spending, the mood and ideation. Everything was about Max, his needs and wants and progress. Max himself was an awfully cute little guy, with curly hair and pouty lips and an expression that conveyed an essential *shtunkdom*.*

He was also a tyrant. His version of "playing" with his four-month-old little brother consisted of pounding on the baby's car seat and yelling into his face. (Erin took one look at this behavior and said, "If he comes anywhere near Josie acting like that, he's going to get smacked.")

Anyway, at some point Max wanted to go to the park, so we packed up and headed to the park. Just outside the park, we passed by a man sitting on the sidewalk with a battered cardboard sign that read: "Homeless Vet. Please Help." He had a giant Starbucks cup for change.

As homeless vets go, this guy looked to be in OK shape. I put him in his late thirties, Hispanic, and pretty well groomed. It was as if he'd gussied himself up for his visit to the prosperous suburbs. All of which made our brief encounter that much sadder and awkward.

Actually, "encounter" is overstating the matter. It was more like a very self-conscious non-encounter. The guy didn't say anything to us as we passed by. He didn't even look up. Nor did we say anything to him, or offer him money. Only Max stared at the guy (as kids will), trying to figure out why an adult man was sitting on the sidewalk and why he had a blanket thrown over his shoulders (it was a pretty warm day) and what his sign said.

His parents said nothing and Erin and I said nothing and

---

* *Shtunkdom* (of Yiddish origin): exuding the qualities of, or personifying, the *shtunk*, loosely translated as a "little stinker."

Max, despite his curiosity, said nothing, either. When I asked his mother later if we should have somehow acknowledged the homeless dude, she said, "He's got a whole life to figure out how the real world works. Why spoil his childhood?" I could see her point. I feel the same impulse to shield my daughter from ugliness. How does one explain class inequalities or addiction or war trauma to a little kid, anyway?

At the same time, I could see Max absorbing a lesson. When a strange man is sitting on the sidewalk, and your parents ignore the man, you should do the same thing.

To be fair: these friends of mine aren't heartless people. They're good lefties who give to charity and believe that regressive tax cuts are bullshit and moaned over the Bush Idiocracy as much as the rest of us. But it seemed to me, as I thought about how this little scene had played out, that they were inadvertently serving the agenda of the Bush Idiocracy, which is predicated on denial.

The essential appeal of conservatism* in this country—aside from its naked pandering to the primal negative emotions of fear and grievance—resides in the notion that Americans need not face any of our common crises of state, need not even cop to their existence.

Their political house of cards is built on denial. Denial of global warming. Denial of the looming fossil-fuel shortage. Denial of our massive foreign debt. Denial of our shameful economic disparities. And on and on.

The whole goal is to keep the electorate fat and happy, to

---

* I am using this term loosely. I don't mean actual conservatism, as articulated by the nineteenth-century political philosophers. I don't even mean the "conservatism" of Ronald Reagan, which was predicated on fiscal discipline and a smaller, less invasive government. I am referring to conservatism as espoused by the right-wing talk show hosts.

assure us that—despite all evidence to the contrary—our superabundant lives are sustainable, we can have it all, the economy will keep growing forever.*

What I saw with Max was basically the origins of this mind-set. His parents (and I) were trying to protect him. But, within that process, we were denying both the true state of the world and also our own moral responsibility for others. We were, in that sense, hiding behind his innocence.

Which is precisely what Madison Avenue wants us to do. They want us to approach parenthood with the bunker mentality, so they can sell us the decor. They do so by cannily exploiting those new-parent hopes and anxieties, trying to convince us that we can safeguard our children through the retail cure. Thus the cavalcade of new products intended to keep your baby safe.

And believe me, we've seen them all, because dozens of catalogs began mysteriously appearing in our mailbox the moment we brought Josie home from the hospital. Erin recently found this item in one of them: a helmet to be worn by children just learning to crawl.

It's not just a matter of keeping your child safe, though. Today, you also have to make sure that he or she is not "falling behind" in the great developmental race to be the next Baby Einstein.

This is the hidden cost of parenting in the information age: it has a tendency to make parenting seem like a competitive undertaking. Every time we take Josie to the pediatrician, we get a report on her "percentiles," meaning how she ranks in terms of her weight and height. When we visit with other babies, I

---

* This critique applies to the Democrats as well, who have shown the same essential willingness to traffic in these shameful myths.

find myself comparing Josie to them, hoping she's developing more quickly than her peers.

Wanting the best for your child is perfectly natural, particularly for newbie parents. What I'm getting at is the underlying mind-set, a mind-set that is parochial to the point of solipsism. In other words: why should I care about the Family of Man when I've got my own kid to worry about?

I fear that education is the arena where this tension will come to a head.* My history here is again a product of my parents' values. For most of our childhood, we lived in the lower-income part of an affluent town, Palo Alto. Our parents sent us to the public elementary school closest to our house. I'm not sure they would have had the money for a private school, but they probably could have sent us to a public school in a "better" neighborhood. The point is that they believed in the public school system, which meant you made do with the school closest to your home.

It wasn't the worst thing in the world for us to be exposed to kids from poorer backgrounds, even if that meant withstanding a little bullying.† Heck, that was part of our broader education in How the World Really Operates. And though it's true that I gave away a lot of lunch money, I did love my grade school. I even cried on the day I graduated.

But I sometimes try to imagine what I would do in my parents' place. If I knew she was being bullied, would I allow Josie to attend our local elementary school? More to the point: would Erin? I'm pretty sure the answer is no. In fact, Erin

---

* Erin has already started fretting about getting Josie into the right preschool. (As a reminder: Josie is barely one year old.)

† I spent most of second grade in mortal fear of Keith Minnis, who beat me up once a month or so.

already has announced that she's not sending Josie to a school that doesn't challenge her intellectually.

Many of our friends have gone the private-school route, for the same reason. They believe in supporting the public school system—until their kid needs a more challenging math curriculum.

I realize that when the time comes for Josie to head off to school, I'll want to make sure she's happy and learning. But parents of my generation have a tendency to worry too much about every little aspect of their child's emotional and intellectual development. One of the main reasons for this overprotectiveness is that families have become so atomized.

In our race to get ahead, we've grown further and further removed from the natural support system of an extended family (and older relatives who might chill us out by knocking some common sense into our heads).

Erin and I, for instance, don't have a grandparent, or an uncle, or even a cousin, living within a hundred miles. We see Erin's folks maybe once a month, mine three times a year, at most. We're more or less on our own as parents. All of which leaves us vulnerable to the anxieties described above.

And how do we, as loyal Americans, respond to these anxieties? We pull out our credit cards. Objects that would have seemed odd even ten years ago—the Rainforest Jumperoo leaps to mind*—are now standard domestic props. I won't even get started on the eight-hundred-dollar strollers, though I must mention that our neighbors across the street recently brought home a battery-operated mini-Escalade for their five-year-old.

---

* And it leaps to mind because—to my shame, and in a moment of weakness—we purchased this obscene monstrosity for our daughter.

It's easy enough to mock these excesses, but it's much harder to fight the larger tide of materialism. After all, as Erin often argues—as the sharps on Madison Avenue know she will argue—"it's for the baby." Ah, guilt-free shopping! Is it any wonder the registers sing so loud at Babies "R" Us?

But as every parent knows, these products aren't just for the baby. They are for the parents, to make us feel like competent caretakers, to reassure us, and, perhaps most of all, to make our lives more convenient.

That's the other crucial dynamic in play here. Having a baby is not, as these things go, a convenient experience. It runs against our national inclinations. To cite a rather unfortunate personal example: my wife and I bought our daughter that miserable Rainforest Jumperoo not because she needed it, but because plopping her in it was more convenient for us.

An even better example: diapers. For years the makers of Pampers and Huggies have relied on our native American sloth to pimp us their landfill cloggers. Erin and I nearly fell into this trap. We wanted the ease of disposables, particularly in those exhausting early months. To her credit, Erin found a cloth brand that she dug.*

But our lust for convenience really goes beyond the products. It's a mind-set, a national religion at this point. And it's what makes so many socially concerned parents retreat from their best impulses, and head into the bunker.

A final example, and then I promise that my little sermonette will be over.

---

* I realize that a single mom working two jobs isn't in a great position to choose environmental good over convenience. But for those of us who have the time, and the will, to do a bit more laundry, there's really no excuse.

A few months ago, Erin and I heard about an antiwar rally happening in our town. It was one of those days where we were both pooped by mid-afternoon. But we got to talking about the idiocy of the war and about the way in which future generations would be paying the fiddler's bill, and that got us fired up enough to overcome the inconvenience of dragging our asses up and out of the house.

So we schlepped Josie to the center of our little New England town. The gathering was nothing dramatic, just seventy or so concerned citizens holding up signs at a busy intersection.

And I suppose there's an argument to be made that Josie could have been harmed by all the car exhaust, or frightened by the noise—if, in fact, Josie were frightened by anything. But the reaction that people had was fascinating. They didn't just smile at Josie. They smiled at us, and nodded. One woman, a veteran of such rallies, said, "It's so good to see families out here, not just us old peaceniks."

In the end, I was glad we brought Josie, because her presence there was a powerful reminder that the effects of war aren't limited to those who can fight, or protest. Despite the cynical effort to outsource the fighting of our wars to this country's underclass, the war itself will take a toll on all of us—and on Josie more than on her elders. She's the one, after all, who will be paying for Bush's demented imperial adventure.

As we walked back from the rally, I got to thinking about how close we had come to bagging it altogether. It had felt so tempting, so convenient, to stay home. But in the end, our lust for convenience is a sucker's game. And it's worse than that. It's an affliction we will pass on to our babies, at precisely the wrong historical moment.

Because let's face facts: as Americans, we've been able to coast on our own superpower status for the last half century.

But the scientists and economists and historians can be ignored for only so long. My wife and I may be able to escape the worst of global warming and the end of cheap oil and our massive national debt. Our daughter will not.

And so it is incumbent upon us—more than on any previous generation—to face these challenges. Not to allow Wall Street and Washington to lull us into a false sense of security, even if, as parents, security feels so precious to us.

Becoming a parent is essentially about expanding emotionally, feeling more than we did before. It should awaken our empathy—not in some fleeting, phony-ass Oprah way, but as rational moral actors. We owe our babies more than a safe, well-appointed bunker.

I'm not suggesting that we should shirk our emotional duties to our babies—the central duty being to love them unreasonably—only that our ultimate duty to them is to face the world as it truly exists, to recognize the trouble we're in as a species, and to take action against that trouble on their behalf.

There are a thousand different ways to do this. Lead a more sustainable lifestyle, obviously. (Consume less. Drive less. Start a garden. Abstain from Pampers.) Become politically involved, rather than surrendering to apathy. Even, as in the case of my father, be willing to put your own liberty on the line for your beliefs.

Above all, these actions require a radical shift in our mindset as parents. We have to recognize that caring for our children, far from granting us a free pass, requires us to make the concrete sacrifices associated with a social conscience. In the face of leaders who like us best as indulgent children, we must strive to be adults who teach our sons and daughters how to be adults, each and every day.

A TALE OF TWO FATHERS

DAVID GESSNER

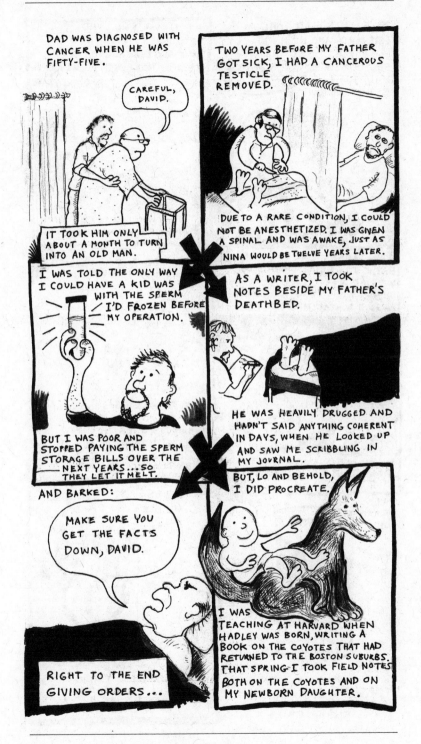

ONE LATE NIGHT WHEN I WAS SIXTEEN, I BET MY FRIENDS I COULD DO ONE HUNDRED PUSH-UPS.

FLYING HIGH NOW

WE WERE IN MY ROOM UPSTAIRS AND MY SISTER CRANKED THE ROCKY THEME.

WHEN HADLEY WAS THREE WEEKS OLD WE ALL WATCHED THE VERY LAST EPISODE OF BUFFY.

BUFFY AND HER FRIENDS WERE DOOMED, THE APOCALYPSE HAD COME... BUT THEN THEY CON-JURED A SPELL...

I REMEMBER ONE SCENE THAT HIT ME AS HARD AS ANYTHING I'VE READ IN SHAKESPEARE.

THE MUSIC WOKE MY FATHER. STILL HALF-ASLEEP, HE BANGED INTO THE ROOM, SLAMMING THE DOOR OPEN AND KICKING ME AROUND PUSH-UP SIXTY-TWO.

THERE WAS AN INSECURE TEN-YEAR-OLD GIRL ABOUT TO GET STRUCK OUT AT THE PLATE.

THEN CAME THE SPELL AND GIRL POWER SWEPT THE WORLD. THE GIRL SMILED TO HERSELF AND STEPPED CONFIDENTLY INTO THE BATTER'S BOX.

WHAT I DID NEXT I STILL CAN'T BELIEVE. I THREW MY FATHER UP AGAINST THE WALL IN FRONT OF MY FRIENDS.

I LOOKED OVER AT HADLEY AND I BAWLED AND BAWLED AND BAWLED.

THINKING BACK ON THAT NIGHT, I'M HAPPY I DON'T HAVE A SON.

NATURE WAS A STRONG BOND, BUT FAMILY WAS A STRONGER ONE...

BEFORE HE DIED, MY FATHER AND I RETURNED TO OUR ANCESTRAL HOME IN THE EAST GERMAN TOWN OF AUE.

GESSNER PLATZ

THE WALL HAD JUST FALLEN, AND AFTER FORTY YEARS OF CALLING THE TOWN SQUARE "KARL MARX PLATZ," THE LOCALS HAD RETURNED IT TO ITS ORIGINAL NAME.

EVERY SUMMER HADLEY AND I VISIT MY FATHER'S GRAVE, NEAR THE OSPREY NEST ON CAPE COD. HALF OF HIS ASHES ARE BURIED THERE.

DAVID GESSNER

BELOVED OF FAMILY AND FRIENDS

HADLEY HAS A BEAUTIFUL FACE THAT CHANGES LIKE THE WEATHER. SHE IS A MIX OF MY WIFE AND ME...

BUT WHEN SHE FURROWS HER BROW SHE IS PURE GESSNER.

MY FATHER HAD COME TO GERMANY TO BUY THE COMPANY HIS GRANDFATHER HAD ONCE OWNED. THERE WAS AN ARCHIVE ROOM INSIDE THE COMPANY AND THERE I STUDIED GENERATIONS OF GESSNERS.

ERNST   HEINZ   PAUL

MOST OF THE MEN WERE INDUSTRIALISTS, LIKE MY FATHER, BUT EVERY NOW AND THEN AN ARTIST...

THE COMPANY WAS BANKRUPT AND NEEDED A SAVIOR. WHEN MY FATHER STOOD IN FRONT OF THEM, THE WORKERS CHANTED HIS NAME.

GESSNER! GESSNER!

AND I KNOW HIM, AND MYSELF, WELL ENOUGH TO KNOW HOW MUCH HE LOVED IT.

HOW WILL HADLEY MAKE HER NAME? WHO KNOWS? AT THE MOMENT SHE LIKES NOTHING MORE THAN SITTING AT HER TABLE WITH CLUMPS OF CLAY...

AND THEN THE SEA CAT DOVE DOWN DEEP...

DIRECTING WHAT SHE CALLS HER "CLAY MOVIES."

MY FATHER WENT CRAZY ON CHEMO. THE HOSPITAL ROOM SPUN, GOLF BALLS FLEW OUT OF THE TV, AND HIS VENETIAN BLINDS TALKED TO HIM.

GESSNER, CAN YOU HEAR ME?

WHEN HE SPOKE, IT WAS IN EITHER A SOUTHERN OR GERMAN ACCENT.

THE NEW LANGUAGE THE DRUGS GAVE HER CONTINUED ON THE WAY HOME.

THESE LIGHTS ARE SO COOL!

WHEN HADLEY WAS TWO, WE WENT TO SEE THE MOVIE MADAGASCAR, AND SHE BEGAN CALLING ME "MELMAN," THE NAME OF THE HYPOCHONDRIACAL GIRAFFE.
THEN SHE BROKE HER COLLARBONE AND THE DOCTORS GAVE HER MORPHINE. UNTIL THEN, SHE HAD NEVER SAID THE WORD "COOL" BEFORE.

YOU'RE THE COOLEST, MELMAN.

TURNED CRANKY AND OLD AFTER THE CHEMO, MY FATHER YELLED AT MY MOTHER. A NURSE WHO SAW THIS SCOLDED HIM.

YOU SHOULD BE NICER TO YOUR DAUGHTER.

THE MOST POWERFUL MOMENT OF MY LIFE WAS HIS LAST.

HADLEY EMERGED FROM NINA BLOODY AND SQUALLING.

I CARRIED HER AROUND THE CURTAIN AND INTRODUCED MY WIFE TO HER DAUGHTER.

ELEVEN THOUGHTS ON BEING THE FATHER OF ELEVEN-MONTH-OLD TWIN BOYS

DARIN STRAUSS

1.

Everyone with a TV or some movies under his belt knows about the start of fatherhood—knows the stations of that particular cross: blue hospital scrubs, handshakes/tears, y'all be careful on your way home now, OK?

Thing is, if you've never actually lived that initial parenting moment, and then do—if you experience that atmosphere of shrieks and moans, that nausea-enforcing blood and that five-hundred-words-a-minute doctor language—there's a good chance you'll miss how it's all really profound and sacred, and beautiful. I did.

I don't like to think I'm unprecedented in this. I see our central nervous system as a kind of vintage switchboard, all thick foam wires and old-fashioned plugs. The circuitry isn't properly equipped; after a surplus of emotional information, the system overloads, the circuit breaks, the board runs dark.

That's my one parenthood regret, so far.

2.

In 2000, I wrote a novel called *Chang and Eng* about famous identical twins; in 2007 my wife gave birth to identical twins. And at the very time that I was spending my children's first days in a postnatal intensive care unit (the boys were born three and a half weeks prematurely), I had to scan the proofs of my forthcoming book *More Than It Hurts You*, which is in some part devoted to children's hospitals: to that frightening world of oscilloscope blips and ventilator beeps, to the cosmic creepiness of a baby ICU. The novel follows an eight-month-old baby; my own babies turned eight months old the week the book finally came out. You get the idea.

Reading my own attempts to describe what happens in such a complex nerve center right when it was actually happening to my young family made for a weird vibe, something about portents getting charged into reality. It sounds hokey. (But so much about parenthood sounds hokey. This is why everybody hates stories about others' kids.) Anyway, all this stuff added to the vertigo there in the ICU, to that hard-to-describe thing all glazed new fathers have, the sense of a deep incongruity to it all. My babies seemed not to be real—yet alone my—children. (That everybody hates stories about others' kids probably explains my own fear about, and the obvious hard time I'm having so far with, this essay.) What my babies seemed to be, rather, were tiny special effects that some audience at home, watching the sitcom of my life, would get a kick out of. "This space case is getting kids?" they would say. "*Him?*"

3.

These sorts of humdinger events—births, weddings, even deaths, I imagine—are so familiar to us that they seem banal, which makes for a whopper of a contradiction. The banality comes in part from our having caught these scenes on TV many times (read above); but there's a reason we've seen them so often: they're in fact the opposite of banal. They're in fact so inherently un-banal that they're probably the dramatic motor in one of every ten narratives we come across. I doubt people in pre-TV generations felt this banal/humdinger paradox. I bet they, on a gut level, felt the bigness of all their big events.

Anyway.

This paradox stuff and the quirky similarities between my sons (Beau and Shepherd) and what I'd been writing about dulled, for me, the reality of their existence.

4.

The first day we got them out of the hospital, all was chaos. One baby would cry while the other tried to sleep; then they'd switch roles. It was a twenty-four-hour wail-fest. My wife and I took them to their first pediatrician's appointment, and the entire way there we laughed the laugh of the terrified. This wasn't parenting; it was Keystone Cops stuff, Farrelly brothers mayhem; it was, surely, not doable for much longer. And we were only at the first day.

In the doctor's office, Beau had dirtied his diaper. (Oh, one other thing: don't you hate the gag-making nicety of our children's phrases? Why do we have to talk like babies when we talk about babies? Why do I blanch from writing, "He crapped himself?" *Why?*) So, I took my son into the men's room, feeling ready to change my first diaper. I did it, to my surprise, fairly successfully. I simply laid my son on the changing table and scrubbed his butt clean. Problem solved. Next, I bent to throw away the browned Huggies baby wipe; when I stood, Beau had crapped himself again. Everywhere. Onto the heretofore clean diaper; onto the changing table itself. Onto, at least a little bit, the floor. I panicked. Before had been minor league stuff, not Keystone Cops at all. Now this was, literally, a comedy shitstorm.

Laying one hand on Beau to keep him from slipping, I contorted myself so my fingertips might reach the door. Now in a sort of gymnast's candlestick position (hand *A* opening door; hand *B* on baby's tiny chest), I yelled to my wife, with even less sangfroid than it reads on the page: "Honey, Jesus, come quick! There's an emergency with the baby!"

"*What?*"

She ran over in what seemed two floorless strides, her face gone the way of any new mother's at hearing the words "emergency" and "baby" in the same sentence. "What's wrong?"

I explained in agitated voice that Beau had gone number two, and there were no more diapers or wipes.

Next there came one of those moments when you notice someone you love sizing you up, as if for the first time. The eyes narrow a bit, there's a pull on the brow, and the person looking at you points out, without a word, how far your shares have dropped in her index of cool people. "Where," my wife said evenly, "are you?"

Now, this surprised me. We were standing two feet apart at the moment in question. "The men's room," I said. (Duh.)

"And what is a men's room designed for?" she said—with the deliberateness of someone explaining to a Zemblan tourist that he's on the uptown A train when, in fact, he wanted the downtown F.

I waited. I waited for the electric bolt of comprehension. It never came.

"Bathrooms," she was saying, "are the one place in the whole building designed for just these kinds of emergencies." And she walked away, holding our other crying son.

"Right," I thought. "I'm in a *bath*room."

Using toilet paper and water, I got the mess out of the way. First real step toward fatherhood.

5.

What makes writing about babies difficult is that everything about them is known and clichéd and sentimental, and yet true. At first, you see your children through a pall of helplessness. They cry, and they eat, and they shit, and you bust your hump trying not to hinder them in that. And they give you nothing in return. *And* they look like Winston Churchill on the nod. My initial thoughts were similar to what my friend Melissa Guion says she felt on her first night home with her mewling, hungry, clinging baby: "Fuck this noise." But then, once you're at your most sleep-needy, once you think you can't clean another shit-flecked buttock or make it through another three a.m. feeding, the child looks at you for the first time; I mean, looks at you in a way that registers a kind of recognition. The gaze sharpens, the mouth bends smileward. And then you're done for.

For me, getting my boys to laugh became an addiction. What were they laughing at? At three months, they didn't speak, they couldn't crawl, they barely seemed to acknowledge each other's existence—but something you would do (blow out your cheeks to play mouth-trumpet, or hum into their bellies) would make them crack up. This is a selfish and embarrassing and transparent admission, but here goes: making my children laugh at my "jokes" was the way I first began to love them.

It's different for women, I think. When the boys were a minute old, my wife held up Shepherd and asked, "Don't you love him so much?" I didn't really understand how she could ask such a thing. *That* purple squirming howler? "He seems nice," I said.

Men, I think, need to be won over. For me, it was Shepherd's laugh—a raucous, yelpy, nonhuman gurgle that can run for minutes. And with Beau, it was his outlandishly soulful smile; I know it's hard to believe, but there's a decency and a poignant sweetness apparent in his face. You can just tell he's already a kind and slightly vulnerable person. These boys still haven't said a word to me, but I believe that they (along with my wife) are my best friends in the world. I know. It makes no sense.

6.

As you read in thought number two, the babies were eight months old when my third book came out. I had to leave them to go on a twenty-two-city book tour. This was nice (the publisher was willing to send me all over) and terrible (I'd be leaving the kids for the first time). After three weeks on the road, I got to see them for a few days before I had to head off again. My wife and sons had been staying with my parents-in-law, and when I walked into the twins' bedroom, they showed me an expression, a blank glint of: "I don't know who you are." This was a heart-hurting moment. I kept waving and smiling, trying all the old prods. Nothing worked. Then Shepherd looked sideways at me for a second, and fired a quick toot from his mouth. That laugh was as if he'd said: "Oh, yeah—*this* clown." It was better than nothing—a lot better, actually.

7.

As a very young kid I was as thin as soup-kitchen consommé, unathletic, given to homesickness. In the fifth grade a little girl called two of my friends and me "the Shrimp, the Blimp, and the Wimp"—and the phrase stuck. (I had one short friend and one heavy friend, so you can guess which name they hung around my neck.) My skinniness kept me in an internal slough of unease.

My own father, on the other hand, was a killer high school and college athlete (1962 Mason-Dixon Hurdles Champion; basketball prodigy at American University). Dawn Steel, the first woman to run a movie studio, knew my father back when and wrote about him in her memoir *They Can Kill You but They Can't Eat You*. She called him, if I remember correctly, a "paragon of elegance and style." Even as a senior at Great Neck North, he had a Nike swoosh of gray hair just above his brow. A born lady-killer. But he's also kind to a fault. He didn't want to be one of those fathers who push their children too hard. As a result, he didn't teach me how to play basketball. Or, rather, when he saw I wasn't good at it, he stopped teaching me. I suppose I hold a slight grudge about this. (To be fair, he *was* my Little League coach; I spent a lot of time in the outfield, spinning around, looking at the cool effect that my spinning had on my view of the grass and three-leafed clovers, etc.) I do remember the one and only time my dad taught me how to play ball. With a grunt, nine-year-old me heaved shots underhand.

At this blacktopped outdoor court, the orange-painted hoops had chain nets that jangled, if your shot went through, like house keys: an addictive sound. Once, to my surprise, my dad blocked my shot. And when he swatted away my desperate hurl, the outdoor ball made a cartoon, Road Runner-ish *ping!*

It's unfair, but this is the memory I keep coming back to. Me throwing the ball, my father slapping it away. It's unfair; my father is kind, and we're still close, and he did a good job raising me, and he made a tough call—the call not to pressure me to be an athlete. But I wish he'd taught me how to play basketball for real—more than that one time—and I wish that my memory of the one time wasn't that. Now that I'm a parent I want to call him and apologize for what's on my mind. It's unfair.

They fuck you up, your mum and dad. They may not mean to, but they do.

8.

To get specific about what's downright cheesy in fatherhood— or about writing on fatherhood—it's that becoming a dad shows you that love is the fundament of all existence. You feel like some Republican candidate at the GOP Convention just for saying this stuff.

All the same: I love my wife; I have, though not with the same seriousness or for as long, loved other women before her—and I love (some of) my other relatives, too. But being a parent is like taking an SAT on love: a more concentrated, stressful, more important test.

My wife and I and both our kids were sick last week—the normal, fluish, change-of-season bummer. And, bad as I felt, I caught myself saying, "I hope the kids get better soon." Now,

again, I love my wife. (Do I sound like Bob Dole yet?) But if
it had been only the two of us who'd had chapped nasal philtra
and thermometers wedged in our mouths, I don't think I'd have
wished that she would be the first one to shake off our flu. Not
to get all preachy about it, but that's parenthood, I think: wanting your kids to feel relief more than you want yourself to.

9.

The reason I thought the audience at home, watching the sitcom of my life, would think, "Why is this clown getting kids?"
is that I'm a chronic fuckup. I have trouble paying bills on time,
I often go out of doors with dumbly mismatched socks, etc. My
wife, for good reason, hates it. This July, I killed four hours
looking for my car in the La Guardia parking lot.

Maybe it's an occupational hazard. The novelist Italo Svevo
is said to have come home alone from a trip to an amusement
park to which he'd taken his son. "Where's the boy?" his wife
asked (in Italian, of course). "Oh, no!"—Svevo grabbed his
coat and hat. "I'll be right back."

But 2008-vintage men don't get to be Italo Svevo. I care
for the boys alone from 6:50 a.m. to 8:30, when I leave to go
to my office to write, and I come home early, every day, to
have them from four to seven p.m. I usually wheel them in
our double-wide Urban Buggy to the swings in Brooklyn's
Prospect Park. The day before yesterday, however, it rained;
our stroller seats had become tiny twin reservoirs. I decided
to try getting the boys to the park anyway. I somehow managed to carry them both—my grip on Beau's pants loosening
as he bit into the dorsal-venous network of my left hand, Shepherd holding my shoulder and throwing his head back like a
dance partner impatient for the dip—to my upstairs neighbor's

apartment. "Can I borrow your stroller?" I asked the neighbor, who has an infant of his own. He let me take *two* strollers.

"Great!" I thought. "I'll just push them side by side." This was a mistake.

The wheels of the two vehicles kept crossing; Beau was too small for his stroller and just missed doing a face plant onto the sidewalk. Curbs were a challenge (which one to lift first?), the passing of every car a kind of Sophie's choice.

There's supposed to be a coherent end to this point, to good old #9 here; something in the spirit of: but I'm getting better every day and with extra diligence blah blah blah. The truth is, it's hard to stop being a fuckwit when you've always kind of been one. But you love your children and you do the best you can and hope nothing goes wrong.

10.

If you're going to have more than one kid, I highly recommend going the twins route.

When I heard we were having identical boys, I panicked. Too much work! But it's sneakily great. You get all the hard (sleepless, messy) stuff out of the way in one stroke. Which is like paying for a house up front. And your kids are always on the same developmental clock; you won't be breast-feeding one and potty training the other. Also, and this is a big plus, they have a built-in friend. Even in this preverbal present, my sons hug and crack each other up when we try to put them to bed. It's heartwarming. And I know you cringed when you read that—the brightest-neon cliché there is—but it fits, because when I see Beau make Shepherd laugh, and then the two of them start to snuggle, my heart is a spurting hot-water bottle everywhere in my chest.

11.

At first they looked like no one, puffball things, the only human detail being their eyes, and even those—just blue marbles set in dough—lacked the quickness of thought. But watching them become people is like looking at a fossil record: picking out what of our faces has endured in theirs. My wife's high regal forehead is there, and the shape of my mouth is. It's a reminder: we're all pretty much Mr. Potato Heads, having been thrown together out of a narrow kitty of nostrils and ears and tempera-ments in some embryological playroom.

And they already have distinct personalities, which is, I suppose, a testament to the mystery and magic of Self.

When I catch one of the boys focusing the cloud of his nascent personality—Shepherd bashfully looking at his brother for approval, Beau trying to make someone laugh by pulling a funny face—I feel the need to rush out and embrace them, as if to scoop the boys away from oncoming traffic. I don't know why it's so urgent. But most of the time I sit without moving, hoping they won't even notice I'm in the room. It's silly, and hard to put words to, but it's almost as though I've convinced myself that if I can be quiet and still to the point of seeming not there, they'll stay this age forever, and so will I.

REMEMBER THE BANANA

BROCK CLARKE

Before I became a father, I wasn't at all sure I wanted to be one; I wasn't sure I wanted to have a son (I never even thought of wanting, or not wanting, to have a daughter, maybe because I had two brothers and no sisters and so couldn't imagine living with a woman who wasn't my mother, or then, later, my girlfriend, and then, later, my wife). One hears this kind of stuff from men my age (I'm thirty-nine years old) all the time, to the point where you wish these guys had been so afraid that they actually *hadn't* had a son, so they wouldn't be able to yammer on about the time when they weren't sure they wanted one. One wishes that each and every one of them had had a vasectomy. One wishes that each and every one of them had become a public high school principal who, as a role model for his students, decided not to just preach his school's Abstinence Is the Most Effective Birth Control policy, but to practice it. Forever. One wishes that, if they really wanted to exercise their right to procreate, they would then be forced to surrender their right to talk about it. One wishes never, ever, ever to be told by another thirty-nine-year-old white, middle-class, highly educated man who treats every subject, no matter how serious, with flip irony, except the subject of fatherhood, which he treats with sickening reverence, that he was afraid to be a father, that he wasn't sure if he was *ready* to be a father, *really* ready, but then again, he adds, is anyone *really ready* for something that will end up being the very best thing he has ever done or ever will do? One wishes these guys would be assigned a parole officer of a sort, someone who, once a week, would force them to blow into a specially rigged BabyBjörn that would be able to tell with 100 percent accuracy whether, since they last took the test, they'd bloviated on the subject of fatherhood. One wishes that these guys, if they failed the test, would be forced to move from Brooklyn (according to the *New York Times*, all of these guys live in Brooklyn) to, say, anywhere else in the United States, thus ensuring that they would forget all about the subject of fatherhood and instead hold forth on the subject of Brooklyn, how they miss it so much.

But mostly, one wishes that one wasn't one of these guys. But one is, and I am. I am fond of Brooklyn, for instance, even if I've never had enough money to live there. As I said, I wasn't sure I wanted to be a father, wasn't sure I wanted to have a son. But now that my son is born, I do love him, a lot, more than anything, and I've been known to talk about it. For instance, I like to talk about the time I stayed up until four in the morning reading Cormac McCarthy's novel *The Road*. By the time I finished the book (as everyone knows by now, *The Road* is a heartbreaking story about a father and a son who decide, since it's the end of the world, that it would be a good time to take a long walk to the beach, and along the way they end up trying to avoid a whole bunch of people who want to eat them) I was weeping. Weeping and weeping. Weeping about what it means to have a son, to be a father, to be a man. So I got out of my bed, went into my son's room, and climbed into bed with him. At which point he woke up, sat up in bed, looked at me, and said, "What are you *doing* in here?"

I didn't answer him. But I didn't get out of his bed, either. I just lay there for a while, thinking of the time, twelve years before, when my grandfather died and we (my family, but not my son, who hadn't been born yet) had his funeral, and then buried him, and then gathered back at my grandfather's house to drink and reminisce. This was in Connecticut. The house has been in my family for five generations. I went upstairs to change out of my funeral clothes and my dad was standing in the middle of the room (the whole upstairs is just one big room), halfway changed himself: he was in his underwear, and was still wearing his oxford shirt and tie and dress socks. He was crying. I don't know about you and your dad, but when I see my dad crying I want him to stop, immediately. So I went over and hugged him, even though he wasn't wearing any pants.

"Hey, don't cry," I said.

"I'm sorry," he said.

"What for?" I said.

"I'll never be as good a father to you as my father was to me."

Now, this was news to me. I always thought my father was an excellent father, certainly way better than I deserved. When I was teenager, for instance, I got drunk and walked on a dozen cars parked on the street and got arrested and fined. Why I walked on the cars, I don't know. The only reason I can come up with was that the cars were on the way from where I was to where I wanted to be. In any case, I was arrested and then released. Somehow I managed to keep the news from my dad for a couple of months, and by the time he found out, I was two states away—at my grandparents' house in Connecticut, in fact. He called me on the phone, mid-afternoon, and told me I'd have to pay the fine (the bill for the fine was sent to him, which is how he found out about the whole thing). I told him I would. I made sure he knew I was ashamed. "Good," he said. And that was about it. He didn't even yell. But I knew how upset he was about the whole thing. I knew this because it was my grandmother's birthday that day. My father normally called her around five to wish her happy birthday. But he didn't call at five, or six, or seven. By seven thirty, I knew my grandmother had noticed, because she was watching *Wheel of Fortune* in a distracted, worried way. So I called my father and said, "Don't forget to call Grandma. It's her birthday."

"Jesus," my father said. "Thank you, Brock." Which I thought was pretty incredible, since I'm the one who had gotten drunk and walked on the cars and gotten arrested and fined for it and caused my father to get so upset that he almost forgot to wish his own mother happy birthday. We hung up, and then my father called right back for his mother. After he did that, I got on the phone and he thanked me again and told me he loved me. That's what I mean when I say he was a better father than I deserved.

I was thinking of this when my father apologized to me for not being as good a father to me as his father was to him. I couldn't come up with one thing he'd done to me in his role as a father that he shouldn't have, or one thing he'd done that he should have done significantly better. I thought maybe, in his grief, my father was confusing me with one of my two brothers. It's possible they had a grievance that I didn't. Once, for example, my father drove my youngest brother home from school. My youngest brother was young at the time, and maybe a little sensitive, although he insists he wasn't sensitive now or at any other time, so apparently this—being accused of being sensitive—is one of the things he's sensitive about. In any case, my father was driving him home, and decided to take a different route than the one they normally took. My youngest brother noticed and asked him, "Where are we going, Dad?"

My father didn't answer for a second. Then he looked over at my youngest brother sitting in the passenger seat and said, in his best movie villain voice, "Lonnie, I'm not your real father." My father claims not to know what he was thinking when he said this. But it was pretty funny. Everyone thought so, except for my youngest brother. Thinking about this now, it might have been this incident that made my youngest brother so sensitive in the first place. Thinking about this now, I seem to remember that my youngest brother, before my father jokingly told him he wasn't his real father, was actually a tough little guy, like a prepubescent Edward G. Robinson but with curlier hair.

Anyway, when my dad was saying he had never been as good a father to me as his father had been to him, maybe he was really meaning to apologize to my youngest brother. I meant to mention this to my youngest brother after my dad had put on his pants and I had changed out of my funeral clothes and we had gone downstairs. But then we started drinking and someone told a story I'd never heard before, about my grandfather eating dry dog food and how nutty that was, and then there was an argument about whether it would have been nuttier if he'd eaten wet dog food, and then someone wanted clarification and asked, "You mean, with his *hands*?" and one thing led to another and I forgot to tell my youngest brother that our dad had probably been apologizing to him when he was apologizing to me. I only hope my mentioning it now, here, isn't too late to do him some good.

It should be noted here that the guys who one wishes would stop talking about how they never wanted to become a father but are so glad they did fall into two camps. One camp is the camp filled with guys who never wanted to become fathers because their fathers were terrible and they were afraid they'd be terrible fathers to their sons, too. The stories coming out of that camp are much more interesting and dramatic than those coming out of the other camp, and therefore implausible, and I won't talk more about them here. Because I'm clearly in the other camp, and here is my point: I wasn't sure I wanted to have a son because I knew I wouldn't be as good a father to him as my father had been to me. I hadn't thought of that before my father brought up the subject, but once he did, I couldn't stop thinking about it. Thinking about it didn't stop me from having a son (there are, of course, prophylactics that prevent guys like me from having sons; but if only there had been a prophylactic that prevented us from thinking about having sons and then talking about it, we'd all be a lot better off), but it did stop me from enjoying the prospect. I worried about it for years, long before I had a son. I read John Edgar Wideman's terrifying stories and essays about his son going to prison for murder, and I worried about that, worried that somehow I would drive my son to prison (I mean this both figuratively and literally: sometimes, in my nightmares, I actually would drive my son to the prison gates and he would get out of the car and wave to me, like I was just dropping him off at school or camp or the mall, before walking through the gates and having them clang shut behind him), all because I was not as good a father to my son as my father had been to me.

Whatever it was, I knew something would happen. I was terrified of it. I really was. I even mentioned this to my father. This was maybe three years before my wife was even pregnant. I don't know how the subject came up. It probably didn't. I probably just blurted it out. I told him how afraid I was to become a father. I was afraid I'd hurt my son, somehow, in some way, and wreck his life. My father looked at me like I was a lunatic. "You can't be scared of something that doesn't even exist," he said. This, of course, is a ridiculous thing to say. But I knew then that this was another way I wouldn't be as good a father to my son as my father had been to me. I would worry about things that I shouldn't. I would talk about things that didn't need to be talked about (my father, for instance, uttered that one sentence on the subject of his father and him and me, and only that one sentence, that one time). I would make things worse just by talking about them. I was one of those guys. Please, I said to whoever was listening when I found out my wife was pregnant, please don't let me be one of those guys.

My son was born. He was beautiful. I loved him. I held him in the hospital. I held him at home. I held him, and waited.

I waited a year, maybe a little bit more. We were moving, from South Carolina to Ohio. I remember this because there were boxes everywhere. My son was in his high chair. He was shirtless, because he hated bibs and we didn't want him getting his shirt all dirty. I was feeding him. When I say I was feeding him, I don't mean I was putting food on a spoon and then putting it in his mouth. I mean I was handing him a banana and he was supposed to put the banana in his mouth. This was my understanding of how one-year-olds were supposed to eat their food. My son had another understanding, though. He kept taking the banana and throwing it on the floor. The floor around the high chair was covered with a tarp for this very reason. Still, it made me mad. My son must have thrown the banana on the floor ten, twelve, fifteen times. My wife was in the other room, packing boxes. But she could hear me telling our son, "No. No. No. Do *not* do that."

"Is everything all right in there?" she wanted to know.

I didn't answer. I picked the banana up off the floor and handed it to my son. With my eyes I told him, "You know what to do with this. You know what I expect you to do with this."

My son broke the banana in two. He looked me in the eyes. With his left hand he threw the smaller, squishier part of the banana down and off to the side a little; it landed on an open box of dishes, smearing the top dish. With his right hand he threw the other, bigger, more solid part of the banana at me. It hit me right in the chest, then rolled down my T-shirt and into my lap. I picked it up with my right hand. I looked at my son. He was looking back at me. His eyes were big and happy. I could see how happy he was. And then I threw the banana back at him. Hard. It hit him right in the chest, and made a loud noise, a big, wet, painful-sounding *smack*. "What was *that*?" my wife wanted to know from the next room. I didn't answer. She'd find out soon enough, when my son started crying and she came into the room and I told her what I'd done and she saw the red banana-shaped mark on his white, white chest. But before that happened, it was just my son and me. He was sitting in his high chair, me in my low one. My son's mouth was hanging open, but he wasn't crying yet. He was still looking at me with his big eyes, but they weren't happy anymore. Maybe he was seeing what I was seeing. Maybe he was seeing the time, years and years later, when I'd be apologizing for not being as good a father to him as my father had been to me. And my son would remember the banana. He would remember it because I was one of those guys who would talk about it, endlessly, as part of the story of my journey from not being sure I wanted to be a father to not knowing what I'd do without my son. My son would remember the banana, and when I said to him, "I'll never be as good a father to you as my father was to me," he would think, and maybe even say, "You know, maybe you won't."

So that was the answer to my son's question, when he woke up to find me crying in his bed after reading *The Road* and asked me, "What are you doing in here?" I was saying I was sorry. I was saying I was sorry that I'm so much like those guys we all hate, instead of being more like my father. I was saying I was sorry for not being as good a father to him as my father is to me. I was saying I was sorry for denying him a chance to plausibly deny the truth of that statement. I was saying I was sorry for throwing that banana at him six years earlier. I was promising never ever to do anything like that again. Except I wasn't brave enough to say any of those things. Finally, I was speechless. Instead, I kissed my son on the forehead, climbed out of his bed, and went back to my own.

THE POINTS OF SAIL

SVEN BIRKERTS

The nerve of fathering is woven through the moment—and here and now is the place to start. Late July of 2008, Cape Cod. We have come down almost every summer for the last twenty years. This time we are staying in Truro, my wife Lynn, our son Liam and his friend Caleb, and I. Our daughter Mara will take a few days off from her job next week to join us, arriving when Caleb leaves. There will be three days when we are all four together, the basic unit, taken for granted for so many years, but now become as rare as one of those planetary alignments that I no longer put stock in. *This*, though, I do put stock in. The thought of us all reassembled reaches me, wakes me with the strike of every blue ocean day.

It's mid-afternoon and I'm in Provincetown, sitting on a deck on the bayside, at one of those rental spots. Liam and Caleb have persuaded me to rent two Sunfish sailboats so that they can sail the harbor together. Caleb has been taking sailing lessons all summer at home, and Liam had some a few years back, though as was clear as soon as they launched out ten minutes ago, he has forgotten whatever he learned. As Caleb's boat arrowed toward the horizon, Liam's sat turned around with sails luffing, and I watched his silhouette jerking the boom and tiller this way and that until at last he got himself repointed and under way. I was smiling, not much worrying about the wisdom of letting him out in his own boat—he's fourteen and as big as I am—though I did take note of a smudge of dark clouds moving in behind me.

Once Liam joined up with Caleb, the two little Sunfish zigged and zagged for the longest time in the open area between the long pier and the dozens of boats anchored in the harbor and I fell into a kind of afternoon fugue watching them. The book I'd brought lay facedown on the little table where I sat. I tracked the movement of the boats and half listened to two men behind me talking about the perils of gin and various hangover remedies, and every so often I stood up to stretch and to glance up at the sky. Shielding my eyes with my hand, I panned left along the shoreline, past the clutter of waterfront buildings and pilings toward Truro and Wellfleet.

I don't remember what year we first started coming to the Cape regularly. We had been down once or twice for shorter visits before we had kids. Massachusetts was still new to us— Lynn and I are both Midwesterners—and going to the ocean felt like an adventure, a splurge. Fresh seafood, bare feet in the brine. What a sweet jolt to the senses it all was. And isn't this one of the unexpected things about getting older: suddenly remembering not just the specifics of an event, but the original intensity, the *fact* of the original intensity?

Those first times have mostly slipped away, replaced—overruled—by the years and years, the layers and layers, of family visits. The place, which is to say the *places*—the many rental spots in Wellfleet and Truro, including some fairly grim habitats early on—has become an archive of family life. Driving along Route 6 in either direction, I have only to glance at a particular turnoff to think—or to say out loud if Lynn is beside me—"that was the place with the marshy smell," or whatever tag best fits.

All of which is to say that this whole area, everything north of the Wellfleet line—which for me is marked by the Wellfleet Drive-In—is dense with anecdote. I have this storage box with its twenty-plus years of excerpts, all of them from summer, all from vacations away from our daily living and therefore of a kind, a time line separate from everything else. "That first summer we . . ." Except that memory obeys not time lines, but associations. Shake the photos in the box until they are completely pell-mell, then reach in. That dark path by the Bayside rental fits right next to the place with the horses, and that in turn fits next to the field where we threw Frisbees. Like that. So when I shade my eyes and follow the shoreline, I am not so much seeing the things in front of me as pointing myself back. I am fanning the pages of a book I know, not really reading, just catching a phrase here, another there.

But now I turn again, I look across the tables on the deck and over the railing and out along the line described by the pier to my right. I see the two Sunfish, Caleb's with the darker sail heeling nicely into the wind, cutting toward the open water past pier's end, Liam's lagging, not quite right with the wind, but at least making headway. And I check over my shoulder to see how the clouds have gained, feeling a first tiny prick of anxiety. The boat rental people said the bay just past the pier was fine, but they also said they were a bit shorthanded today, that they wouldn't be taking their boat out quite as much to patrol. This flashes back to me as I see Caleb's boat slip out of sight behind the end of the pier, though I find that when I sit up straight I can follow the top part of his blue sail—accompanied, some distance behind, by Liam's, which is red.

We came those first summers when Mara was little, just the three of us, so often renting on a shoestring and ending up in some places that in retrospect seem rankly depressing, but at the time, when we were in them, were mainly fine. We ignored or joked about smells and bugs and cupboards lined with floral sticky-paper and those molten-toned seascapes bolted to the walls. We took pride in making do, and I think now that we had endless patience for the clattery busywork of being young parents, the stroller pushing, the pretend playing, all the up and back repetitions. I remember one summer we set ourselves up in a box-shaped little house—it was one of a dozen or so—on a hillside near Wellfleet. And in our largesse, before ever even setting eyes on the place, we invited my mother to visit for a few days, with Lynn's sister to arrive as soon as my mother left. It turned out that there was barely room for all of us in the living room, with its huge picture-window fronting the road. It rained most of the week. I was beside myself with boredom. But I also wanted to be a good father. I played and played with Mara, trying to make her vacation a happy one. Alas, we had nowhere to go. My only diversion was a box of dominoes found in the closet. I sat Mara down on the floor beside me and we built towers. Over and over, piece by ticking piece, always the same basic design. How high could we make it? And how irritated I got if Mara knocked one of my good towers down. I was building for myself, desperate to stay amused. Somewhere we have a Polaroid of the two of us sitting beside our prize construction. Looking at the photo, I think what a stunning, unbelievably sweet little girl she was—and how ridiculous it was for me to get so serious about stacking those bones.

What kind of a father was I? I know that I tried to be different from my own father, who all through my childhood maintained that he loved us—and clearly did—but who also told us, often, that we would appreciate him only when we were older and more intelligent. *Then* we would talk. But I could not imagine having that kind of detached deferral with my own child. I wanted entry to Mara's world, a role in shaping her mind, her sense of things. I wanted to get as close as I could.

My problem was that I had no idea how to proceed. I was never one for playing. The sight of a spinner on a gussied-up board game or of some molded plastic doll—these things filled me with fatigue. I hated almost all toys; nor could I endure the infantilized pretend chatter that was the required accompaniment to all forms of parent-child play, at least from what I'd observed. "Snuffy is a *niiiiiice* kitty . . ." Yikes! I could finally do only what I knew to do, what I liked to do. I could talk. I invented characters, told stories, created plot situations that grew into one another and became more and more elaborate over time. Steffie and Kevin, their friend Lenny, the villains Moe and Joe, Steffie's rival Cherry Lalou—and the world they lived in, the street, neighborhood, town . . . I worked hard at these, the adventures were good ones—so I thought, anyway—full of surprises, resisting pat endings but still upholding a basic picture of a moral universe, a triumph of idealism over low impulse. And Mara loved them. Every night, or whenever we had time together, she would beam at me: "Tell me a Kevin and Steffie, Dad." This went on for years.

Mara is almost twenty now. She is taking a break from college, living with roommates in an apartment in Belmont, ten minutes from where we live. She has a forty-hour-a-week job in a stationery store in Harvard Square, though she barely makes ends meet. She is, by her own admission, unsettled, experiencing vivid and frightening dreams and moods that can suddenly plummet and leave her feeling sad and exposed. The sensations she describes are familiar to me—they reach all the way back into my own young years.

I wasn't thinking about Mara just then, as I stood again on the deck to stretch, but I was very much aware of her. Her funks, the tone of her recent phone calls, knowing that she would be coming soon. I peered out at what I could see of the bay but all these things were there in my peripheral awareness.

I was having my first real doubt now. I could still see the tips of both sails, moving toward the other part of the bay, just above the edge of the pier, clean little shark-fin shapes. But the sky was definitely darkening and the wind was picking up slightly, and the farther out Liam took his boat, the less confidence I had in his bluster about knowing how to sail. I turned around to see if there was a clock in the rental shed. The girl who worked there had left her counter and was standing on a crate, shading her eyes and peering at the harbor. She must have picked up on my agitation, because just then she said: "They'll be fine—but they shouldn't go too far out." I nodded. They would know that, I told myself. Then: they're fourteen-year-old boys, they *won't* know. I looked back quickly to make sure I saw the sails.

Liam has always been different from Mara. Six years younger, he is made from other material. Whereas she is delicate, slightly wan, he is fleshy and boisterously solid. He always has been. Since preschool he has never not been the biggest boy in his class. Barely into his teens, he has already caught up to me, and I am not small. The other night I told him to stand up straight against a wooden beam in the Truro house. I put the top of a DVD case flat on his head and drew a faint line. Then I told him to do the same for me. We had to laugh—we were the thickness of a pencil lead apart.

Given his size and his point-blank confidence, I tend to forget his age and essential vulnerability. When I have to face it I can get overwhelmed. He could hurt himself, cry a child's tears. Or be in danger. The worst was years ago. He was seven or eight years old, at summer camp. Lynn and I got a call at noon one day that we should come get him, that he was in the infirmary, having what appeared to be an asthma attack. We hurried over to bring him home, worried, but also thinking he had just overtaxed himself. We told him to rest in his room. Suddenly he was standing at the top of the stairs, red in the face, making a noise that was almost a bleat, terror on his face. He couldn't breathe, he was choking for air. Without hesitation we sat him down there on the top step and called the doctor, who told us to get an ambulance right away. Which we did. And moments later—time was a jumble—I was behind the wheel of our car, following an ambulance across town, hurtling through red lights, my calm life gone into a hyperventilating freefall that would not stop until more than an hour later, when a doctor came out to assure us that Liam's breathing had been stabilized and that he would be fine.

How long it took—maybe years—for that shock to ebb fully, for some trace of that anxiety not to be there every time he went outside to play, daily breathing treatments notwithstanding. I think of the way we look at our children when we are afraid, the way we read their eyes to see if they are telling us everything, and the terrible sense we have of their fragility, which for me goes all the way back to the very first night we brought Mara home from the hospital and set her up in a little crib. I remember how I just lay there listening to the breathing sounds, sure that if I tuned them out for an instant they would stop. A superstition: much the same as how I used to believe that if I relaxed my will for an instant while flying the airplane I was in, it would instantly plummet. Life has taught me much about my fears and about my grandiose presumptions, but only gradually.

Liam and Mara, what a strange distribution of personalities—no, what a pair of souls. I have to think in terms of souls where my closest people are concerned. To think of them as personalities diminishes them, a personality being something one can put a boundary around somehow. Liam and Mara could not be more different, in who they are and in what each drew forth from us as parents. We never had a program or a plan. I have never had a clear instinct for what kind of father to be, not in terms of what I should be doing, modeling, instructing. I have somehow trusted to being myself. Maybe a better version of myself—kinder, more attentive, and more consistent in my responses than I might be if I did not feel the responsibility of children.

My idea—and feeling—of being a father has changed from year to year, if not from week to week. The father of a newborn is very different from the father of a toddler or a school-age child or a preteen or . . . Is there anything constant in it, besides the love and care—the great givens—the fact that I would do anything at any time to ensure their safety and well-being? But in terms of who I *am*—well, it stands to reason, doesn't it? The father of newborn Mara was thirty-six, the father of teenage

Mara was fifty, and the man looking out for some trace of his teenage son is slowly pushing sixty.

I keep an image that I refer to from time to time to orient myself, from an afternoon moment on a Wellfleet side road some years ago. We had a weeklong rental, an upstairs apartment in a frowsy old house that had been divided up to accommodate people just like us. The yard was grassy, though, and shady, and the house was on a nice stretch of road to walk, and nearby we had discovered a small horse-farm, which became a popular destination for keeping the kids amused. We would stand by the roadside, pressed against the wooden fence, and watch the horses being exercised in the corral. Mara might have been ten or eleven that summer, Liam four or five, and I somewhere in my late forties. I do all this approximate figuring because my epiphany—I think it counts as one—had everything to do with ages and proportions.

It was the very end of a beautiful summer afternoon, the light beginning to slant. But though I was vacationing, I was also trying very hard to get some writing done, to bring a book project around to completion. It was because I wanted to think, to stew in my own notions, that I begged off when Lynn and the kids started off down the road on another walk. I waved them off, I remember, and then sat myself down on a steep, grassy verge in front of the house and watched. They were moving slowly, one or both kids dawdling. I sat and stared at them, and as I did I felt come over me, gradually, the clearest and sweetest melancholy. It was as if I had suddenly moved out of myself, pulling away and rising like some insect that has left its transparent shell stuck to the branch of a tree. It was as if the needle on the balance had drawn up completely straight; the string I plucked was exactly in tune. I watched my wife and two kids walking away from me down the road and I got it. I was exactly in the middle—of the afternoon, of the summer, of an actuarial life, of the great generational cycle. Outlined against the horizon in front of me were those three shapes, and behind me, imagined on the opposite horizon, were my own two parents, both still alive and in health, just coming into their seventies. I was in the middle, at once a son, a father, and something else: a man with plans and projects in his head, no one's person. It was the frailest and most temporary alignment, and the sensation just then of everything holding steady, hovering in place, exalted me, just as the knowledge that it had to change filled me with sorrow. I took a breath and swallowed my metaphysics. I headed in to use the bit of time I had to do my work. For if parenting held any practical lesson for me, it was that I had to learn to stake out time, to filch every little scrap I could.

Something's happened just now, here, between one glance and the next. There were two sails in view beyond the line of the pier, but when I look I see only one. The blue sail. Caleb's. Fatherhood compresses into a single pulse, long enough for me to jump off the edge of the deck to the sand and start jogging around the ropes and old buoys to where the pier meets the shore, and when I reach that point I duck and go under to get to the other side, where I can see. As I straighten up I see just the one boat, and I can't get a clear picture of the rest. There are other boats, sailboats, bobbing at anchor, just masts. I scour the water surface between—nothing. I am not afraid, exactly, but definitely anxious. Liam can swim, he has a life vest, he is right there somewhere. And yes, yes, there—I center in—I spot something moving right next to one of the anchored boats. A small commotion. Caleb's Sunfish appears to be heeling around in that direction. Liam has obviously

tipped over; he is there fussing in the water next to his capsized boat.

I know, sure as anything, that he will not be able to right
the thing by himself. And Caleb won't be able to do much.
Still not worried, I also realize I should tell the girl at the rental
shack so that she can send someone out to give him a hand.

When I get back, the girl is standing on her crate with
binoculars. She is ahead of me. "I've got Jimmy on his way to
check it out." When I turn, a small launch is chugging toward
pier's end. "He'll just bring them in," she says. "It's getting
kind of blowy out there." And so it is. A glance up reveals that
our blue day has gone completely cloudy and that the water is
getting choppy. I return to my chair to wait.

There is no guide to any of this. Kids get older in sudden
jumps and with each jump the scramble begins. Strategies that
worked so reliably one day are useless in the face of the new.
Moods, secrecies, distances, brash eruptions. You know things
are shifting when you suddenly find yourself choosing your
words, reading cues like you never had to before. I had thought
the family, our blustering foursome, immutable until Mara arrived at adolescence. Then she changed. She grew moody, and
these moods were not something she could leave at home when
vacation time came. This altered everything. It marked out
before and after. *Before* was all of our innocent routines: walking to the beach, walking to the pond, or getting ice cream or
lounging in front of a rented movie cracking jokes. *After* was a
new unknown that threw so much about family life into question. Who were we that this young person would find a thousand reasons not to be with us, who was she to take us in with
evaluating eyes, to wander off on self-errands that left the rest
of us wanting? "Family" now felt like something picked apart.
What had happened to our invincibility?

To be a parent, a father, was suddenly to contend with the world washing in. Or adulthood. Adulthood is a force that no wall of childhood can ultimately withstand. Fatherhood has its first incarnation as a presiding and protecting. Later it becomes a kind of brokering. We start to run interference between the world as we know it and the world as our children are learning about it. If early parenting is about the fostering of innocence and the upholding of certain illusions—to give the child's self time to solidify—the later stage of parenting asks for a growing recognition of sorrow, cruelty, and greed, of the whole unadorned truth of things, the truth that the child, now adolescent, will encounter; but the recognition is marked and annotated and put into perspective.

The last few of our Cape summers have made me feel this acutely, more than our daily-world interactions. The idea of vacation is so imbued with heedlessness and innocence—the stock imagery of families relaxing together—that any small sadness or disaffection is amplified. The kitschy menu board at the clam shack seems to mock us, as do the shop-window posters, the happy blond groups bicycling along the beach road. For there is our teenager moping in the backseat, or on her beach towel, or lying curled up in bed as if nothing in the world is worth the exertion of sitting up. At times the daily business left behind can seem like the real vacation, the place to get back to.

I'm on my feet again. Foreground and background—my thought and my immediate awareness—seem to merge as soon as the procession comes into view from behind the pier. The launch with two silhouettes—one of them Liam's. And then, behind, the Sunfish with sail down, on a tow. Caleb's blue-sailed boat trails behind. All's well, I think, shaking my head. The girl

from the rental desk makes her way down to the beach. I wave
to Liam, wait for some nod. But though he seems to take me
in, I get no response. He is sitting up very straight in the back
of the launch, looking the way prisoners always do in movies.

I jump down from the deck and join the girl on the beach.
Jimmy has unhooked the Sunfish and pushed it toward shore;
he turns the boat to dock it at the pier. Liam remains upright
in his seat. He doesn't respond when Caleb passes the launch
on his way in.

A few minutes later, he moves toward me along the pier,
his life vest still buckled tight. He looks pale, and when he
draws closer and I reach to touch his shoulder, I catch something new in his expression. He's afraid.

The story comes out in jags, and not right away. First we
all have to gather together again. Lynn arrives from her errands
around town and we mill around for a few minutes collecting
our things. And then the four of us are back on the main street,
scouting for a restaurant where we can sit. Only when we get
a table and sit does Liam open up. It jars me. He switches into
an edgy sort of agitation, not like him, talking fast and using
his hands. I'm expecting some dramatic bluster, but I'm wrong.
"I thought I was going to drown," he says. The voice itself, the
tone, is flat. I know he's serious. "I was in irons—facing right
into the wind—and then I got pushed into this other boat."
We're at our table on the enclosed patio of a big bayside restaurant, paying full attention. In the five minutes since we arrived
the sky has gone black—the wind is shaking the plastic around
us, the first drops trailing down.

It's not until we've placed our order that the whole story finally comes out. And now I start to put it together, the way he
was sitting in the launch, the look on his face when he walked
toward me. I get the surface of it, then I get more. And even

now, as I write, I'm feeling still other layers. I feel the shadow of the wing—the dread—as I did when he was talking. Liam could have drowned; it could have happened. He will need to tell it again and again to us before that look on his face goes away.

He was doing fine, he claims, until he passed the pier and found himself headed toward the moored boats. "I started to get scared," he says. The boats were coming up fast, and he tried to turn. "I messed up." I stare at his hands, big and red. "I got turned around and all of a sudden I was in irons." I can see he likes the phrase. "My boat got pushed back into this other boat and then my tiller got caught in its rope." He pauses to get the sequence straight, and takes a breath. I think how I'd seen none of this, only the triangular peak of his red sail stalled in the distance. He explains how he was trying to work the tiller free with one hand while using his other to jostle the boom back and forth in hopes of catching some wind. And then—

"I don't really know what happened, something screwed up. I got the tiller free but the boom whipped around and all of a sudden it pulled the rope around my neck." That was when it happened. His boat had heeled over with a rush, jerking him into the water—with the rope suddenly around his neck. The force of capsizing instantly tightened the noose and as the mast pulled down to the water he could barely get his hand in between the rope and his throat. He was being pulled down by the boat. He panicked, thinking he was drowning. And then somehow, he doesn't know how, he slipped his head free.

He told his tale a number of times that night, getting his version the way he wanted it, gradually putting the picture outside himself, giving it over to us. As we listened, we all did that primitive thing. We kept reaching over to touch him. I put my hand on his, Lynn leaned her head against him, Caleb tapped his shoulder. The three of us were making him real again, planting him in our midst, taking him back from that "almost."

"You could have drowned, my God"—we said it again and again as the rain hammered down. And we talked about it for the rest of the night. We hovered around, bringing the "almost" in close and then fending it off again. I thought of myself there on the deck, oblivious, and could not resist extrapolating: a big obvious message about how it is between parents and their children—between any people who are close, really—how it snarls up together, all the vigilance and ignorance, luck and readiness, love and fear. We know nothing.

Four days before we have to leave the Truro house, Mara arrives. We are the basic unit at last—Caleb took the ferry back to Boston the day after the sailing episode. Reunion is sweet. But the ground feeling, the joy, of having everyone together in the same place, with nothing on the schedule except trips to the ocean and the making of meals, is overlaid with darker tones. Mara is still in her mood, it's obvious. She tells us that she has been having bad dreams and feeling anxious every night. I see her on the couch, reading a magazine, looking for all the world like a young woman relaxing with her family, except that something in the shoulders, the tilt of the head, gives her away.

Mara gets through the first night easily enough. In fact, she sleeps like she hasn't slept in a long time, dead-weight sleep. Sleep like I have not had for decades. She told me to wake her early, that she would join me for my walk, and once I've had my coffee I try. But after a few separate prods I give it up. I go alone all the way down the long hill to the deli-market to buy the papers. Heading back, I think about our long season of morning walks. It lasted for years, that season, and I remember it often. How we moved in companionable solitudes, rarely breaking into talk. We walked almost every day, miles at a time. She told me once, later, that she did it to keep me from being sad. I may have been doing it for the same reason—we were tunneling the mountain from opposite sides. But then our morning schedules changed and we tapered off.

I open the sliding door off the deck quietly—everyone is still sleeping—and I drop the *Times* and *Globe* on the kitchen counter. I see Mara sprawled on her bed much as I left her. I pause in the doorway and study her. I forget in which Greek myth one of the gods drapes a cloth woven from gold over a sleeper's body, but I think of that as I stand there. I see how her face goes all the way back to first innocence.

Mara does seem happier now. Being away, or being with us, has given her a lift. She starts to crack wise, which is always a sign. And she is eager to go shopping with Lynn in Province-town. That next day they disappear for a few hours. And then in the late afternoon we all go to the beach. The tide is low, the light spectacular. Lynn and Liam take their boogie boards down to where the waves are breaking. Mara wraps herself in a towel and reads Nabokov's *Ada*. I just stare, first to the left where the beach gradually merges into dune line, then, with a visceral pleasure—"There is nothing like this," I think—over to the right, where the flat sand reaches into the faintest mist and the shoreline at every second takes that quicksilver print of water, and where silhouettes stand and wade and swim in the distance.

Mara doesn't go in the water this afternoon, or the next. There was a time when she would just *fling* herself into the tallest waves she could find. She would yowl and shake herself and do it again. I feel, though, like something about all this water is beginning to reach up to her now, like she might be almost ready to push up off her towel and march down. But not yet. We sit side by side and watch Liam, our appointed stone gatherer.

Lynn asked him to find some large ocean stones for her garden. Liam likes this kind of thing, a task. He has his big goggles on and every few seconds we see him go arsey-turvey into the waves, and then up he comes, arm lifted high, clutching the next prize, which he stops to inspect for a moment and then either hurls to the shore or releases back into the water. The Sunfish episode has receded. This is in keeping with his style. If for Mara life backs up and grows scary, for Liam it catches, pauses, and then rushes on again. They are so very different, and I look from one to the other as if recognizing that essential fact. It's the kind of thing I might say out loud to Lynn, but she's not here. She's out swimming—I see her paralleling the shore, a small moving shape down to my left. I would tell Mara, but Mara is all at once up. While we were both sitting there watching Liam, the moment came. She has dropped her towel and is on her feet. With a quick over-the-shoulder glance she tromps down the sand and right to the water's edge. No running back and forth to work up to action. She pushes her hair back behind her ears and steps thigh-deep into the water. A flinch—I feel a sympathetic shock—and then she's in, under, three seconds vanished, and up with a thrust. And in again. I want to shout something, but I don't. I wish for the cold salt to scour her clean.

Liam, I see, has noticed his sister in the water. This makes him happy. I can tell. He turns away from the rock project and goes dolphin-bounding toward her. He loves company, and the company of his sister especially. When she can be gotten to. He wants to cruise the waves with her now, standing by her side. Nothing in common between their body types—he dwarfs her. But they are brother and sister, something in the way they stand side by side tells on them. They share humor—it's invisible, but I recognize it—and care. They share a certain brashness, too. When the big wave they've been waiting for arrives, they push into it with the same slugging lunge. Two heads, and then, right when the wave thins to breaking, two tumbling oblongs flashing against the green.

Contributors

Steve Almond is the author of five books, the most recent of which is *(Not That You Asked)*, a collection of essays.

Rick Bass is the author of twenty-four books of fiction and nonfiction, the most recent of which is *The Wild Marsh*, to be published by Houghton Mifflin Harcourt in July. He lives in western Montana with his wife and daughters.

Richard Bausch is the author of eleven novels and seven story collections. He lives in Memphis, Tennessee, and teaches at the University of Memphis.

Charles Baxter is the author of five novels, the most recent of which is *The Soul Thief*, and four books of stories. He lives in Minneapolis, where he teaches at the University of Minnesota.

Daniel Baxter is a structural engineer and lives in Cleveland, Ohio.

Sven Birkerts is the author of eight books, the most recent of which is *The Art of Time in Memoir: Then, Again* (Graywolf Press). He edits the journal *Agni* at Boston University and is Director of the Bennington Writing Seminars.

Jennifer Finney Boylan is the author of ten books, including the memoir *I'm Looking Through You: Growing Up Haunted*, published by Doubleday/Broadway (Random House) in 2008. Her 2003 memoir, *She's Not There*, was one of the first bestselling works by a transgender American. She has appeared widely on various television and radio programs, including *The Oprah Winfrey Show*, *Larry King Live*, and NPR's *Marketplace* and *Talk of the Nation*. She has been the subject of documentaries on CBS News' *48 Hours* and the History Channel. In 2007 she played herself on several episodes of ABC's *All My Children*. Her nonfiction appears regularly in *Condé Nast Traveler* magazine and on the op/ed pages of the *New York Times*. A professor of English, Jenny teaches at Colby College and lives in rural Maine with her family. Her new young adult series, *Falcon Quinn* (Bowen Books/HarperCollins), commences publication in 2010 with the first volume, *Falcon Quinn and the Black Mirror*.

Rick Bragg has written three memoirs, *All Over but the Shoutin'*, *Ava's Man*, and, most recent, the third book in the trilogy, *The Prince of Frogtown*. He worked at several newspapers before joining the *New York Times* in 1994. In 1996 he won the Pulitzer

Prize for Feature Writing for his work at the *Times* and later became the newspaper's Miami bureau chief. Bragg has received more than fifty writing awards in twenty years, including a Nieman Fellowship at Harvard University and, twice, the prestigious American Society of Newspaper Editors Distinguished Writing Award. He is now a professor at the University of Alabama's journalism program in its College of Communications and Information Sciences.

Brock Clarke is the author of four books of fiction. His most recent—the bestselling novel *An Arsonist's Guide to Writers' Homes in New England*—was a Booksense number one pick, a Borders Original Voices pick, and a *New York Times* Editors' Choice book, and will be reprinted in ten foreign editions. His short fiction and nonfiction have appeared in *One Story, Virginia Quarterly Review, New England Review, Georgia Review, Southern Review, The Believer, Ninth Letter,* and the annual Pushcart and New Stories from the South anthologies. He's a 2008 National Endowment for the Arts Fellow in fiction, and he lives in Cincinnati, where he teaches at the University of Cincinnati.

Anthony Doerr is the author of three books, *The Shell Collector, About Grace,* and *Four Seasons in Rome.* His short fiction has won three O. Henry prizes and has been anthologized in *The Best American Short Stories, The Anchor Book of New American Short Stories,* and *The Scribner Anthology of Contemporary Fiction.* Doerr lives in Boise, Idaho, with his wife and two sons.

Clyde Edgerton is the proud father of Catherine, Nathaniel, Ridley, and Truma Edgerton. Catherine is a member of the band Midtown Dickens, and the others are just getting under way. Edgerton teaches in the MFA program at the University of North Carolina Wilmington. He is the author of nine novels and one memoir. A book on fatherhood, birthed through the essay in this volume, is scheduled for 2011 from Little, Brown.

Nick Flynn's *Another Bullshit Night in Suck City* won the PEN/Martha Albrand Award for general nonfiction, was short-listed for France's Prix Femina, and has been translated into thirteen languages. Flynn is also the author of two books of poetry, *Some Ether* and *Blind Huber*, both published by Graywolf Press. He has received fellowships from, among other organizations, the Guggenheim Foundation and the Library of Congress. His poems and essays have appeared in *The New Yorker, Esquire, The Paris Review*, and the *New York Times Book Review*, as well as on public radio's *This American Life*. His film credits include "field poet" and artistic collaborator on the Oscar-nominated documentary *Darwin's Nightmare*. He teaches one semester a year at the University of Houston, and spends the rest of the year elsewhere.

Ben Fountain lives in Dallas. He is the author of the story collection *Brief Encounters with Che Guevara* (Ecco/HarperCollins), which won the 2007 PEN/Hemingway Award.

David Gessner has worked as a cartoonist for the *Harvard Crimson, High Country News*, and the *Boulder Weekly*. He is working on a graphic memoir called *Wormtown*, which is set in his hometown of Worcester, Massachusetts. In his nongraphic life he is the author of six books, including *Sick of Nature, The Prophet of Dry Hill, Return of the Osprey*, and *Soaring* *with Fidel.* He is the winner of the Pushcart Prize and the John Burroughs Award, and his work has appeared in many magazines and journals, including the *New York Times Magazine*, the *Boston Globe, Outside, The Georgia Review, Harvard Review,* and *Orion.* He has taught environmental writing at Harvard, and currently lives in North Carolina with his wife and daughter.

Sebastian Matthews is the author of a poetry collection, *We Generous* (Red Hen Press), and a memoir, *In My Father's Footsteps* (W. W. Norton). He co-edited, with Stanley Plumly, *Search Party: Collected Poems of William Matthews.* Matthews teaches at Warren Wilson College and serves on the faculty at Queens College Low-Residency MFA in Creative Writing. Matthews also co-edits *Rivendell*, a place-based literary journal, and serves as the creative director of Asheville Wordfest.

Neal Pollack is the author of the bestselling parenting memoir *Alternadad*, and the founder of Offsprung.com, an internet community and humor magazine for "parents who don't suck."

Davy Rothbart is the creator of *Found Magazine*, a frequent contributor to public radio's *This American Life*, and author of *The Lone Surfer of Montana, Kansas*, a collection of stories. His work has also been featured in *The New Yorker*, the *New York Times*, and *High Times*. He lives in Ann Arbor, Michigan.

Brandon R. Schrand is the author of *The Enders Hotel: A Memoir*, the 2007 River Teeth Literary Nonfiction Prize winner and a summer 2008 Barnes & Noble Discover Great New Writers selection. His work has appeared or is forthcoming in *Tin House*, *Shenandoah*, *The Missouri Review*, and numerous other publications. He has won the Wallace Stegner Prize and the Pushcart Prize. A two-time grant recipient of the Charles Redd Center for Western Studies, he lives with his wife and two children in Moscow, Idaho, where he coordinates the MFA Program in Creative Writing at the University of Idaho.

Jim Shepard is the author of six novels, the most recent of which is *Project X*, and three story collections, the most recent of which is *Like You'd Understand, Anyway*, which was nominated for the National Book Award and won the Story Prize. His short fiction has appeared in, among other magazines, *Harper's*, *McSweeney's*, *The Paris Review*, *The Atlantic*, *Esquire*, *Granta*, *The New Yorker*, and *Playboy*. He teaches at Williams College.

Darin Strauss is the international bestselling author of the novels *Chang and Eng* and *The Real McCoy*, which were both *New York Times* Notable Books. Also a screenwriter, he is adapting *Chang and Eng* with Gary Oldman, for Disney. The recipient of a 2006 Guggenheim Fellowship in fiction writing, he is a clinical associate professor at New York University's graduate school. His most recent novel, *More Than It Hurts You*, was published in 2008 by Dutton. He lives in New York with his wife and two sons.

Michael Thomas was born and raised in Boston. He received his BA from Hunter College and his MFA from Warren Wilson

College. His debut novel, *Man Gone Down*, was selected as a Top Ten Best Book of 2007 by the *New York Times* and a Notable Book of 2007 by the *San Francisco Chronicle*. He teaches at Hunter College, and he lives in Brooklyn with his wife and three children.

Acknowledgments

I commend Abigail Holstein, my excellent guide, for her perfect admixture of saltiness and sophistication, a combination I have always imagined the best New York editors possess. She has served this book and the writers within it well. I salute Daniel Halpern—for saying yes, and for helping to bring this book into the world.

Liz Farrell was there from the very beginning. Without her boundless enthusiasm and know-how, this would not have happened. She deserves more credit than I can convey here.

It can be a vulnerable thing, writing about one's fatherhood. So I'm grateful for the generosity of the writers collected here, who allowed me to persuade them to do so anyway, especially those four who started the project with me: Anthony Doerr, Rick Bass, Steve Almond, and Charles Baxter.

My gratitude as well to those persons whose

assistance was invaluable at points early and late: Clay Ezell, Jessica Purcell, Suet Chong, Allison Saltzman, Alison Forner, Christopher Silas Neal, Speer Morgan, and, in particular, Kim Barnes.

Special thanks to the following rock-solid individuals . . . for friendship and support in rough seas: Jeff Jones, Gary Williams, Matthew Vollmer, Michael Shilling, Wesley Bullock, Kyle von Hoetzendorff, Tony Perez, and Cheston Knapp, aka C$; for sharpening my thinking, both about this book and about fatherhood: Brandon Schrand, Nate Lowe, Bryan Fry, and especially Mark Cunningham; for a welcome harbor: the peerless community of writers and students at UNC Wilmington; for their love: Daniel, Pamela, Andrew, and Phillip George.

If all goes well, fatherhood will be a lifetime occupation. But for me it would feel a paltry and hollow one without the mother of Lucille Paley George. Whatever's more than thanks, whatever's more than love, I give to Meg, who on an August Sunday evening just after six o'clock delivered the gift I cherish above all others, a feat I've been doing my best to live up to ever since.

While commissioned for this anthology, the following essays appeared previously, sometimes in different form, in the following publications:

Ben Fountain, "The Night Shift," in *New Letters*, Spring 2009.

Charles Baxter, "The Chaos Machine," in *The Believer*, February 2008.

Anthony Doerr, "Nine Times (Among Countless Others) I've Thought About Those Who Came Before Us in My Brief Career as a Father," in *Missouri Review*, Spring 2009.

Rick Bass, "Notes from Adolescence," in *Southern Review*, Fall 2008.

Sven Birkerts, "The Points of Sail," in *Ecotone*, Winter 2008-09.

A version of Davy Rothbart's essay, "Zeke," was first featured as "I'm the Decider" on the public radio program *This American Life* on March 9, 2007.